EARLY TERMINATION

EARLY TERMINATION

A PROBATION CASE FILES MYSTERY

CINDY GOYETTE

LEVEL
BEST BOOKS

Author Photo Credit: Jon DEmilio

First edition

Cover art by Michael Verdun

This book was professionally typeset on Reedsy.
Find out more at reedsy.com

For Brittany, the queen of snark

Praise for Early Termination

"A rollicking ride through the gritty world of feisty Probation Officer Casey Carson, a fantastic character with a heart as big and vast as the Arizona desert she calls home. When her probationers keep stacking up as homicide victims, Casey realizes that someone is sending her a message, and they're dead serious about it. Now, she must unravel the sinister plot before she becomes the next victim. A complex, entertaining story that includes a secondary theme of romantic frustration simmering in the background, and a twisty ending that ensures we'll see more adventures from Casey Carson. A great read! Five thumbs-up!"—Kerry Peresta, author of the Olivia Callahan Suspense series and *Back Before Dawn*

Chapter One

In probation work, there's no such thing as a routine day at the office. This morning, flashing red and blue lights guided me to the crime scene. Pulling up behind the coroner's van, I parked my Jeep Wrangler and took a deep breath.

Coroner meant someone was dead. Not a good start to my day, but even worse for whoever I'd been called here about.

As I climbed out of my Jeep, I adjusted my sunglasses and surveyed the area. Yellow crime scene tape blocked off the entrance to the canal. Red tile rooftops peeked over six-foot walls that separated the waterway from the middle-class sea of stucco on either side. The canal, about ten feet wide, snaked smack in the middle of a dirt pathway that residents used to get their steps in.

September was drawing to a close, and I appreciated the sign of cooler weather that would drop below one hundred degrees for the first time in months. Ninety degrees might seem hot to some, but in Arizona, it was sweater weather.

I walked up to a uniformed cop and held out my badge. "I'm with probation. Detective Ramsey asked me to come."

Police reaching out to us wasn't unusual, but a crime scene call wasn't routine. My curiosity mixed with dread.

The cop glanced at my identification. "Ms. Carson. Welcome to the shit show. Don't touch anything." He held the tape high so I could pass. I ducked underneath and secured my badge to my belt so the other officers could tell I belonged there.

Lots of Tempe Police blue uniforms and forensic staff mulled around the area, but I homed in on the tall, balding man standing close to the water. He had on plain clothes—khakis and a plaid shirt with the sleeves rolled up. I figured he might be Ramsey, so I walked over to him.

He scribbled something on a small notepad and glanced at me as I approached. "You the PO?"

I nodded and dropped my gaze to the mound covered by a tarp at his feet. I wasn't fond of seeing dead bodies. I was a PO, not a cop, for a reason.

"Thinking this might be one of your charges, Ms. Carson," he said. "I gotta warn you, it's not pretty. He was in the water for a while, and birds and god knows what else got to him. You got a strong stomach?"

No. At the mere thought of seeing the body, my breakfast threatened to make a reappearance, but I wouldn't admit that. "I'm fine. Why do you think he was on my caseload?"

Ramsey shrugged. "Someone stuffed your business card in his mouth."

I gulped air. "You're kidding."

"Nope. You ready?" Ramsey reached down and pulled the sheet back before I could respond.

A bloated, green face, missing chunks of cheek, greeted me. Bulging eyes looked skyward. Bran flakes swirled in my stomach and crested in my throat. Without a word, I ran to the canal and vomited so hard I thought I'd hack up a vital organ or two.

"You okay, ma'am?" Ramsey sounded bored.

I wiped my mouth on my sleeve and straightened. Memories of the same man, alive and animated, flashed in my mind. Not so long ago, he'd been proud of accomplishing a solid month of sobriety. Now, I hardly recognized him. "Could you put the sheet back?" I said, keeping my back to the body on the ground.

"Sure."

I waited a moment to give Ramsey time to cover the corpse and for me to compose myself. But that would take a while, and the detective didn't seem like he had a lot of patience. The relationship between police and probation was fickle. We often needed each other, but POs were on the lower end of the food chain.

When I finally turned around, Ramsey tapped his pen against his notebook. "So, you know the guy, or what?"

"Brian Johnson," I said. "He was on abscond status. Haven't seen him for a few weeks, maybe a month. He was doing well, but then he stopped reporting. He probably relapsed. I was gearing up to request a warrant for probation violations. What do you think was the cause of death?"

Ramsey shrugged again. "Too soon to tell, but most people who die of natural causes don't end up in a canal or send a message like your business card does. They preserved it in a plastic Baggie, so we'd get the point no matter how long it took to find him."

I felt even sicker. Could the message have been for me? "Couldn't you ID him through fingerprints? I thought you had all kinds of tech gadgets for that."

"Sure," Ramsey said. "But then I wouldn't have seen your reaction. Plus, some of his fingertips are missing, and what's left probably isn't usable. Dental records take time." He pulled a business card out of his shirt pocket and handed it to me. "Call me if you think of anything else I might need to know."

I turned back to the canal and vomited until I had nothing left to give.

Chapter Two

Back in the solace of my Jeep, I clutched Ramsey's business card and tried to bring my breathing back to pre-heart attack level. Eyes shut, I hoped for Zen, but Brian Johnson's ballooned face floated before me. Jerking my eyes open, I shook my head to clear the image.

Brian was an okay guy. Like most of my charges, he had a drug problem. When he was high, he made poor choices—like stealing cars—which was why he was on probation. When sober, he had a sharp wit and a kind heart. Last time I saw him, he even made a large payment toward the restitution he owed. Relapses weren't uncommon, and I figured that was the reason he'd stopped reporting. But he'd been in the canal, not out terrorizing the community. I felt guilty for thinking the worst of him, even if it was an occupational hazard.

Why was my business card stuffed in his mouth? Had to be a message to me. But what was the message? I gave my card out all the time. Everyone I supervised got one. I also left them on doors when I did fieldwork and no one was home. Family members often got one, as did attorneys, treatment providers, and other community partners. Support staff at the office also handed them out if anyone asked for one.

My phone buzzed in my pocket. A text from Tony Romero, the new officer I was training.

Thought u were meeting me at the office @ 9. I'm ready to go.

I rubbed my forehead. Normally, watching Tony fumble his way through his probationary period was a good distraction. The job wasn't for everyone, and I was coming to realize it probably wasn't a good fit for him. Because his dad was the manager of the community service unit, Tony's shortcomings were often overlooked. I was given the task of shaping him into a decent PO or finding an infraction strong enough to justify letting him go.

I started my Jeep and sent Tony a text message saying I was on my way. I tried to concentrate on the day ahead of me, but all I could think about was my newly deceased probationer and what his death had to do with me.

The probation office sat across from Central High School in downtown Phoenix, which didn't quite cover the thousand feet sex offenders needed to keep between them and any schools. But buildings were expensive, and the department couldn't always be picky.

I had a cubicle on the second floor with the rest of my unit. Entertainment was abundant as we watched the goings-on at the campus below us. Though I'd been out of high school for years, I could spot the mean girls from fifty feet away. Most of what I saw made me feel old, even though my thirty-first birthday was still a few months off.

Once I arrived, I stopped by my supervisor's office to fill her in on my trip to the canal that morning. But the dry-erase board hanging outside her door said Alma wouldn't be in until that afternoon. Brian Johnson would not get any more dead; I could wait to chat with her then. Back at my desk, I found Tony sitting in my chair, yucking it up with Claire, who had the cubicle across from mine.

Eyeing Tony's boots perched on the edge of my desk, I raised an eyebrow. "Make yourself at home." I dropped my messenger bag on the floor next to a stack of files.

Tony lowered his feet to the floor. "Ah… Let me finish the field list."

He stood and scurried back to his cubicle several spots back. I'd talked to him about working instead of socializing before, but I obviously had to revisit the subject. I wasn't trying to be a killjoy, but he was behind in his work and needed to learn about priorities.

"Lilian Harrison's been trying to reach you," Claire said. "She sounds upset."

"What else is new?" Lilian was the eighty-year-old mother of my least favorite client, Eric Harrison. She called me several times a week, usually hysterical and claiming Eric was running amuck. She was a sweet old lady, but the problem was that whenever I went to the house to see what was going on—which was often—she didn't remember that she'd called and sometimes even accused me of harassing her son. I faulted dementia, but I couldn't ignore her calls in case there really was a problem.

I played my messages, and sure enough, six of them were from Lilian. "Eric's going to kill me," she said, wailing into the phone. "You've got to do something."

I tried to call her back. If she was really in danger, which I doubted, she should call the police, not me. But I got her voicemail.

After deleting the last message, I looked up to see Tony staring down at me. "I mapped out our day." He held out a list of directions from an internet map site, which gave us the most succinct route to take.

"We need to swing by Eric Harrison's first," I said.

Tony let out a giant sigh. "He's not on the list. Do I have to do a new map?"

"No. We'll adjust. Not a big deal." I fought to keep the annoyance from my voice. Being flexible was a huge part of the job. Plans were often upended when a client's crisis popped up unexpectedly.

I couldn't fathom why Alma thought I'd be a good trainer. I had the patience of a puppy without the happy-go-lucky attitude, and I wasn't exactly known for my coaching skills. I wondered if I was supposed to benefit from the experience as much as Tony or if it was Alma's idea of a joke.

I swung my gear bag over my shoulder. Inside was my baton, bulletproof vest, and any paperwork we might need. My pepper spray and handcuffs were clamped to my belt. Some POs carried firearms—I wasn't one of them. Guns had a way of falling into the wrong hands. And since one was used to end my mother's life, I had an even stronger aversion to them. Most days, I tried not to think about that.

"Let's go." I headed toward the door with Tony in tow.

Lilian and her son lived in a ranch-style house in an older section of west

Phoenix. It desperately needed a remodel and probably hadn't had a good cleaning since I was in diapers. Lilian kept the heavy curtains on all the windows shut. Since most of the lightbulbs were burnt out, I always kept a flashlight in hand, even if it was mid-afternoon.

Eric said he lived with his mom to help around the house and even got paid by the state to be her caregiver. The joke was on the state. The place had fallen into even worse disrepair in the six months I'd supervised him.

Tony and I made our way to the front door after he called in our location on the radio. "Stand to the right side of the door so they can't see you until they've opened it," I instructed as he knocked.

He opened his mouth to say something, but the look I lasered his way seemed to make him think otherwise. He adjusted his stance and sighed.

Lilian answered. Her wrinkled face was tear-streaked. "Casey," she whispered. "He's lost his mind. He wants me dead so he can have the house." She leaned forward. "I took him off my life insurance policy, but he doesn't know it."

Her secret was safe with me. I wasn't about to stir the drama pot. "Can we come in?"

She stepped aside, and we entered. I clicked my flashlight on and shone it around the living room. "He home?"

"In the kitchen."

I waited a beat. "Anybody else here?"

She shook her head no.

Normally, I would have asked more questions, but Lilian wasn't exactly a reliable source of information. I'd hoped Tony would jump in and show me any PO abilities he'd kept hidden so far, but he remained silent.

I walked to the kitchen, with Tony and Lilian behind me.

Eric stood at the sink with his back to us. He was a pretty big guy—and not in a muscular way. His physique attested to the time he'd spent on the couch. Probably with donuts. He tipped his head back as he sucked something down from a brown bottle. When he placed the container on the counter, I noted it was a forty. Several more empties littered the counter as well.

I looked at Tony and made a cuffing motion with my hand against my wrist, so he'd know my intention. A blank look settled on Tony's face. *Cripes.* I'd have more luck asking Lilian for help.

"Eric," I said. "Please turn around."

Eric's shoulders tightened, and he cracked his neck before slowly turning to face us. Bloodshot eyes watered, his face was flushed, and sweat glistened on his brow. The odor of alcohol radiated off him. Eric was drunk. I knew from his history that he was a mean drunk. Because of this, he wasn't allowed to drink.

Eric needed to go to jail.

Our agency didn't allow us to make arrests without police assistance unless there were immediate safety concerns, which meant we needed to manage a call to dispatch so they could send an officer. And we needed to do so without putting Eric on alert.

A collection of scary knives clung to a magnet on the wall behind him. That and the rookie PO at my side turned my *"oh-shit"* radar up a notch.

I motioned toward the door. "Let's talk in the other room."

"What the fuck," Eric said. But he complied and walked past me and Tony into the poorly lit dining room where his mother met us, wringing her hands.

I wanted to call for backup, but since Tony was clueless about my plan, I searched my brain for a way to make the call without Eric getting wise.

Eric saved me the trouble. "I'm going to jail, aren't I?" His words came out slurred.

"I'm exploring our options," I said, hoping to keep him from freaking out. I looked at Tony and made a gesture toward the radio. "Call it in."

Eric took a step toward his mother. "Can I at least hug my mom goodbye?"

I was losing control of the situation and kept my eye on the exit in case we had to run. Tony had his thumb on the radio mic but looked confused about what to say.

Eric stepped forward and wrapped his arms around his mom. He whispered something in her ear, and she reached for the waistband of his jeans. She moved his shirt out of the way, revealing the handle of a gun.

Her gnarled fingers wrapped around the grip. I sprang into action, but before I could reach them, she'd pulled out the gun and passed it to her son.

Shit.

"Gun!" Lurching forward, I shoved Lilian out of the way, then tackled Eric, taking him to the ground before he could raise the weapon. As we fell, Tony jumped on top of us.

Not helpful.

Fumbling for control of the gun, I snatched it out of Eric's hand and held it above my head. "Get his hands," I said to Tony, my voice cracking.

Tony pinned Eric to the ground as I rolled out of the way and pushed the handgun under a hutch. With that out of reach, I fumbled for my handcuffs while Tony struggled to control the flailing Eric. Eric's elbow clipped me under my chin before I was able to grab his arm and hold it to the floor with my knee. Cuffing one wrist, I reached for the other just as Tony got a hold of it.

Handcuffs in place, I sat back on my haunches and caught my breath.

Eric squirmed beneath Tony's weight, cussing, but we'd restrained him, and he was no longer a threat. Tony straddled him and rode him like a bucking bull until Eric ran out of steam. Panting, I rubbed my aching jaw, then, still slightly out of breath, I keyed the radio and requested backup.

In the dim light, it took me a minute to locate Lilian, lying on the floor beside the dining room table. She squinted at me, sweetness draining from her face like something flushed down the toilet—replaced by an evil I'd only seen in horror films. "You broke my goddamn hip," she said, spittle coming out of her mouth. "You're gonna pay, you bitch."

Chapter Three

I massaged my jaw as a patrol officer folded Eric into the back of his car. Tony stood next to me on the front porch.

"That was something," he said, adjusting the badge hanging around his neck that had gone cockeyed during our struggle with Eric.

I took in the surrounding scene. Three police cars, a fire truck, and an ambulance. The paramedics were still inside, tending to Lilian, who hadn't stopped screaming at me until I left her house. Neighbors poured onto the street, adding to the commotion. A Channel 6 News van pulled up, and Suzy Vega—a well-known crime reporter with a vendetta against law enforcement—got out.

"How the hell did she find out about this so fast?" I said under my breath.

"She's sleeping with a detective," the cop walking by said. "Hypocrite."

Was he talking about the reporter or the detective? Guess it worked either way.

I didn't want to talk to Suzy Vega. In fact, department policy prohibited it. We had an information officer to handle the press.

Suzy's cameraman stretched as he got out of the van and opened the back. He loaded a bulky camera onto his shoulder and followed Suzy to a place she pointed to in front of the house.

I slid my cell out of my pocket and scrolled through my contacts for my supervisor's number. Alma answered on the second ring.

"I've got a situation here," I said.

"I'm listening." Alma didn't like paperwork or surprises. Today was not her lucky day.

I filled her in on what had transpired. "It all happened so fast," I said. "Good news is we disarmed Harrison before anyone got hurt."

"Anyone but his elderly mother," she said.

Right. "That was an accident. She handed Eric the gun. She was in the way."

Alma sighed.

"Oh, and Channel 6 is here. Perhaps you should alert the Information Officer."

"Jesus," Alma said. "How the hell did they get wind of this so soon?"

"Rumor has it Vega is sleeping with a detective."

"Shit. Not Vega. She's going to rip us to shreds. Did your ex-husband tell you that?"

My turn to sigh. She meant Betz. Detective Barry Betz. I'd been trying to stay away from him since he helped me out of my last disaster and had let it slip that he still had feelings for me. I had to admit, he wasn't alone in those thoughts. But we'd divorced for a reason—although that reason was now murky in my mind. His sister, Lieutenant Jasmine Faulk, had let me know she wouldn't stand for me toying with her brother's heart again. Jasmine scared the crap out of me.

And then there was Marcus—or, as I referred to him in my head, His Hotness. The kiss he'd planted on me a few months ago still set butterflies loose in my stomach whenever I thought of it. While Marcus was back in New Jersey, tying up loose ends, we tried to get to know each other better over text messages and late-night phone calls. While I explored this new relationship, I swore off contact with Betz, so I didn't muddy the waters. For the hell of it, I swore off wine at the same time. I wasn't doing so well with the wine thing, but I'd stayed away from Betz. I'd only turn to him as a last resort.

"Jesus," Alma said before I could answer. "I just put Channel 6 on. This is running live. What happened to your hair?"

I reached up and ran my fingers through it, then turned my back to the camera.

"Is your jaw red?" Alma said. "And tell Tony to wipe that stupid grin off his face."

I grabbed Tony's arm and spun him about, so he also had his back to the camera.

"Get out of there," Alma said.

The front door to the house opened, and the paramedics wheeled Lilian out on a stretcher. As she passed us by, she shook her fist at me. "That's the one. The one who busted into my home without a warrant and assaulted an old woman." Her quivering voice was worthy of an Oscar.

I took Tony's arm and dragged him to my Jeep. Suzy ran alongside us, the mic in her hand. "Officer Carson, I have documents that prove you've been harassing this family for months," she said with authority. "Care to comment?"

For a moment, I froze. I would later learn that I looked like a deer in headlights before the camera, but for now, I resisted the urge to put her on a stretcher, like the mean old lady behind us who continued to shout about how unfairly I'd treated her.

"Contact our information officer." I leapt behind the wheel of my Wrangler and put the Jeep in reverse, backing away before Tony could climb into his seat. That, too, was caught on video and would come back to haunt me. I slammed on the brakes and forced myself to breathe as Tony jumped in and buckled his seatbelt. Then, scraping the bottom of the dignity bowl, I held my head high and narrowly missed a patrol car as I careened down the street.

"Smooth," Tony said.

I couldn't help but give him the finger. And although that was blurred out when I later watched the news, only a moron would have missed it.

Chapter Four

Back at the office, everyone gave Tony and me a standing ovation. Once word got out that we were on the news, everyone had booted up their laptops to watch. Sometimes, I hated the internet.

"Way to go, Case," Andy Bell said, still clapping. "Glad you have the mad skills to take out an old lady."

"Stuff it, Bell." I walked past him to Alma's office.

Alma sat at her desk, wrapping her long dark hair into a bun on top of her head and then letting it fall. She habitually played with her hair when she was stressed. Knowing I caused her anxiety added to mine.

Alma's boss, Roxy Rich, sat on the couch under the window. Roxy always wore short skirts and had an afro that added a good six inches to her already tall frame. She crossed her toned legs, her top foot swinging with her high-heeled shoe dangling precariously on her toe. "Close the door," she said.

Not good. I shut the door and leaned against it.

"You should get checked out medically. Your jaw is swollen," Alma said, as she swooped her hair into another bun.

I reached up and rubbed the sore spot. I'd been through worse. "I'm fine. Nothing a little makeup can't hide."

Alma shook her head and cleared her throat.

"We read your case notes," Roxy said. "Seems like the mom called you almost daily to complain about her son."

"Sometimes several times a day," Alma added.

"She and her son have been sending letters to Channel 6 claiming you weren't doing your job. Weren't responsive, that sort of thing," Roxy said.

13

"Son said you weren't fair to him. Discriminated against him."

That pushed my buttons. "Based on what?" My voice rose, and I fought to keep it under control. Guilty people got defensive. Yet here I was, defending myself. I prided myself on being a damn good PO and didn't appreciate my work or ethics called into question. "How could I discriminate against him? He's my race, about my age."

"We're not sure," Alma said. "We just know what Vega told the information officer."

I paced the few feet in front of the door. "This is total BS."

"It may be," Roxy said. "But Suzy Vega has a hold of it, and she's on a mission. We need to make sure our ducks are in a row. Our information officer wants to talk to you, by the way."

That should be fun. Truth was that I liked most of my clients, but not all. Harrison fell into the latter category. Mostly because he deflected responsibility for his behavior like a talented goalie. But I tried to keep my attitude in check and treated him like everyone else. My eye rolling was internal. I thought I had a pretty good relationship with Lilian. Apparently, a broken hip changed her impression of me. Or I misread her. She'd been complaining to Channel 6 about me, after all.

"In the age of police brutality, we have to be extra careful," Roxy added.

While we weren't police, we were sworn in as officers. And when we wore our gear, some people couldn't tell the difference. "I was being careful." I gave them a blow-by-blow description of what had happened. I felt stronger when I was done. Everything was by the book. "I had no intention of arresting Eric without backup," I said. "But when the gun came out, it was a matter of personal safety, and I had to act, or I might not be standing here. Same goes for Tony."

"We need you to write all that down," Alma said. "Step by step. Then I'd like you to take a few days off."

"Administrative leave?" I swallowed the lump in my throat. I'd been down that road before and never wanted to take that trip again. Last time, everything had worked out in my favor, but it had been humiliating to turn in my badge, even if it had only been for a few days.

"It hasn't come to that," Alma said. "I'm just concerned about you, all you've been through.... And you're overdue for time off."

Roxy stood and smoothed her skirt. "At least cool off for a few. Take a walk around the block. And send Tony in. We want to talk to him, too."

I rubbed my arms and looked around, trying to ground myself. "Fine." I turned and left the room. Closing the door behind me, I took a moment, leaned my back against it, and regulated my breathing before I faced my coworkers. My phone buzzed in my pocket. A text from Alma. *Call someone. Just to be safe.*

She meant my union rep, and she, as a manager, wasn't supposed to suggest that. But Alma had my back as much as she could. I wasn't so sure about Roxy. I'd heard that she'd held other officers' feet to the fire before, and I knew she could make my life miserable if she wanted to.

Chapter Five

The stares of my coworkers burned a hole through my back as I made my way to my cubicle. I told Tony Alma wanted to see him and grabbed my bag.

"You okay?" Claire asked.

I nodded. "Just hate the scrutiny."

"They making you write an incident report?"

"Yeah. I'll do it in a bit." I positioned my bag on my shoulder.

Right now, my priority was to get out of the building and away from the questioning glances of my coworkers as quickly as I could. Alone, I might be able to think straight.

In the sanctuary of my Wrangler, I put my head back and closed my eyes. The episode at Eric's house played on a loop in my head. His mom, exposing the gun and handing it to her son...me, shoving her out of the way...Lilian's face twisted and mean as she spat hateful words in my direction.

I missed my mother every minute of every day, but at times like this, the void her death had caused was overwhelming. I wanted my mommy.

I drove to the nearest drive-through and bought myself a bucket of Diet Coke. Alternating deep breaths with big gulps, I found the nearest park and stopped under a tree in the outermost corner. Unzipping the window of my ragtop, I pulled it down, hoping the fresh air would calm me.

Deep in thought, I jumped when my phone buzzed in my pocket, alerting me I had a text message.

Missing you, Sunshine. Heading your way.

Marcus. He nicknamed me that tongue in cheek—I wasn't known

for brightening people's days. His use of the moniker let me know he understood me. I could be cranky, and it hadn't run him off.

I slumped in my seat. Normally, a message from His Hotness made my day. The distance between us made flirtation fun and without consequences. But thoughts of rekindling whatever we'd started last summer only added to my angst. We'd shared a couple of passionate kisses and had almost died together at the hands of Diablo—one of Phoenix's most dangerous gangs.

He'd come through for me when I'd needed him most. How could I not be attracted to that?

But I hardly knew him. At the time, I'd been excited to explore the possibilities, wondering what could come next. Now it seemed real. He was on his way—maybe even moving here.

It was possible he'd fallen in love with the desert, and not me. Although the intimacy we'd shared was not for sissies. Plus, he'd promised to return before he went home to New Jersey to tie up some loose ends. The feel of his touch was never out of my mind. Then again, neither was Betz's.

Safe travels, I texted back. Picturing him mounting his Harley and riding across the country, shoulder-length creamy brown hair blowing in the wind, made my stomach flutter. A model in a cologne ad had nothing on Marcus— he was hotter than my steering wheel on a sizzling August day. How would I be able to say no to him and take it slow as I planned? Thankfully, it would take a few days for him to make the cross-country trip. I prayed I could sort out my feelings by then.

I took another drink, and my phone buzzed again. Thinking it was Marcus, I glanced down. Betz. I swallowed hard. Damnit. I thought my hiatus from all things ex had cured me, but as I opened his message, I could barely breathe.

Really, Case? Beating up an old lady?

I rolled my eyes. *Not funny.*

Saw it on the news. Seriously, you okay?

Other than hyperventilating? *Fine.*

K. Let me know if you need anything.

Will do. But I had no intention of running to Betz. Not this time. He was a safe place, sure, but I needed to learn to take care of myself. My dependence on him had been part of the problem I was coming to learn. And I didn't like him telling me what to do. Eventually, we'd butt heads. We always did. Ah, the reason we'd divorced. I knew it would come to me.

I dropped my phone in the center console and started my Jeep. I'd promised to meet my sister, Kate, at my niece's swimming lesson. I could use a good dose of Kate.

I parked in front of the Ahwatukee YMCA and grabbed my messenger bag. As I stepped outside, Detective Ramsey's business card fell to the ground. With what had happened at the Harrison's, I'd almost forgotten about Brian Johnson and his decomposing face. Now that image was back in my head, and I realized I hadn't mentioned the death of one of my charges to Alma.

I tossed the empty soda cup in the nearest trash can and perched myself on the low block wall a few feet from the door. Fishing my cell out of my bag, I called Alma's direct line. Without preamble, I filled her in on my early morning trip to the Tempe canal.

"More?" she said. "You have more bad news?"

I cleared my throat.

"So, we don't know the cause of death?" she said. I pictured her playing with her hair.

"No. The only reason they called me is that they found my card." A little tidbit that weighed heavy on my mind. I also suspected Ramsey had a sick side and wanted to watch me squirm, but I kept that to myself.

"Jesus," Alma said. "What a day you've had. You okay?"

Define okay. "I'm fine."

"You're not fine. Stop saying you're fine. You never really dealt with that whole Diablo nightmare last summer. Or that they will probably try to seek revenge for that whole debacle with your cousin. Or your mom's death. You have like a gazillion vacation hours. Why not take some time for yourself?"

My left eye twitched. "Relaxing makes me nervous." A vacation alone was as appealing as childbirth. Both things might be in my future, but I couldn't see them happening anytime soon. Maybe if I had a partner to share such life events, I'd be in more of a hurry. But decisions about having children were one reason Betz and I had split. And Marcus was more of an idea than a boyfriend. However, I didn't feel like spending time alone and letting my thoughts run wild. Work was a good distraction.

Alma's reminder about Diablo slapped me in the face with the truth—I'd never be able to relax. I may have been somewhat responsible for several of them going to prison, or at least they saw it that way. With most of the original gangsters out of commission, I figured I had a little breathing room. But I knew through one of our gang POs that Diablo was reorganizing, and I'd been warned that someday they'd come for me.

Usually, I went with the I'll-deal-with-it-when-it-happens approach, but it was always hanging over my head.

After yet another promise to Alma that I'd take good care of myself, I tossed my phone back into my bag, hoisted it on my shoulder, and walked through the locker room and out to the pool.

My sister sat on a chase lounge, jostling two-year-old Ethan in her arms. My four-year-old niece, Ashley, enthusiastically waved to me from the pool. I returned the greeting and plopped down on the chair next to Kate.

Perfectly put together in white shorts and a black tank top, Kate's blonde bob bounced as she soothed her son. She reached into her bag, pulled out a tube of sunblock, and tossed it to me.

I caught it. "Thanks, but I'm good."

"Said the last skin cancer patient," she quipped. "Put it on. Especially your face."

I knew better than to argue. She was a mom through and through. Squeezing a drop on my finger, I rubbed the cream onto my nose and cheekbones, wincing when I touched my tender jaw.

Kate pushed her sunglasses to the top of her head. "What happened to your face?"

"Nothing."

"It's red and swollen." She gave me her best death glare. My niece and nephew would not get away with a thing.

I sat back and stretched my legs out in front of me. The September sun was still intense at the height of the day, and the heat burned through the fabric of my jeans. "Guess you didn't see the news. I was on camera, and it wasn't my best work."

"Spill it."

Kate didn't like my job. As I gave her a succinct version of events, she brought her phone out and Googled the story before I could finish. Suzy Vega's voice grated on my last nerve as, on camera, she accused me of abusing my authority. Lilian wailed in the background.

The mothers sitting around us turned to stare.

"Turn that down," I said, hissing.

Kate ended the video and shook her head while tapping Ethan on his back. "I hate your job."

"Noted."

"You just got off admin leave not long ago. How can you have so much go wrong in a year?"

Ouch. "Thanks."

"Sorry. I just wonder what it's going to take to persuade you to go into a different line of work."

I stared straight ahead. We'd had this conversation before, and it always got my dander up. If I didn't know that Kate had my best interest at heart, I would have avoided her. "I love my job," I said, as I had a thousand times before. "Anyway, end of conversation. I heard from Betz today." She didn't know about Marcus. I could only take so much well-intended advice.

That got her attention. "And?"

"He was just checking on me. Saw the story on the news."

"You going to see him?"

"No. Anyway, he didn't suggest we meet." Maybe he was trying to stay away from me, too. Although I had moments when it took every ounce of strength I could muster to keep my vow to put Betz where he belonged—in my past. This was one of those moments.

"Remember," she said. "You guys divorced for a reason. I love Betz, but your relationship didn't work because you couldn't agree on anything. As far as I can tell, that hasn't changed. You need someone a little less intense."

"Betz isn't intense."

"He is around you. You made the guy a nervous wreck."

"Why did I come here today?"

"Because you needed a reality check."

She was right. I could count on Kate to keep me on track, but I was too tired to listen to her point out my flaws. Best to change the subject. Again.

"How's Hope doing?" Hope was our cousin. After that whole Diablo thing, she was going through a rough patch and was staying with Kate and Kevin until she got back on her feet.

"She's understandably down. But she's out there every day looking for work. It's hard with her record and being fired from the probation department, though. How's Joy?"

I got the more challenging cousin in the deal. Hope's sister, Joy, was a handful. But she had a house back in Boston and would return to it in the morning, giving me my peaceful life back. "Her bags are packed. Looking forward to some quiet time."

"I bet."

Lesson over, Ashley lifted chubby legs out of the pool and smacked wet feet against the decking as she ran my way. "Auntie Casey," she cried.

And boom, thirty pounds of wetness hurled herself onto my lap. I didn't care. I wrapped my arms around her and kissed her slimy cheek. "Great job, Fish. Dory would be jealous."

She laughed and wiggled out of my hold, going straight for her mother's purse and a bag of crackers. At least I rated above a snack. I wasn't maternal and preferred puppies to babies, but my niece had my heart.

My sister threw a towel at me, and I wrapped it around Ashley as she smacked crackers between her lips. Kate stood, balancing her belongings and her son on her person, as we all walked to her Subaru in the parking lot. I hoisted Ashley into her car seat while Kate secured a now-sleeping Ethan.

"High five," I said, palm colliding with my niece's before I shut the door.

"Come for dinner this weekend," Kate said. "I already invited Dad."

"Okay." I waved until they were out of sight. The half-hour of normal was a welcome break, but as I stood alone in the parking lot, the events of the day lay heavy on my shoulders once again.

Chapter Six

J oy greeted me at the door with a crushing hug. "Oh, Casey," she said. "I saw the news. Good Lord, do you still have your job?"

I wiggled out of her embrace and took a step back. My cousin had a certain fashion sense and owned nothing that didn't have a plunging neckline or fat-sucking spandex. Today, she wore super short shorts and a lime green top that left little to the imagination.

When I'd left that morning, a pile of suitcases waited at the door. I planned to drop her at the airport in the morning. The pile was gone.

"Um…where are your bags?"

"Surprise!" She threw her hands up in the air. "I postponed going home. I'm not leaving you in your time of trouble."

I couldn't catch a break if it was Velcroed to my hands. I struggled to keep my expression neutral, but my mouth dropped open just the same. "Really, Joy, not necessary. I'm fine."

"Of course you are," she said. "But I'll be here just in case. Anyway, I have a date."

Ah, the real reason she didn't want to leave.

"And Hope needs her little sister."

If I thought I could talk her out of staying, I would have given it a shot. She'd come through for me when the shit had hit the fan during the Diablo debacle, so on some level, I owed her. But I really wanted my privacy back.

Joy sashayed ahead of me into the kitchen. "I made dinner," she called over her shoulder. "Chicken cordon bleu with those tiny potatoes and green beans."

23

Not long ago, Joy had lost over one hundred pounds, but since she'd arrived at my house, she'd been cooking up a storm, and her waistline was starting to give up the fight. A win for me. It was nice to come home to a good meal.

She had set the table, and two glasses of red wine were waiting. I was touched by her effort. It was nice to feel pampered for once. At the sink, I scrubbed up, then picked up a glass of Merlot and took a satisfying sip. If Diet Coke was coffee to me, wine was crack.

"Oh, Honey," Joy said. "Sorry, I wasn't clear. Your plate's in the microwave. I set the table for my date. I was thinking you could eat in your room."

"What?"

"I have a date," she repeated loudly, treating me as though I were slumped in a chair and drooling on myself.

"You expect me to stay in my room? In my house?"

"I'd do the same for you if you ever had a date." She put her hands on her hips and puffed out her bottom lip. Were we really going to debate this? After the day I'd had?

Before either of us could argue our point, the doorbell rang. Joy jumped up and down like a five-year-old at Christmas.

I grabbed her arm. "Who's your date?"

"You'll see." Joy pulled away and hurried to the door.

I took the stolen glass of wine and followed.

Joy smoothed her tank top and pulled the door open.

I almost dropped my glass when I saw Jerski standing there. Pete Pajerski, or Jerski as he'd been dubbed by most who knew him, was a probation officer, and he'd shared an office with Hope before she got fired. He wasn't the last person I wanted to see on my doorstep, but he was on the list.

"What are you doing here?" I said before I could sort it out.

Joy wrapped her arms around him and planted a kiss on his cheek. Question answered.

"He's your date?" I still couldn't wrap my mind around it.

"He is," Joy said, beaming.

Jerski stepped inside. "Nice job today, hotshot," he said to me. "I wouldn't want Suzy Vega snooping around my caseload. Hope you've got your ducks in a row."

I wanted to punch him, but I took another swig of wine instead. Joy sending me to my room suddenly seemed like a good idea. I made my way back to the kitchen, grabbed my dinner out of the microwave, scooped up the bottle of wine, and shut myself inside my room. It was going to be a long night.

Chapter Seven

I started most of my mornings with a run. It cleared my head, kept me sane, and helped me stay a size six despite my love of wine and bagels. Dressed in shorts and a T-shirt, I wandered into the kitchen in search of my shoes while pulling up a playlist on my phone.

Jerski sat at the kitchen table, a mug of coffee before him. He'd stayed the night. *Gag.* I'd burn the bed if Joy ever went home.

"Good morning," he said in an unbearably perky voice.

"Morning," I grumbled.

He added a splash of creamer to his cup. "I've been meaning to call you."

I put one earbud on. "Why?"

"Did you forget what a great team we made? I'm your ride or die."

More like he was going to die if he didn't stop pushing my buttons. Jerski had helped me when Hope was missing, and Diablo was after me. He hadn't been my first choice of a partner; he didn't make that list. But he was the only one available, and he'd come through for me when I'd needed him most. I'd thanked him at the time. What else did he want?

"I was thinking," he went on. "We should do some field work together. Now that I'm dating your cousin, we should get to know each other better."

I forced a smile. Jerski's buzz-cut hair, army fatigues, and kick-your-ass demeanor conflicted with my style. Plus, it seemed like he was getting to know Joy very well without my help. "I'm training a new guy. Not much time to work with anyone else," I said. Besides, I preferred to work alone. And Jerski got on my last nerve. Having him in my house was bad enough. I didn't want to be stuck in a car with him.

"I'll send you an invite," he said, ignoring my excuse.

I shrugged. I'd decline until he got the message.

Joy emerged from the guestroom wearing a skimpy negligee. *Good God.* I grabbed my Nikes and headed out the door.

For four miles, my thoughts bounced with each step. Brian Johnson, Eric Harrison, his angry mother, Suzy Vega, and Diablo invaded my mind, deflecting contemplations of Joy and Jerski and whatever they were doing in my kitchen. Alma had strongly suggested I contact my union rep. I wasn't ready to do that just yet. Reviewing what had happened at the Harrison house, I'd done things by the book. It was unfortunate that Lilian got hurt, but that was on her son. He'd put us in the situation. I didn't see why I'd need union help.

I tried to distract myself by thinking about Marcus, but that led to thoughts of Betz.

So much for running keeping me sane.

Jerski's car was gone by the time I made it home. In the house, I heard the shower running in the main bathroom. I closed myself in my room and got ready for the day.

It was eight-thirty and time for me to head to work. Pulling my cell off the charger, I glanced at the screen. A message from Tony. I rolled my eyes. I was trying to stop doing that and had even started an eye-rolling jar. Most of the jar was filled with IOUs because who had that much cash around? But today, with no witnesses, I figured this one didn't count.

I read Tony's message, which was about ten minutes old. *Got a situation here. Call me!*

My call history told me Tony had called sixteen times in the last half hour. A knot formed in the pit of my stomach as I got back to him.

When he answered, I could barely hear him above the yelling in the background. "What's going on?"

Breathless, Tony said, "I stopped...for coffee...on my way...way to work. Shut up!"

This wasn't good. "What the hell's going on?"

"You're hurting me!" another voice yelled.

"Tony?"

A car door slammed. "Anyway," he said, still winded. "I saw Henry Coffman. He was...standing on the corner...he has a warrant, you know."

This was getting dicey. "Go on."

"So, I rolled down the window and said, 'Hey, Coffman.'"

"Yeah?" I headed toward the garage. It sounded like this might be Tony's last day at work.

"So...he runs. I remember you said not to chase people. So, I stayed in my car and followed him. The guy's not in great shape. It only took a few blocks for him to run out of steam."

Putting my phone on speaker, I laid it on my chest and put the Jeep in reverse, backing out of my garage. "And?"

"I cut him off with my car, jumped out, and subdued him. He's in the back seat right now. Shit!"

"What? What's happening?" I sped down the street.

"He's trying to kick out my window. Stop that, you asshole! You want to add destroying property to your charges?"

I had to yell to be heard over the commotion. "Where are you?"

"Northern and Seventh Street."

"Stay there! Call the police. Don't lay another hand on Coffman. Just sit tight. I'm on my way."

I pushed the end button and tossed my phone on the passenger's seat as I took the entrance ramp onto the highway. I'd told Tony to never chase a fleeing subject, yet he runs after him with his car? We don't chase people with cars. Tony had just violated most of the department's policies on making an arrest. And he wasn't even supposed to be working alone. For goodness' sakes, he was out buying coffee. He didn't have his gear. Not to mention the bazillion safety violations he'd racked up.

I was pretty worked up by the time I arrived at the intersection.

Three squad cars surrounded Tony's Kia in the Circle K parking lot. I pulled up behind them and held out my badge as I approached on foot.

Someone had kicked out the rear passenger window of Tony's car, and glass littered the ground. Tony waved me over as he talked to one of the cops. Coffman sat on the curb, hands cuffed behind his back while an officer stood guard. When he saw me, he spat on the ground. "I'm suing you and your fucking rookie."

I rolled my eyes. Damn. I was going to have to get a bigger jar.

A female cop intercepted me before I made it to Tony. "You his training officer?"

As much as I didn't want to claim him, I nodded.

"I don't envy you," she said. "He's a bit gung ho. Granted, Coffman's a jerk, and he has an outstanding warrant, but he claims your boy hit him with his car, then jumped him."

I cringed.

"Thing is," she said. "There's a dent on the car that backs up Coffman's story. No witnesses, though. Gonna give your boy the benefit of the doubt, but I'm not saying it won't come to charges later on."

If she called him "my boy" one more time, I'd scream. "I understand," I said.

"Oh, and this might interest you. Coffman has a wad of cash I've only seen on drug dealers and strippers."

"Great." Coffman was on supervision for selling meth. He'd been doing better but must have returned to his old tricks. I'd address that with him next time we talked.

The cops took Coffman away, leaving me with Tony, who was still amped up. "Meet me at the office," I said. Dealing with Tony was now Alma's job. I was done.

"What?" he said. "No, good job, Tony. No fist bump? I caught a wanted fugitive."

I bit my lip. Best not to get into it with him on the street. Not with witnesses. Besides, this was higher than my pay grade. Alma could handle it. "I'll see you there. Don't stop for anything."

I left him standing there with his mouth hanging open and hurried back to my Jeep.

Chapter Eight

Inside Alma's office, I closed the door behind me and leaned against it. "Tony's got to go," I said. "And if you disagree, you need to find a different training officer. I'm done."

Alma gave me a blank stare. "Don't you ever have good news?"

I threw myself on the sofa and cradled my head in my hands. "He chased down one of my guys on warrant status, bumped him with his car, tackled him, and stuffed him in the back seat of his personal vehicle before calling me. He wasn't even on duty."

"You're kidding." Alma stood and paced the room. "Did he hurt the client?"

"Don't think so, but Coffman's threatening to sue us."

"What did the police do?"

"About Tony? Nothing yet, but they aren't making any promises about his future with them."

"That's just great." Alma collected her hair on top of her head. "I needed this. I already have Lilian Harrison calling me from the hospital every hour. She wants your badge."

"Yeah, I figured."

"Please write up an incident report on Tony's latest misstep. And I still need one for the Harrison mess. About Tony, I'll notify Roxy and see what she wants to do."

I pushed off the couch. "I'm getting good at incident reports. Harrison's is done. Check your email."

I'd made it to the door, my hand on the knob, when Alma said, "Did you call the union?"

31

My shoulders sagged. "No."

"Wouldn't hurt."

I opened the door and walked back to my cube, feeling the weight of her words. I'd been through enough that I'd started to change my long-held stance that only guilty people needed the union. Things had gone so quickly when I needed them last time; the situation resolved itself before they could do me much good. But it had been slightly comforting knowing they were there for me. I just didn't want to become a frequent flyer.

As I approached the row of cubicles that made up Alma's unit, Tony was reenacting his takedown of Coffman to a crowd of fellow POs with most of them egging him on. He didn't have a clue. I almost said something, but then remembered that I'd washed my hands of the matter.

There was no way I'd be able to concentrate and write an incident report worthy of Tony's firing with this crowd. Scooping up my laptop, I grabbed my messenger bag and headed toward the door. Hopefully, the Joy and Jerski show wouldn't be playing when I got home, and I'd be able to get some work done.

All I wanted to do was go home, write my reports, and drown my sorrows in Diet Coke. But Detective Ramsey had other plans. His SUV boxed in my Jeep. He stood outside his vehicle, arms crossed, watching me approach behind dark sunglasses.

As I got closer, he picked two cups of coffee off the hood of his vehicle. "How about a break?" he said.

Talking to a detective about a dead client wasn't my idea of a break. And coffee was no Diet Coke.

I opened the rear door of my Jeep, laid my laptop and bag on the floor, and closed the hatch. I turned to face him. "What can I do for you, Detective?"

He tried to pass me a cup of coffee, but I waved it away. "Appreciate the offer, but I'm not a coffee drinker."

Ramsey shrugged and settled one cup back on the hood of his car. "Good thing I don't mind it cold. I drink gallons of the stuff. Don't see how you can live without it."

"I get my caffeine in other ways."

He nodded.

I leaned back against my Jeep and checked my watch. I'd hit afternoon traffic if I didn't leave soon. "Any news on Johnson?"

"Homicide."

No surprise there. "What happened?"

"He was shot in the back. Body was in such bad shape from being in the canal, it wasn't initially obvious."

I winced, remembering how decomposed his body was. I didn't know him well, but nobody deserved to die that way.

"You know anyone who'd want him dead?" Ramsey said.

I thought for a moment. "Johnson was a meth addict. Most of his friends were drug users and involved in the system. Nothing jumps out at me, though." But my business card suggested someone wanted the murder tied to me. "I'm sure you've heard of Diablo. They may have it in for me." I told him about the situation several months ago that started with a run-in with one of their members, Javier Ramirez, and how he might hold me responsible for his present accommodations at the Arizona Department of Corrections.

"Impressive," Ramsey said.

Not how I'd describe what had happened.

Ramsey took a sip of coffee, then placed his cup next to the one he'd brought for me. Withdrawing a notebook out of his pocket, he scribbled a few notes, then met my gaze. "Mind if I take a look at Johnson's file?"

I didn't see the harm in that. "Sure."

I led him back through the employee entrance, and we climbed the stairs to the second floor, where my cubicle was. Tony continued to hold court. One hard look from me, and he rushed back to his desk while the other POs dispersed. I knew how to clear a room.

Brian Johnson's file was in a pile of warrants I needed to write for clients who'd failed to report and I couldn't track down. Johnson had been AWOL for a while, and a recent trip to his last known address showed me the apartment was vacant.

I sorted through the files and pulled his from the middle of the stack. I couldn't let Ramsey take the file or make copies without a formal request, but I wanted to cooperate with his investigation. I opened the folder and laid it flat on my desk. "What do you need?"

"Whatever you've got."

"My notes are electronic, but clients fill out a form when they report. I keep those in the hard file." Brian hadn't provided a wealth of information. I read Ramsey the last address he'd given, which wasn't good. "He reported working at a taco place as a dancing chicken," I said.

Ramsey raised an eyebrow.

"Yeah," I said. "Who knew that was a thing."

"You ever verify the job?"

"I saw the chicken costume once when I did a home visit, but that was a few months ago. I left a message with his boss in an attempt to find him before I did the warrant, but I never heard from him. I read Ramsey the employment information, and he wrote it down.

"He have a girlfriend, family, anything like that?"

I paged through the file. "I don't believe so. His parents washed their hands of him because of his addiction. Far as I know, they're back east, and he hasn't had contact with them in years."

Ramsey made a few more notes, then closed the cover of his notebook and tucked it into his pocket. "Let me know if you remember anything else."

"Will do."

I tossed the Johnson file into the early termination pile. There were a few ways to get off probation early. The most common way was to complete all court-ordered conditions while staying out of trouble. Another way was to die, but that was a much less popular option.

I escorted Ramsey through the building, and we parted ways at our vehicles. Someone had shot Johnson in the back. It sounded like a hit to me, but I wasn't the one who had to figure out why he was killed or who did it. Instinctively, I reached for my phone to text Betz and see what he thought. Then it came back to me, my pledge not to complicate things. Divorce should be final, after all. I dropped the phone on the passenger seat and headed home.

Chapter Nine

Settled at my dining room table, I worked on the incident report about Tony and his cowboy antics. In my opinion, he was dangerous in a position of authority, and he should find a job that was a better fit. Wanna-be cops rarely made good POs. There was a law enforcement side to the job, but it was equally mixed with social work. It wasn't always easy to walk the tightrope between holding people accountable and cheering them on. Everyone struggled with it at times, but those who were more interested in kicking down doors and hauling people off to jail were no longer welcome in most law enforcement agencies. Even police departments were trying a kinder and gentler approach to keeping law and order, even if the media suggested otherwise.

I finished my report and electronically sent it to Alma. I hated to think of anyone losing their job, but Tony was a liability and needed to go before someone got hurt. Still, I was glad it wasn't my decision. One reason I never thought about going into management. But, if I had to be honest, it was mostly because I wasn't good at being politically correct. I called shenanigans when I saw the need. That didn't always go over well.

It was almost six o'clock when I powered down my laptop. Scooping the last bottle of Merlot off the wine rack, I headed to the kitchen, making a mental note that a trip to the wine shop would have to happen soon.

Holding my glass, I settled on the sofa and clicked on the TV, absently scrolling through the channels. I came to rest on the evening news. Suzy Vega stood beside a charming older woman, who seemed sympathetic, using a walker for support.

Suzy shoved her mic in the woman's face. "So, your grandson told you a probation officer ran him down with his car and tackled him on the street?"

Oh crap.

"That's right. He was no threat to anyone. He was simply walking home."

From a drug deal.

Suzy took her turn. "And your grandson went to jail while the probation officer went free?"

"That's what happened."

The camera zoomed in on Suzy. "Those same probation officers arrested another probationer yesterday, leading to an elderly woman being hospitalized with a broken hip." A video clip of Lilian Harrison leaving her house on a stretcher while me and Tony stood on the porch played. Then Suzy's face appeared large on the screen. She stared into the camera like she was challenging me. "I did a little digging. We at Channel 6 have learned that the male officer involved is in training, so the fault for any improper use of force lies mostly on the training officer. At this news station, we remain committed to the people. I pledge to stay on this story of abuse of power by the probation department."

The coverage went back to the anchor desk and the weather. I clicked off the TV and sent Alma a text. I hoped I would not be behind Tony in the firing line.

Chapter Ten

I was at the office by eight-thirty the next morning. Alma sat at her desk, Roxy was on the couch, and I leaned against the wall. Alma had texted me the night before asking that I show for an early morning meeting titled "damage control."

I probably got three hours of sleep.

"It seems Lilian Harrison has, over the past month, written several letters to Suzy Vega. She complained you weren't responsive to her pleas for help about her son. Vega claims she didn't put much stock in them until the unfortunate incident the other day," Roxy said. "The episode with Tony Romero yesterday has further stoked the fire."

I glanced at Alma. She nodded in encouragement.

I cleared my throat. "I responded to Lilian. Most times, she didn't remember what she'd complained about by the time I got there. And she called almost every day, several times. Even if this were my only case, I couldn't possibly be more responsive."

"And your case notes reflect that," Alma said. "We just want you to know what's going on since Vega has wind of this."

Roxy uncrossed her legs and then re-crossed them. "We've decided to let Tony go. Because his father's a manager with us, we thought it was only fair to alert him first. So, Tony probably knows. We asked him to be here at nine."

I checked my watch. So, any minute now. I didn't want to be here when the conversation took place. "You done with me?"

Roxy shook her head. "We want you to go through his caseload and see if

38

there are any problems. We trust you not to share this with your peers."

"Of course."

"Our information officer wants to talk to you," Alma said. She held out a sticky note, and I took it from her. Alma's tiny printing covered the paper with a phone number and a name.

"Okay."

"He'll make a statement to Vega. You're not to talk to the media," Roxy said.

"Got it."

Back at my cubicle, I busied myself with reading my email. Out of the corner of my eye, I saw Tony walk by, on his way to Alma's office. He stared hard in my direction, but I pretended not to see him.

About ten minutes later, Tony, followed by Alma, went back to his desk. From her directions, I could tell she was watching him pack. "You can't take that," she said. "Just personal belongings."

Tony sighed so loudly that I could hear him from my desk three cubicles away. I put my earphones on and turned up the song that was playing.

Tony's escort from the building was swift. I kept my head down. When he'd gone, I hurried to the empty conference room where I could get a good view of the parking lot. Closing myself inside, I stood by the window and looked through the slats in the blinds. Tony's father, Luigi, leaned against a black Toyota, arms crossed and a look of disgust on his face. Tony dropped a box in the trunk and got into the passenger's seat. Luigi looked up at the window and squinted. Before I could duck out of sight, our eyes connected. Then he turned back to the car, got in, slammed the door, and sped out of the lot.

So glad that was over.

I laid the sticky note Alma had given me on the table and gave the information officer, Don Street, a call.

"I looked at your case notes," he said. "I need you to tell me what isn't written down."

"It's all there. Eric generally reported when he was supposed to. There were no known violations until Wednesday, when I found him drinking at home. I'd planned to call the police to help with the arrest, but then the gun came out, and I had to act."

"Mr. Harrison says you didn't treat him fairly."

"Not true. I directed him to complete the conditions of his probation. Substance abuse treatment, community service, payments on his probation fees, that sort of thing. I went to his house more than I typically would for a client, but that was because his mother was constantly calling me to complain about him."

"Okay," Don said. "Got it. Your notes are very thorough, and I appreciate that. Makes my job easier. If you think of anything else, call me. Hopefully, this will all blow over when Vega realizes there isn't much of a story to work with."

Fingers crossed. I thanked him and disconnected.

My personal cell pinged in my pocket. I withdrew it and looked at the screen. *What are you doing tonight?*

Betz. My stomach flipped.

Why?

There's someone I want you to meet.

Huh?

No answer. I paced around the conference room table, holding my phone in my hand. My first thought? Betz had a girlfriend. Why on earth would he want *me* to meet her? I knew I should take the high road, but I felt sick to my stomach. My head told me that wasn't fair—I had no claim on him. My heart told my head to shut the hell up. Last time I saw Betz, he dangled a bit of hope that we could get back together. I'd acted like I didn't notice, but I thought about it all the time. Without a response from me, had he given up and moved on?

After five laps, I gave up and stuffed my phone back into my pocket. I had work to do.

Settled at the mess that used to be Tony's desk, I grabbed a legal pad and made a to-do list. It didn't surprise me that Tony was behind in most aspects of his job. I'd been working on time management with him since he'd started four months before.

I had a hard time concentrating, though, and checked my phone every few minutes, hoping Betz would get back to me. Who the heck did he want me to meet? And why did the thought that he'd gotten on with his life get under my skin? But my screen remained blank.

Two hours later, I had a three-column list of Tony's cases. One for warrants that needed to be completed, one for expirations that were overdue, and one for court reports. I accessed his calendar to see when he had his next office day scheduled. Tony directed half of his caseload to report in one day. I planned to cover that. It would be a long day.

Reports to the court were the highest priority—judges were sticklers for timeliness. I gathered those files with plans to stay up late to get the bulk of them done. I couldn't stand having a ton of work hanging over my head. As I stood, a torn piece of paper fell out of one file and fluttered to the floor. I picked it up. Suzy, followed by a local phone number.

Suzy wasn't a common name, not spelled that way. Hoping it was Suzy Homemaker, or Suzy anyone, as long as it wasn't Suzy Vega, I dialed the number.

"Channel 6 News," a cheerful voice said.

I hung up.

Why would Tony be talking to Suzy Vega? Was it before or after the episode at the Harrison house? On the drive back to the office that day, once I'd calmed down, I'd treated the situation as a training opportunity and told Tony about the department's information officer and how he would handle the press.

It wouldn't be the first time he'd ignored my tutelage, but it made me mad just the same. If he broke the policy and spoke to Suzy while he still had a job, what would he say now that he'd been fired?

A quick trek to Alma's office and her dry-erase board told me she'd be in meetings the rest of the day. Back at my desk, I sent her an email detailing what I'd found, along with a plan to get Tony's work done, or at least cover the emergencies.

With my laptop in my bag, I headed home, praying I'd have the house to myself.

Chapter Eleven

After stopping at the grocery store and stocking up on Diet Coke and Merlot, I turned down my street. Betz's black 4Runner sat at the curb. My heart galloped into gear.

There didn't seem to be anyone in the SUV. If he was inside the house, that meant Joy was home and had let him in. Crap. Double crap.

With resolve to be nice and welcoming to Betz's new "friend," I pulled into the garage, grabbed my shopping bags, and entered the house through the kitchen.

A tan ball of fur bounced against my legs, causing me to stumble. The dog barked, sniffed, thumped its tail, and its nails clacked on the tile floor. A dog circled between my feet and tripped me. I crashed into the counter before the dog scampered back into the living room.

What the hell?

Last time I checked, I didn't have any pets.

If my wine bottles broke, there'd be hell to pay. Cute or not.

I left my groceries on the counter and headed to the living room.

Betz and Joy stood talking. A dog zipped around the room like someone was chasing him.

Betz smiled when he noticed me. Cute himself. No girlfriend on his arm. Thank God.

"Is this who you wanted me to meet?" I said, watching the dog stop to scratch himself.

"Casey," Betz said. "Let me introduce you to Felony."

"Felony?"

"Some patrol guys found him and a few others in a dumpster. Can you believe that shit? Anyway, they named him. You should see Miss Demeanor."

I scanned the room for the "others" and was comforted to only find one dog.

"So, you brought him here?" My voice squeaked.

"We talked about you getting a dog."

"No. *You* talked about me getting a dog. I remember saying it was a bad idea."

"But he's adorable," Joy said. "And you need a companion, what with being single and having no friends."

I rolled my eyes. Damn. Another dollar for the jar.

"Give it a try," Betz said. "If it doesn't work out, I'll take him after Jasmine moves out. She's allergic."

"And when is she moving?"

"Soon," he said.

He'd been saying that for months. "I don't have time for a dog."

"Sure, you do," Joy said. "Like I said, no friends."

She obviously didn't know how cranky I was with all the crap at work, or she'd be smart enough to keep her mouth shut. But I couldn't commit assault in front of a cop, ex-husband or not.

"I took Felony to the vet," Betz said. "Seems to be some kind of Cocker Spaniel mix. He's had shots, a bath. Besides, you could use some protection after that whole Diablo thing."

He didn't have to remind me that Diablo wanted me dead; it was never far from my mind. It didn't matter that most of them were behind bars. There was no shortage of them. "Doesn't look like much of a guard dog."

The Cocker Spaniel in him was endearing, yet something seemed off. His snout stuck out a little too far, his curly ears were too short, and his skinny legs were lanky. Of course, he was a mix. No one would throw a purebred in the dumpster. They were worth too much.

Felony laid on his back and wiggled like he had an itch he couldn't reach. Didn't look like he had much going on in the smarts department. And he didn't appear traumatized by being abandoned.

"Still, he'd bark if someone came to the door like he did when you came home," Betz said.

An alarm would probably be easier…and cheaper. And it wouldn't have to be walked and fed. But then Felony sat up and cocked his head like he was waiting for my reply. That face could melt an iceberg.

I could have said no to Joy and even Betz. But those sad puppy eyes? Not playing fair. "For a while," I said. "But I want you to look for a permanent home." I doubted his allergic sister Jasmine would go anywhere anytime soon.

"I can do that," Betz said.

Joy bent down and patted Felony on his head. "Okay, little man. I'll see you later. Auntie Joy has a date."

Of course, she did. "With Jer—I mean, Pete?"

She held up her hand and wiggled her fingers. "Nope. Until this hand has a ring on it, I'm playing the field and keeping my options open."

Why did it sound normal when she said it, yet I felt like a jerk for being interested in two men?

Once she left, Betz stuffed his hands in his pockets and rocked back on his heels. "How've you been?"

I shrugged. "Work's crazy. In fact, I have to write a few reports tonight."

"So, no time for dinner?"

I held back a groan. Saying no to Betz equaled turning down a piece of chocolate cake. Both sweet and delicious, but I'd feel like crap afterward if I indulged. My promise to keep my hands off him protected him as much as me. Neither of us needed to go through the agony of breaking up again, and I understood that would be unavoidable. That didn't mean I wasn't tempted. After the week I'd had, I could really use some love.

I hemmed and hawed so much that Betz got the message without me answering. "Another time," he said. "I'll grab the supplies from the car. Be right back."

Felony ran to the screen door, and, butt wiggling, watched Betz walk to his car. He had already become attached to him. "I feel you," I said.

Betz returned with a twenty-pound bag of dry food, bowls, a dog bed, and a leash. He placed everything on the dining room table and handed me a folder. "His shot records. You'll have to mail in the rabies stuff for his tags."

"Tags? This is getting serious. Not sure I'm ready for a commitment."

"Don't I know it." Betz patted Felony on the head, smiled at me, and walked out the door.

I turned to the dog, who looked at the bag of food and barked. "Oh, so that's how it's gonna be?"

I fed Felony, ate a sandwich, and took the dog for a walk around the block.

Back at the house, I set his bed on the floor and settled on the sofa with my laptop and the files for Tony's reports. Felony took one look at the bed and jumped onto the sofa, snuggling up beside me.

I pointed to the floor, about to yell at him, when he looked up at me with those puppy eyes again. "That's not fair," I told him. I would have to lay down some ground rules. Tomorrow would be soon enough, I thought, as I pet him.

Chapter Twelve

The night stretched out endlessly. Felony had no interest in his bed on the floor, crying his tiny heart out and pawing at my side of the bed instead. Eventually, in my sleep-deprived state, I pulled him into bed with me sometime around three in the morning. His favorite place to settle was on my head. I woke more than once to a mouthful of fur. A few hours later, I woke alone. Panicked, I sat up and grabbed my phone. Switching the flashlight on, I swept its beam around the room.

I spotted Felony, assuming the pee position over my running shoe. Before he could deliver, I bolted out of bed, scooped him up, and sprinted to the front door. Stepping outside, I settled him on the small patch of grass that made up my front yard. While Felony did his thing, I stretched and glanced about my neighborhood. The surrounding houses were dark as my neighbors got a good night's sleep. Lucky bastards.

Movement down the street caught my eye. I squinted and rubbed the sleep out of them and tried to focus. An engine started, and a motorcycle moved toward me. For a moment, I thought Marcus had arrived in the middle of the night, but not wanting to wake me. My heart fluttered at the thought of seeing him again. Then panic set in as I realized I wore my sleep shirt with no bra and morning breath. Not the way I pictured our reunion. But as the motorcycle drove slowly by my house, I realized things were much worse than that.

The rider kept his eye on me as he puttered by, pointing a finger gun at me and grinning as he pulled the imaginary trigger. *Yikes!* I recognized the emblem on his leather jacket right away. A pitchfork. Diablo. They were still gunning for me.

I grabbed Felony, crushed him to my chest, and hurried inside, locking the door behind us. At the living room window, I peered through the slats of the blinds. Taillights got smaller as the bike moved down the street and then disappeared when the driver turned onto the main road.

Message received—they hadn't forgotten about me.

Felony wiggled in my arms, alerting me to the death grip I had on him. "Sorry." I lowered him to the floor and grabbed the baseball bat I kept by the door.

In the kitchen, I turned on the light. The time was only a few minutes past five. A bit early for me, but it was impossible to go back to sleep in my rattled state. Diablo wanted me to be aware that they were watching me. They'd waited for me to spot them. Since the biker had left, there was no point in calling the police. I'd fill Betz in when it wasn't an ungodly hour of the day. He would tell me to get a gun. Usually, I scoffed at the idea, but the dumb luck that had kept me alive thus far couldn't last forever, and a baseball bat and a Cocker Spaniel-mix dog weren't the most reliable sources of protection.

The probation department didn't readily distribute guns. I'd have to go through the arming process. I didn't have that kind of time. I needed to buy one myself and ask Betz to teach me how to use the damn thing.

Having consumed two Diet Cokes, I felt prepared to tackle the day. It was Saturday, a day usually reserved for cleaning the house and running errands. It neared ten when Joy exited her room, stepping over the vacuum cleaner on her way to a hair appointment. Sorry for the inconvenience.

"Don't forget dinner at Kate's tonight," she said, stopping to give Felony a pat on the head before walking out the door.

Joy had bought a beater car, thinking she wouldn't stay in Arizona long, but needing transportation while she was here. She revved the noisy engine before pulling out of the driveway.

I finished vacuuming and tidying up the house, pausing every hour to take Felony out back, baseball bat in hand. So far, he'd only had one accident in the house. Since I didn't own a kennel, I closed him in my bathroom with a bowl of water and hoped I wouldn't come home to too much destruction. I was uncertain of his age, but assumed he was nearing the end of his puppy stage. Regardless, whoever left him for dead obviously hadn't bothered to house-train him.

I'd texted Betz earlier, and as I pulled out of my driveway, he got back to me. I put my earphones in and took the call.

"Had a surprise visitor this morning," I said. Then, I filled him in on Diablo's appearance in my neighborhood.

"We knew they wouldn't let it go," he said.

"Yeah, but over time, I was beginning to relax."

"You should get a gun."

"What, the Cocker Spaniel isn't enough," I said with a chuckle. "Actually, I wonder if you could help me with that."

"Really? You're finally coming around?" I couldn't miss the excitement in his voice. He did care about me.

"Desperate times call for outrageous measures."

"Desperate measures."

"Whatever. Anyway, can you help?"

"I've got the perfect gun for you," he said. "How about we meet for some target practice, and I'll get you all set up?"

"Sounds good. I'm headed to the pet store now."

"How did Felony do last night?"

"He slept on my face."

Betz laughed. "Means he loves you."

"Yeah, well… Keep looking for a home for him."

"Sure. Come by after the pet store?"

"Okay. See you in a few." I hung up and stored my earphones in their case. My heart thudded in anticipation of spending time with Betz. I hoped his sister wouldn't be there. I didn't feel like dealing with her judgment.

The pet store parking lot was packed. Inside, I wandered the aisles. Who knew there were so many fun things available for our furry friends? Before

I even made it to the wall of kennels in the back, I had my arms full of toys, treats, and a little Cardinals jersey that was too cute to pass up. The variety of kennels was too much to take in. I opted for a hard plastic one that would be easy to assemble.

Whoever became Felony's forever owner would at least have a head start.

Stuffing the items inside the crate, I picked it up and started toward the cash registers up front. A woman rounded the corner and collided with me.

"Watch where you're going," she said before I could even meet her eyes.

I gathered a comeback, but before I could deliver it, I stared into the face of Suzy Vega.

"You," she said.

"You," I shot back.

She cleared her throat. "Got a new puppy?"

What gave that away? "Yes." I side-stepped her.

"Wait." She put her hand on my arm. "How about I buy you a cup of coffee?"

"Ah, no thanks. If you have questions, you need to go through the information officer."

"I'm doing a piece on law enforcement brutality," she said, following me. "Your name just keeps coming up. I want to give you the opportunity to give your side of the story."

My jaw dropped. I toyed with the idea of asking her if she'd talked to Tony and if he was contributing to her piece, but Alma's warning not to talk to her flashed like a neon sign in my brain. "Excuse me. Gotta go."

I hurried to the pay station and took several glances over my shoulder as I completed the transaction. Thankfully, Suzy had disappeared back into the store.

In my Jeep, I practiced deep breathing, flexing my hands open and shut. I sat there, waiting until Suzy exited the store with a bag of cat food. She got into a sporty red convertible and drove off. I didn't know why, but I felt compelled to follow her. She knew a lot about me, yet I knew next to nothing about her. Seemed like a good opportunity to level the playing field.

I followed her toward the freeway. As we came to the entrance toward Phoenix, I wrestled with the idea of staying on her tail. Betz's house lay straight ahead, and he was expecting me. But Suzy took the west on-ramp, and I did the same. Just a few exits, I told myself. If she kept going, I'd get off and loop my way back.

But she took the next exit.

The light caught me, and I had to wait while she drove toward South Phoenix. Heavy traffic caused me to lose sight of her. When my turn came, I took a left and got back into the turn lane for eastbound Interstate 10, hitting another red light.

The overpass provided me a view of the buildings on the other side. One of them, a seedy bar. Next to a cluster of Harleys was Suzy's parked car. My throat tightened. Had she led me straight to Diablo? If so, did Suzy meet with them concerning me, or was it merely a coincidence? They could have had a killer Ruben sandwich, for all I knew.

The left turn arrow flashed green, and I had no choice but to get back on the freeway and drive toward Betz's house. My hackles were up. What was Suzy up to? But the last place I wanted to be was anywhere near Diablo. I had to let it go.

Chapter Thirteen

I pulled up to Betz's stucco two-story on the Ahwatukee side of South Mountain. Jasmine was out front, pruning the bushes under the living room windows.

Great. I cracked my neck and got out of my Jeep. "Hi." I tried to sound cheerful, like it was good to see her.

Jasmine turned to look at me, shears bouncing in her hand. Her narrow-eyed stare told me how happy she was to see me. "Casey," she said, curtly.

So, we weren't going to pretend. "Betz inside?"

She nodded and watched me walk past her to the front door. I pressed the bell and waited, my back to Jasmine. Her continued gaze burned a hole in the back of my skull.

I suppressed the urge to explain myself to her, remembering her lecture about my relationship with Betz several months ago. In fact, I often replayed it in my mind. But I wasn't here to mess with her brother's heart. I only wanted to learn to better protect myself.

Just when I couldn't stand the silence anymore, the door swung open, and Betz ushered me inside.

"She hates me." I followed him into the dining room, where several handguns lay on the table.

Betz shrugged. "Nah. She likes you; she's just looking out for me."

"Whatever."

"Anyway." Betz motioned to the guns. "I have a few possibilities. These are nineteens. Good for your small hands."

I held out my hands and inspected them. "My hands aren't small."

Betz held up his and pressed them against mine. A tremor rushed down my spine at his touch, but I saw his point. "Okay."

He dropped his hands. "I like the Glock." He racked the slide and showed me that the chamber was empty and there was no clip in place; then he handed me the gun. I balanced it in my hand.

"How does it feel?"

"Like a lot of responsibility."

"Are we doing this or what?"

I let my finger inch toward the trigger but didn't touch it. "Fine, I guess."

He took the weapon from me and packed it and the others on the table into a duffle bag. "We'll head to the desert. I know a great place for some target practice."

I followed him to the garage, where we got into Betz's 4Runner. Jasmine watched us back out of the driveway and pull away; her gaze reeled me in like a fish on the line that she couldn't wait to gut. I broke contact and studied my cuticles.

"How's Felony?" Betz asked as we started down the street.

I cleared my throat. "He's a monster."

Betz laughed. "Yeah, right. He's growing on you, isn't he?"

"Well, I just dropped a hundred-and-fifty bucks at the pet store, so what does that tell you?" Then I told him about my run-in with Suzy Vega and my thinking that she was in contact with Diablo.

"Hmm," Betz said. "They do hang out there." Deep in thought, he tapped his chin. "Wonder what she was doing there. She's no biker chick."

"She told me she was doing a story on law enforcement brutality. Maybe she's interviewing Diablo about me." I was once the target of a lawsuit filed by a gang member saying I'd assaulted him. The lawsuit was dropped, but the accusation might be brought up again. It would be great for Suzy's story.

Betz rubbed the back of his neck. "If she's stirred that pot, it would explain why they started checking on you. I'm glad you're getting a gun."

My stomach rolled, but I forced a smile. "Yeah, just hope I never have to use it."

"That's always the hope," Betz said. "But it's good insurance."

He turned off the paved road and onto a dirt path. The rutted trail jarred me, forcing me to hold on to the dashboard. We drove about a half-mile and came to a stop in front of a hill that would serve as a backstop for the rounds we were about to fire.

Betz supplied me with earmuffs and clear glasses and fitted me with a holster. Then he went over and over the range rules, testing me and making me repeat them back to him. This felt like school. It wasn't fun. An hour passed, and we hadn't even fired a round. I was hot and cranky; sorry I'd agreed to this.

"Are you even listening?" he said, hands on hips.

I yawned. "When do I get to shoot the damn thing?"

Betz cursed under his breath. "Safety is the most important thing."

"Yeah, I got that."

"Okay." He led me back to his vehicle. "Let's get some ammo."

"Yippee," I said without enthusiasm. I checked my watch. Still a few hours before Kate expected me, and I was a hot mess. I'd need to shower.

Betz showed me how to load the magazine, and then we holstered our weapons. I waited while he tacked a target to a wooden structure that someone had left behind for that purpose. The spent shells at my feet told me we weren't the only ones to use this spot for target practice.

While Betz stood behind me barking orders, I withdrew my weapon, checked my sights, and then, as instructed, slowly pulled the trigger. The first bang startled me, but as Betz talked me through, step-by-step, I relaxed. It started to be fun. Until I thought about my mother meeting her fate at the hands of such a weapon. I shook off the thought and tried to stay in the moment.

Once I emptied the magazine, Betz had me check my surroundings and holster my gun.

We walked forward, checking the target. No tight groupings, but at least I hit the silhouette—mostly in the gut, a few times in the shoulder. No kill shots, but it would get a bad guy's attention. Betz counted the holes twice, then scratched his head. "You missed one."

"Bullshit."

Betz sighed. "You're ornery. We should call it a day. We can try again tomorrow."

I rolled my eyes. "No way. I have things to do."

"I want you proficient if you're gonna carry."

"Next weekend. I can only take so much of this."

We stored our gear and picked up a bunch of spent rounds, leaving the area better than we found it. Betz secured the Glock in its case and handed it to me. "I hope I don't regret this. I'd like you to take a class before you carry concealed but keep it at home. I'll bring a gun safe by tomorrow for you to store it. Don't let Joy near the thing."

I gave him a mock salute and took control of the box. As we drove back to Betz's house I struggled to right my sour mood. I couldn't believe it had come to this. I'd always hated guns, and when my mom met her fate at the hands of one, my revulsion grew even stronger. I saw firsthand how they tore families apart. And I loathed knowing I had enemies out there who might encourage me to use the damn thing.

Back at the house, I thanked Betz for his time and then headed home for a quick shower before dinner at Kate's.

I placed the boxed gun into my nightstand drawer before opening the bathroom door. Felony was passed out on the floor on a pile of shredded toilet paper. My shampoo bottle and toothpaste tube were almost unrecognizable, and a mixture of the contents made the floor slick. One step in the room, and I was flat on my ass.

Felony woke and his nub of a tail wagged so hard his backside wiggled as he climbed on top of me and licked my face.

"You should be embarrassed," I said as I lay in the muck and let him have his way with me. Mess aside, no one had ever been this happy to see me. I was starting to see the appeal of pet ownership. Damn, Betz.

Chapter Fourteen

An hour later, I'd cleaned up the bathroom and Felony and I had showered. I dressed in my usual—jeans and a T-shirt—thinking my wardrobe needed an overhaul. But every time I tried something different, I felt too conspicuous, like lights on a Christmas tree—like Joy. Felony wore his one and only top, the Cardinal's jersey. I didn't care much about sports, but I knew my dad would get a kick out of it.

At Kate's house, I handed her a bottle of wine and tried to check my bad mood at the door.

My niece and nephew shrieked with excitement at seeing Felony. I left them in the great room, playing tug of war with his new rope toy, and joined my family in the kitchen. My dad sat at the table, nursing a mixed drink. My cousin Hope stood at the counter chopping tomatoes, and my brother-in-law, Kevin, seasoned steaks. Joy had yet to arrive. "She bringing a date?" I asked, sidling up to Kate.

"She's bringing someone," Kate said. "Didn't say it was a date."

"I don't think she talks to people unless she can date them." I picked a carrot off the vegetable tray Kate was preparing, and she smacked my hand.

I pulled back and took a bite.

Kate shrugged and set to work opening the wine. Once I had a glass in hand, I went over to my father and gave him a peck on the cheek.

"What's with the bruise?" he said.

I reached up and rubbed the spot, flashing back on the struggle with Eric Harrison. I'd applied makeup to cover the mark, but obviously didn't do a good job. "Just a minor incident at work." My dad was a widower, and he didn't get out much. He never watched the news, and I didn't see the point in alerting him to the series of mishaps that was my life. I got the grumpy gene from him.

I crossed to the counter, where Hope pushed sliced tomatoes into a bowl piled high with field greens. I wrapped my arm over her shoulders. "Have a minute?"

Hope wiped her well-manicured hands on a towel. "Sure."

She followed me outside, where we sat on welcoming patio furniture. I sipped my glass of wine while Hope nursed a bottle of water. She was on probation. No alcohol. "How are things going?" I asked.

She tilted her face to the sun and closed her eyes. A year older than me, she had a certain elegance that seemed to end with her in the gene pool. Kate had it, too, although she was more conservative. I was the plain Jane in the family, while Joy was a billboard for Mardi Gras. "I'm hanging in there," she said. "It's been a lot to come back from." She was referring to her entanglement with Diablo, subsequent arrest, and loss of her job as a PO. It seemed unfair that she faced criminal charges for the whole mess, but she had financially benefited from Diablo's crimes. In her eyes, she felt lucky she'd dodged a prison sentence with probation.

"Kate says you're testing to become a counselor," I said.

"I already took it. I'm waiting for my score. I majored in counseling; thought I should use it. And I have a job offer."

She'd been working part-time at a fabric store, and it wasn't her thing. "Do tell."

"It's for a treatment provider. They work with addicted youth and have a wilderness program. It shows kids that a natural high is better than anything they can get from drugs."

"That sounds interesting." Although I couldn't picture Hope in the woods, I got that she wanted to reinvent herself. "Good luck."

"I'm excited."

The screen door opened, and Kevin went to the grill with a tray of steaks. Hope got to her feet. "Better get back to helping Kate."

I firmly believed that people were more than the poor choices they sometimes made. And Hope had made some doozies. But I knew she was a good person, and she'd been quietly putting her life back together. I respected her for that.

I rose and followed her inside.

We'd just finished setting the table when the side door blew open, and Joy flounced into the room. She held the door with her hip, balancing a sheet cake in her hands. Glancing over her shoulder, she laughed. A woman came in behind her, teetering on skinny heels. Dressed in a silky, pink flamingo-covered halter top and flouncy skirt, her waist-long highlighted golden blonde hair belonged on a woman half her age. Pursed smoker's lips and sagging skin under her eyes told the truth.

The woman walked past Joy and set a casserole dish on the counter. Sweeping hair out of her face, she took in the room.

Joy let the door slam shut. "Meet Millie. Uncle Albert, I just know you're going to love her!"

Oh God, this was going to be good.

If I hadn't known my cousins' mother, I would have thought Millie had birthed Joy. Although they looked nothing alike, their style was the same. Both had that bat your eyes and giggle way about them that made me want to scream.

Millie went right to work on my dad, sliding an empty chair so close to him, she practically sat in his lap. My father had a frightened deer-in-headlights look on his face. He gulped his drink and mouthed *Help me!*

"Hey, Dad," I said. "Can you give me a hand outside for a moment?"

He jumped to his feet, almost knocking Millie to the floor as he adjusted his golf pants, left the table, and followed me.

Outside, he grabbed my arm and steered me toward the back gate. "Let's get out of here."

I laughed. "We're not sneaking off. You just have to set some boundaries."

My dad had been a widower for just over a year. Retired, he spent his days watching game shows and drinking whiskey. Too much whiskey. I worried about him being so lonely, but even I wasn't ready for him to date.

It felt wrong to replace my mom so soon. And Millie wasn't his type. She was Joy's.

He took my chin in his hand and tilted it toward the sun. "What really happened to your jaw?"

"Oh, that." I squirmed out of his hold. "Just a little run-in with an uncooperative probationer." My mom had been the only member of the family who understood my line of work. Everyone else worried way too much, so I tried not to stoke that fire.

"I worked my entire career without a scratch on me," he said. "Don't know why you insist on putting your life on the line."

Not fair. He'd been an accountant. He didn't understand my need for frequent adrenaline rushes. Although I could do without Diablo, one thing I loved most about my job was that you never knew what was coming. No two days were the same. "I've decided to get a gun," I told him, hoping to make him feel better knowing I could defend myself. But just thinking about it made my skin crawl.

"About time," he said. "You know how to pick one?"

"Betz is helping me."

My father's face lit up. He loved Betz. Sometimes, I thought he preferred his company to mine, and I feared I'd lose my father in the divorce. "You two getting back together?"

"Nope. Just relying on his expertise. Come on." I took him by the arm. "Let's go inside and see if Kate needs a hand."

"Just keep that woman away from me," he said, begrudgingly falling into step beside me. "She's a tart."

At dinner, I slid into the seat next to my father before Millie could snag the spot. Grateful, my father squeezed my arm.

I grabbed the wine bottle and topped off my glass before passing it to Millie. She shook her head and waved her hands like I was offering her crack.

"I don't drink," she said. "I'm in recovery."

"Oh. Good for you." I passed the bottle in the other direction, and Joy gratefully took it, pouring herself a glass.

Millie eyed the tumbler of whiskey in my father's hand, judgment obvious. He leveled his gaze toward her, defiantly downing the remaining liquid. This match was doomed.

It was hard to have conversation of any depth, with two small children dominating the room. Dinner was complete chaos as my niece insisted on putting on a show, singing off-key and falling over her feet as she strutted around. A fight broke out when Ethan tried to one-up her. She whacked him on the head with the spatula she used as a microphone. Felony joined in the mix, and I had to chase him around the table to retrieve said spatula. Both kids joined in, cheering Felony on as he ducked out of my reach.

In the end, I left exhausted but happy that I had a place in a somewhat crazy family. I felt a step closer to my father, who had been slowly coming back to me since we'd solved the mystery of my mother's death.

At least my family took my mind off Brian Johnson's distorted face, Lilian's accusations that I was a bully of a PO, and Diablo breathing down my neck.

But as I drove away, I remembered that someone had stuffed my business card in the dead man's mouth, and tension returned, bubbling in the pit of my stomach like a bad burrito.

Chapter Fifteen

Monday morning came too soon. One thing about living with an untrustworthy dog, you don't sleep, not deeply at least. I constantly made sure that he was by my side and not running around my bedroom destroying things or peeing in my shoes. At first light of day, I felt him stir and I jumped out of bed and coaxed him to the back door before he could leave an unwanted present on the floor.

Yes, I'd bought a crate. No, I couldn't bring myself to make him sleep in it.

My phone pinged an early morning message. *Morning, Sunshine. Getting closer!*

My chest tightened at Marcus's words. This was really happening. *Safe travels.*

I liked Marcus. A lot. He was insanely hot, funny, and he kept me guessing. A girl could do worse. And trust me, I had. Not talking about Betz. There was no comparison—it'd be like comparing apples to a ceiling fan—they were so different. Betz was law and order, and Marcus flirted with the dark side like a drunk businessman in a hotel bar. He tried to toe the line, but it seemed like a struggle for him sometimes. A bad boy fighting his natural path. Not sure I had the energy to rein him in.

But his kiss! It ignited a fire in me that still smoldered all these weeks later.

If we were going to have a shot at a relationship, I needed to get my life in order. He'd seen me at my worst last time he was in town. I didn't want him thinking I lived in a constant state of chaos, even if partially true.

Not to mention, Diablo had it in for him too. I'd warned him coming back to the valley might be bad for his health, but he was undeterred.

Booting up my computer, I settled in front of it with a Diet Coke and a banana. A maps app told me it was about thirty-six hours on the road between New Jersey and Phoenix. The calculator on my phone told me the trip would take him about three days at the rate he was going. One of those days had already passed. Did I have time to get it together? Doubtful. But I'd try.

Dressed in my usual jeans and T-shirt, I slipped on my running shoes and lured Felony into the kennel with a trail of treats. His yipping broke my heart, but at least he and my possessions would be safe.

Traffic in Maricopa County started at dawn and pretty much lasted until evening. I needed to pack my patience, but sometimes, my drive was the only time I got to process what was going on in my life.

Calling Detective Ramsey to see if there were any recent developments on the Brian Johnson case was on my to-do list.

I had Eric Harrison's probation violation hearing that afternoon. That should be fun. I'd recommended revocation of his probation to prison. Not a decision I took lightly, but he pulled a gun on me. Still, I knew he'd fight it—nobody wanted to go to prison. Fine by me. That's what judges were for, to make the tough decisions.

Pulling up to my office, I spotted my client, Marjorie Wilkins, standing outside the front door, puffing on a cigarette. I waved to her as I drove by, circling around to the back of the building and parking in the covered lot out back. Marjorie didn't have an appointment, but I'd make time for her anyway. She was trying to get her act together. Sometimes, that was all I could ask for.

After checking in, I went to the lobby and called Marjorie back. Dressed in sweats with her hair slicked back with a headband, she looked like she'd just rolled out of bed.

"What's up?" I said once we were in an interview room.

Marjorie sighed and hung her head. "I'm not gonna lie. Things aren't good."

"What happened?" Last time I checked in with her, about two weeks ago,

Marjorie was thriving in sober living, attending substance abuse treatment, and was working closely with Child Protective Services to get her kids back after losing them to the state because of her drug problem.

Marjorie took a tissue from the box in front of her and wadded it in her hand. "My ex contacted me. I know I shouldn't have gone to see him. We've talked about this…"

I nodded.

"Anyway, we met up, and I ended up using with him. I stayed out past curfew, and now I'm on a thirty-day suspension from the house." Marjorie teared up and dabbed at her eyes with the tissue.

I leaned forward. "First of all, good job for coming in and telling me. I appreciate that."

"I screwed up everything. Now I'll never get my kids back."

"Hold on. Let's not jump to conclusions. We just have to figure out what to do to get you back on track. You're not the first person to relapse. It's not an easy road."

"It's just that I was doing so well."

"You were, and you can draw on that—remember what tools you used when things were going right. Your ex is a trigger for you. Let's start by figuring out what options you have if he contacts you again. Having a plan is half the battle."

We spent the next twenty minutes coming up with a list of more appropriate choices than meeting with negative influences and relapsing. With a referral to a shelter for the next thirty days and a directive to attend daily NA meetings, Marjorie seemed to feel better about her situation. "Thank you, Casey. I know you could have detained me for this."

I stood and walked her to the door. "Come on, we know this is a process. What did I tell you when we first met?"

She stopped and gave me her full attention. "As long as I'm honest with you, you'll do everything you can to help me."

"Exactly."

She pushed on the door, then paused before exiting. "I'm glad you were here and not that guy, Tony. He gives me the creeps."

So, I wasn't the only one who felt that way. "How do you mean?"

"Last time I came in, you were in court. He met with me and told me I didn't deserve to have my kids. Said I would screw up sooner or later."

"Sorry about that. But don't worry, you won't see him again. He no longer works here."

Relief relaxed Marjorie's face. "Thanks, Casey. For everything."

"Of course," I said, pulling the door shut behind her.

I'd seen lots of POs come and go over the years. It wasn't unusual for a probationary employee not to make it to permanent status with the department. In the few instances where I'd been involved, more reasons for letting someone go always cropped up after they were gone. So was the case with Tony. I'd found that out when I went through his files.

It angered me that he'd spoken to Marjorie that way. POs held a lot of power over people's lives. Getting them to buy into the process was the first step toward success. That wouldn't happen with threats.

Then, there was Tony's connection to Suzy Vega. Was he feeding her inside information? I had no way of knowing, but it was something to keep in mind.

Back at my desk, I placed a call to Detective Ramsey. "Any news on the Brian Johnson case?"

Ramsey cleared his throat. "Was about to call you. We found his backpack with a journal inside. Interesting stuff. You able to come by and chat about it?"

I swallowed hard. "Ah...sure." Did he want to see me because I was the only connection to Brian, or was there something in the diary about me?

"How's this afternoon?" he said.

"I have court at one. Can I stop by after?"

"That works," he said, and he disconnected the call.

I spent the rest of the morning recording notes in the system, submitting the reports I'd completed the night before, and returning phone calls. After a quick lunch at my desk, I changed into nice slacks and a button-down shirt. Court attire that I kept in my office. Switching my running shoes for ankle boots, I looked somewhat respectable.

The jail in Central Phoenix housed the courtrooms for probation violation hearings. I parked at a meter and sailed through security, finding the docket hanging outside the door. The Harrison hearing was listed for the one p.m. slot. I went inside.

I was a few minutes early and used that time to confer with Rita, the court liaison officer. "Eric Harrison is contesting your alleged allegations," she said. "But since he has new charges, the judge will most likely set the violation hearing over to track with his new case."

"Who's the defense attorney?"

She shuffled some papers and pointed across the room with her chin. "Alice Koontz. She's new."

I took the seat at the table next to the county attorney, Ken Wonder. His name suited him as he looked like a doll. "Looks like this will be continued since he has new weapons charges pending," he said. "He pulled a gun on you, really?"

"And he was drinking." Failing to obey all laws and consuming alcohol were the only conditions I'd alleged. Somehow, he'd brought payment of his restitution and fines up to date, and he'd recently made a dent in his community service hours, showing he was making some effort. Violating the drinking term seldom led to custody time. The weapons allegation should. Still, since he had new charges pending today was a formality.

Harrison came out dressed in black and white stripes. Deputies led him to the defense table, where he sat next to Alice Koontz, who wore a power suit. They spoke in hushed tones while Harrison looked over his lawyer's shoulder and glared at me.

I wondered if he would have shot me if I hadn't disarmed him. The disdain on his face today had me guessing he would have. That thought made my stomach fold into itself.

Shortly thereafter, the clerk called the court to order, and everyone stood. The attorneys gave their names and bar numbers, before Ken asked that the probation violation case track with the new charges.

I tried to keep my attention on the judge, but Harrison's glare on me felt like a floodlight in my face.

"Next matter," the judge said after setting a new court date a month later.

"Can I say something?" Harrison got to his feet.

His attorney shook her head and placed her hand on his arm. Alarmed, the closest deputy stepped forward, but Harrison held his ground.

"Go ahead," the judge said. "But run anything you're about to say by your attorney first."

"She's part of the problem. I want a new lawyer. She's interfering with my freedom of speech. I also want a new PO. This one's been out to get me for months. I'm fearful of her, and I have the right to protect myself. And I'll be filing a civil suit against her."

Was he kidding? I looked to Ken for help, but he was checking his phone.

"The probation department can handle a request for a new PO," the judge said. "And you can file your motion for new representation." She stood and adjusted her robe. "Let's take a ten-minute break."

The deputy led Harrison away from the microphone and toward the holding room. I didn't like how they pulled me into this. Or that no one defended me or let me set the record straight.

Out in the hallway, I checked the time. It was a twenty-minute drive to the Tempe Police precinct where Ramsey worked. I had plenty of time to get there. I was almost to the exit when I heard my name. I turned to see Luigi Romero coming up behind me. "Got a minute?" he said.

My insides tightened. What did he want? Adjusting my messenger bag on my shoulder, I crossed my arms and waited.

"A heads up would have been nice."

"About what?"

"Tony. If there were kinks to work out, I could have helped."

"Sorry," I said. "Things got out of hand quickly. Did he tell you about Henry Coffman?" Other probationary employees didn't have the clout of having a father looking out for them. I didn't see why Tony should get special treatment, but I kept that to myself. I'd never had a problem with

66

Luigi, and I didn't want to start now.

"Yeah." He scratched his head. "He told me. I know his arrest of Coffman stretched the limits of our policy, but it was your job to teach him about that."

My eyes didn't even roll before bugging out of my head. Was he serious? "I did. He knew he wasn't cleared to act alone. Even if he was, we don't take such extreme measures, you know that. A probation violation warrant doesn't merit that kind of action. Henry wasn't a danger to the community."

Luigi crossed his arms. "We don't know each other well, but I know your reputation. You like to work alone. Maybe being a field training officer isn't for you."

I couldn't argue with that, but it didn't mean I hadn't done a good job. And I didn't like Luigi analyzing my work performance—something he knew nothing about. Like he said, he hardly knew me. "I understand you're upset, but I don't feel comfortable continuing this conversation. Tony's firing wasn't up to me, although I think it was the right move." I squared my shoulders. "You should address any concerns to my supervisor."

Stepping around him with false bravado, I walked out the door.

Chapter Sixteen

I waited ten minutes in the lobby of the homicide unit before Ramsey ushered me inside. "Sorry for the wait," he said before taking a sip from a to-go coffee cup. "Things are nuts around here."

I followed him down the hall to a cubicle at the back of a large room. The desks were mostly occupied, and the chaotic atmosphere jangled my nerves. At his desk, Ramsey pulled a metal chair up to the side and settled in his swivel chair. He balanced a small book in his hands. "Mr. Johnson kept a journal. Looks like it was an assignment given by his substance abuse counselor."

I took the empty chair. Not the first time I'd heard of that requirement.

"It starts out with typical stuff. Cravings, struggles with sobriety, ending old friendships with users, that kind of stuff. But then, toward the end, he talks about being in over his head, but he doesn't say why. Said he was thinking about confiding in you."

Was that why I was here? "He didn't."

"He said more than that." Ramsey leaned back in his chair and steepled his fingers. A coldness chilled his expression. "He wasn't sure he could trust you. Thought you might be in on it."

That didn't sound good. "In on what?"

"That was my question for you."

I tried to keep my expression neutral, but my face seemed to have a mind of its own, and my mouth dropped open. "You can't think…"

Ramsey shrugged. "I'm just telling you what his journal says. Did he ever talk to you about his mistrust of you?"

"No."

"Maybe he didn't get around to it in time. Anyway, he wrote about being followed. He was scared, and he didn't feel safe. Any idea who would be after him?"

Gut punch. If he had told me, could I have helped him and avoided his murder? "No, no idea."

But as I spoke, I remembered something. At our last office visit, Brian had told me he was nervous. He felt like someone was after him. Chalking it up to meth-induced paranoia, I'd asked him to submit a urinalysis. Never got the chance to follow up and tell him the UA was negative and explore if the threat was real. "Um, let me review my notes. There was something... He was worried about being followed. I remember not thinking much of it at the time."

Ramsey nodded. "That would be helpful."

I ran my hands over my thighs, rocked forward, and stood. "Anything else?"

"Not at the moment. I appreciate you coming in. How's Betz these days?"

His question blindsided me. "You know Betz?"

"Went to the academy together."

Okay...but I never took Betz's name. So, how did Ramsey know we were married? Were they that close?

As if reading my mind, Ramsey added, "I looked into you. I know you two were a thing."

Looked into me? I cleared my throat and picked my messenger bag off the floor. "He's fine. I'll tell him you said hi."

Ramsey chuckled. "He'll get a kick out of that, I'm sure."

Feeling unsettled, I followed Ramsey to the exit. My work cell buzzed in my bag as I climbed into my Jeep. Marjorie. I answered on the first ring.

"Hey, what's up?"

"I'm sorry, but I can't stay at the shelter."

I fastened my seatbelt and got the AC going. "Why not?"

"Someone's following me." *Not her, too.*

"Why do you think that?"

"A car kept circling the block as I walked to the building. Then they drove by real slow."

"Maybe they were looking for the address?"

"I don't think so." The fear in her voice was hard to ignore.

"Could you see the driver?"

"The windows were tinted."

I aimed the vent at my face, and warm air choked me. "Who would follow you?"

"I don't know. But it's the second day it happened."

"Where are you now?"

"About a block from the shelter. Hiding in an alley. The car just went by again, but I don't think they saw me."

Maybe Brian Johnson wasn't meth-paranoid, but Marjorie could be. She'd admitted to recent use. Still, I knew forcing her to stay in a place where she didn't feel safe would backfire. And after what happened to Brian, I wanted to be extra careful. "Do you have somewhere else to go?"

"I have a friend…. She's clean, I swear."

"Okay," I said. "Text me the address and check in with me once you get there. Come see me tomorrow. We'll figure something out."

"Thank you, Casey."

"Sure thing," I said. "I appreciate you keeping me updated. Remember our chat this morning and make wise choices, okay?"

"I will." She disconnected.

I stared at my phone, processing our conversation, then headed back to the office where I'd go through the case notes on Brian Johnson.

Chapter Seventeen

S itting at my desk, I cleared my voicemail, then logged into the system to check my case notes. Brian Johnson last reported four weeks ago. As I remembered, he hadn't looked so good that day. After leaving my office, he was supposed to knock out a few community service hours. I checked the Chronos. He had shown up. For the last time.

Subsequent phone calls and text messages from me to him went unanswered—a red flag that he had absconded supervision. Tony and I had gone to his last reported address, finding the apartment vacant. I'd planned to go to his employment as a last-ditch effort to make contact before I requested a warrant. I had it on my to-do list for the day his body was discovered. But then, there was no need.

I scrolled back through his previous file notes, stopping when I saw a chrono Tony had made about six weeks ago.

Guy's a total jerk. All proud because he went a few days without using. Told him I'd be watching him closely. He might get one over on blondie, but I'll hold him accountable.

Blondie?

Didn't he know I could see this? Or that the court or involved attorneys could request these notes? They had to be professional. Tony's father would probably say it was the fault of my poor tutelage; that I hadn't covered this. But I had. Even if I hadn't, some things were common sense—not that Tony had much of that.

The smidgen of guilt I felt over Tony losing his job evaporated. I emailed Alma, suggesting she check the chrono from that day. Because of Brian's murder, I assumed Roxy had already gone through the file, but she hadn't mentioned Tony's gaffe. She probably knew it would piss me off.

I left off the part about Brian saying he didn't know if he could trust me. That I could be in on it. In on what? Maybe I was in the dark, but Ramsey no longer found me credible. If he ever did.

I figured Ramsey would check in with Brian's counselor, the one who had asked him to keep the journal, but I didn't think I'd be overstepping if I did the same. I had a pretty good relationship with Marta at the treatment center, as I sent a good chunk of my clients to her. I found her in my contacts and placed the call.

"Hey, Casey," she said.

"How's it going, Marta?"

"I'm good. Business is booming, which isn't a good thing, but it pays the bills."

"I get it. Did you hear what happened to Brian Johnson?" It had been on the local news, so I knew I wasn't sharing anything confidential. I held back the part about my business card, though, as Ramsey hadn't shared that part with the press, thank God.

"One of my clients told me. So damn sad. He was putting in the work, such a waste."

"Yeah, that's how I feel. He wasn't a bad guy."

"There's going to be a vigil tomorrow night at the park across from the center if you want to come. His murder has hit the recovery community hard."

"I'll do my best to be there," I said. "I'm sure Detective Ramsey has contacted you, just wondering if you noticed any red flags when working with Brian the last few weeks."

Marta sighed. "I got a message to call that detective. It's on my to-do list today. Last time I saw Brian was about two weeks ago. I meant to call you last week before I realized he was dead. I didn't want to terminate him from the program, but he had four unexcused absences, which is the limit."

"He stopped reporting to me, too. Did he mention anything to you about being followed?"

"He did. You think that was true? That's who killed him?"

"Could be. I thought he was using again, but his last UA was clean."

"Same here," Marta said. "I'm going to mention to that detective that we had a problem with a client dealing at our site, which led to a few of our people overdosing. It was Fentanyl, though, not meth, which was Brian's drug of choice."

Poly substance abuse wasn't uncommon. Sometimes, addicts used whatever was available. "Not like he couldn't have switched. Anyway, I'm sure Detective Ramsey will look into it, do a toxicology report."

"That's true," Marta said.

"Did you ever catch the dealer?"

"Nope. But it seems to have stopped around the time Brian went missing."

"Well, that's good. I'll see you tomorrow night."

"Will be good to see you, Casey. Take care."

I spent the rest of the day at my desk, writing warrants on Tony's caseload and requesting Brian Johnson's death certificate to file a petition for early termination of his probation. It was just after six when I packed up to leave. The surrounding cubicles were empty as everyone had gone home for the day.

My laptop and Henry Coffman's file were in my messenger bag. I had his violation hearing in the morning, and it made sense to go directly to court from home. As I walked through the empty building, I heard the door to the stairs and then the outside door open.

I was only a minute behind, but when I got to the parking lot, no one was around. Strange, since I'd heard the door open. But there was another set of stairs that led to the basement. Maybe they changed their mind and went to the lower level.

It wasn't out of the ordinary for POs to work late, but the parking lot was empty except for my Jeep and the two county cars available for fieldwork. The sun had begun to set, and I squinted in the remaining grainy light, looking for signs of life. I was alone.

A chill ran down my spine, and I shook it off. I was probably overreacting, but with a murdered probationer, his killer on the loose, and Diablo mad at me, it was hard not to think the worst.

Hurrying to my car, I locked myself inside, wishing I'd set up the training I'd need to become armed.

Add that to my list of things to do.

The gun Betz had given me, locked up at home, wouldn't do me much good tonight. Arizona gun laws were pretty loose, and one didn't need a license or permit to carry. But Betz wanted me to have more shooting time under my belt before I lugged the thing around, which made sense.

Brian Johnson wasn't the first probationer I'd lost to violence. The risky lifestyles many of my clients led often put them in harm's way.

But my business card stuffed in Johnson's mouth flashed like high beams on a dark road—this time, it was personal.

Chapter Eighteen

I circled the block before pulling into my garage, making sure no motorcycle-riding vengeful gang members were watching my house. Passing through the garage and into the kitchen, I found Joy standing at the stove cooking something that smelled so delicious, it made my stomach growl.

"Please tell me Jerski isn't coming for dinner." Felony greeted me with a wagging tail and insistent licks. Dropping my bag on the kitchen table, I turned my attention to the dog before looking up at Joy.

She shook her spatula at me. "Jerski? You call him Jerski? That's not very nice."

I shrugged. "Fits most days." Crossing over to the stove, I peered over her shoulder and into the pan, where she stirred a mixture of tomatoes, basil, and garlic. "That looks good."

She shoved me aside with her hip. "You can have some, but it has to simmer for a while. Millie and Uncle Albert are coming over in a few."

"Together?" My dad *and* that woman from the other night? I tugged on my ear. I must have misunderstood.

"After you left, they got to talking. Hit it off."

"You're kidding."

"You know I'm psychic. I wouldn't have brought her over if they weren't a good match."

I'd forgotten about my cousin's self-proclaimed psychic abilities and how she hadn't been right about a damn thing so far.

The doorbell rang, and Felony strutted to the front door. Joy laid the spatula on the spoon rest. "That will be them."

I grabbed her arm. "Let me get it. We have to be careful about opening the door."

"Again?" she said. "I thought those mean gangsters you pissed off went to prison."

"Not all of them. We need to be extra vigilant for a bit."

Joy sighed and returned her attention to the sauce while I made my way to the front door. Felony had beaten me there, his butt wiggling with excitement. He probably would greet gangsters or family the same way—so much for Betz's promise of a guard dog.

I spied my father's bald head through the peephole. Behind him, Millie smiled. *Oh, boy.*

I opened the door and ushered them inside, scanning the street for Diablo before closing the door. They both fawned over Felony before giving me a second-rate hello. Fair. I didn't greet them with as much enthusiasm as Felony did.

"You have a lovely home," Millie said, taking in the room.

I looked over her shoulder at the living room, full of thrift store and garage sale finds. It had a cozy, lived-in look that suited me. I could count on one hand the number of times my dad had stood in the room. Since my mother died, he'd become a homebody, his only outings to the local bar or liquor store. I wondered what magic Millie had conjured up to get him out and about.

"Have a seat," I motioned to the sofa.

Millie sashayed her way over and settled her bouncy butt on the couch. My dad followed and sat down beside her. "Smells good in here."

"Dinner will be ready in a few," Joy said, entering the room. "Can I get anyone a drink?"

"Scotch, neat," my dad said.

Millie laid a hand on his arm. "Now, Albert, I thought you were going to take a break from the hard stuff."

My dad hung his head. "Water then."

Millie nodded. "Make that two."

Maybe Millie wasn't so bad, after all.

"I'll get it," I said, leaving the room.

Back in the kitchen, I scooped food into Felony's bowl and made sure he had fresh water. After depositing two glasses of water on the coffee table for my dad and Millie, I stepped out back and took a call.

Felony followed.

Marjorie.

"Hello?"

"I need your help," Marjorie said, out of breath and a hint of hysteria in her voice.

"Where are you?"

"At my friend's…. Someone…. Someone's outside. Oh, God, they're trying to get in."

"Call the police."

"The police? I'm calling you."

I struck my palm to my forehead. "I'm not the police. They can get there faster than me. Call them and call me back when they get there."

"Okay."

I hung up and paced. Felony watched me with curiosity.

I sat on the patio chair, my legs twitching with nervous energy. Felony lost interest in me and did a sniffing tour of the yard. A few minutes later, I took a call from an unknown number. "This is Casey."

"PO Carson?"

"Yes."

"Officer Ruby here. I'm with your client, Marjorie Wilkens, and her friend Bertha. They claim someone followed them home and was creeping around the yard. By the time I got here, no one was around, but there are pry marks on the back door the owner says are new. Ms. Wilkens is having a bit of a crisis. Not sure what I can do for her. Her friend plans to stay somewhere else tonight but can't bring your client along. I don't feel comfortable leaving her here alone, but I have to get back on duty. Anything you can do to help?"

I checked my watch. After seven. We had little housing available to us, especially for women. And definitely not after hours. We'd already tried the shelter, but Marjorie didn't feel safe there and was on suspension from the other housing we had. "I agree, she shouldn't be alone. Give me the address, and I'll head over." Hopefully, I'd think of something on the way.

I disconnected and returned to the living room where Millie was telling a story that had my father slapping his thigh doubled over in laughter. Happy tears streamed down Joy's face. "Sorry to miss out on the fun." And the mouth-watering aroma emanating from the kitchen. "But duty calls. I'll be back as soon as I can."

Joy gave a dismissive wave, and Millie continued with her story. They wouldn't miss me.

Only Felony seemed to notice I was still in the room. When I opened the door to the garage, the dog snuck past me and sat eagerly at the door to the Jeep. "Guess you can come." I took the leash off the hook by the door. "Let's put your guarddog skills to the test."

Chapter Nineteen

The drive to North Phoenix was smooth, with light evening traffic. Felony sat in the passenger seat, watching out the window like he wasn't sure he trusted my driving skills. He seemed used to traveling by car, though, so that was good.

Stopped at a light after exiting the freeway, I popped my Air Pods in and placed a call to Ms. Cody, an ex-client of mine who had a heart the size of Maricopa County. After battling addiction herself, her new mission was to help women in recovery. A few minutes of catching up, and I gave her the lowdown on Marjorie's predicament.

"You bring that poor thing over here. I just took an apple pie out of the oven, and I've got ice cream to top it off. Guestroom bed is ready and waiting for company."

"Thanks, Ms. Cody. You're a lifesaver."

I disconnected and pulled into a convenience store parking lot, where I entered my destination into my GPS before completing the rest of the drive.

The address Officer Ruby gave me belonged to a well-worn bungalow with territorial weeds and a chain-link fence that was caving in on itself. "You stay," I said to Felony as I exited the Jeep, locking the door behind me.

I picked my way over a broken concrete walkway and rang the bell. The windows were dark, but I spotted a flash of light as the curtains slightly parted. A moment later, the door cracked open, and a slice of Marjorie's face stared out at me.

"Just me," I said. "Why don't you step outside? I have a dog in the car, and I don't want to leave him."

"Let me grab my bag." Marjorie disappeared for a moment, then came out with a battered backpack slung over her shoulder.

Seated in the Jeep, with Felony moved to the back seat, Marjorie gave a heavy sigh. "Thanks for coming to get me. I've never been so scared."

"It's okay." I started the car. "I've got a safe place for you to stay tonight. Let's get out of here before that guy comes back. You can tell me exactly what happened on the way."

Marjorie darted nervous glances down side streets as we made our way out of the neighborhood. "So, here's what happened," she said as we turned onto the main road. "Bertha and I came home, and this guy pulled in behind us in the driveway. He had a crowbar in hand. We ran inside and locked the door. He tried the handle and then went to the back door, where he tried to pry the door open. I called you and then the cops. Bertha yelled that the police were on their way, and he took off. He was gonna kill us, I'm sure."

"How horrible," I said.

"Scared me half to death. I think it was the same car that's been following me."

I stopped for a light. "Did you give the officer a description of the car?"

Marjorie nodded. "We didn't get the plate. Just that it was a black sedan. Bertha was too scared to stay in her own house that night. I feel awful for bringing this crap to her door."

I checked my rearview mirror. No one was following. Hopefully, the patrol car scared them off. "Who do you think is after you?"

Marjorie worked her hands in her lap. "I have no idea. I didn't recognize them."

"Well, you should be safe at Ms. Cody's," I said. "But I want you to be extra careful until the cops figure this out. Don't go anywhere alone."

"No problem." She checked the side mirror and went ramrod straight. "Hey, that black car has been behind us for a while."

I glanced in my rearview mirror. Sure enough, a nondescript black four-door was on our tail. I switched lanes and slowed down, hoping it would pass us, but it also reduced its speed. Tinted windows concealed the occupants. My mouth went dry.

At the next side street, I took a right turn. The car continued on. The thing about Phoenix is that most streets are on a grid system. A trip around the block would take us back to the main road.

I took the next left. Halfway down the residential street, a car drove toward us. The same black sedan. I kept going, and we passed each other. From my side mirror, I watched the car do a three-point turn, and once again, it was on our tail. "Hold on," I said.

Marjorie gripped the grab bar in front of her, and I took a sharp turn back onto the main street, nearly missing a car already on the road. The blaring horn didn't unnerve me as much as the knowledge that we were being followed by a maniac with a crowbar.

My cell pinged in the cup holder. "See who that is," I said.

Marjorie scooped up the phone while I kept my eye on traffic. The sedan was back on the road, two cars behind us.

"Say's it's Betz," Marjorie said.

I held out my hand, and she passed me the phone. "Hey," I said. "I'm pretty sure I'm being followed."

"Diablo?"

That hadn't occurred to me. "Don't think so. But someone's been following one of my clients. I'm trying to take her somewhere safe, but this car keeps getting on my tail."

"Where are you?"

I sped up through a yellow light, noting the street sign. The black car ran a red to keep up with me. "Just passed Thunderbird. On Scottsdale Road."

"Are there busy businesses you can stop at?"

"Yeah. There's a grocery store." Without activating my blinker, I made a sharp turn into the parking lot. The sedan couldn't react quickly enough to follow me. "Okay, I'm parking."

"Hang on," Betz said. "I'll have a patrol car meet you."

I pulled into a spot and through to the next one, so I wouldn't need to back up if we had to make a quick exit. Marjorie twisted in her seat, nervously checking our surroundings, but I no longer saw the sedan.

"I think we lost them," I said once Betz came back on the line.

"They've dispatched a patrol car. Don't leave until they meet you."

I put my head back against the seat and exhaled. "No worries."

Marjorie had turned white. She was young, early twenties, but still looked like she might stroke out from fear. She pumped her legs up and down like they were motorized. I placed a hand on her arm. "It's okay. Police are on their way."

"I so want to use," Marjorie said.

"But you're not going to. I'm taking you to Ms. Cody's, and you're going to have pie."

"Pie?" she said.

"Pie?" Betz echoed, reminding me he was still on the line.

"Pie," I said. "We're going to calm the hell down and eat pie." A patrol car pulled to a stop in front of us. "Police are here," I told Betz.

"Okay," he said. "Call me when you get where you're going. Don't leave me hanging."

"Promise. And thanks."

"Anytime."

I disconnected and got out to meet the cop. He was an older guy, and he looked at me like I was an inconvenience, but he seemed to soften after I showed him my badge and filled him in. With a plan for him to escort us to our destination, I felt somewhat better. There were dozens of black cars on the road, and each sighting of one nearly gave me heart failure. But within ten minutes, Ms. Cody had us parked securely in her garage, so if our tormenter drove by, they wouldn't see my Jeep.

After texting Betz that we were safe for the moment, I went inside and joined Ms. Cody and Marjorie at the kitchen table where pie was being served.

I stared down at the plate in front of me, tore off a chunk of crust, and slipped it to Felony, who sat patiently at my feet. My adrenaline dump was dissipating, and my nerves were raw. I didn't need a sugar rush. "Can I get this to go?" I said. "It looks and smells delicious, but I don't have much of an appetite right now."

Marjorie seemed to find comfort in the food. Safer choice than meth.

Ms. Cody stood and took my plate to the counter, where she slipped my slice of pie into a plastic container. She added a second piece and snapped the lid shut. "You're lucky to have Ms. Carson as your PO," she said, placing the container in front of me before taking her seat. "She was fresh out of the academy when she was assigned to me. Worked with me until I got my act together, and that took some doing. Been clean ever since. What can I do to help you?"

When Marjorie didn't answer, I said, "Ms. Cody's an unofficial mentor. You can learn a lot from her."

"Tomorrow, we'll go to a meeting," Ms. Cody said. "Don't want this scare to knock you off track."

"Good idea," I said. "Just be wary of black sedans. Marjorie, does your ex drive a car like that?"

She dabbed the last crumb with her thumb and sucked it into her mouth, then pushed her plate away. "Last I checked, he had a red car, but that was a while ago."

Who, then? "I think it's okay for you to go to a meeting, but otherwise, I'd lie low for a bit. And if you see anything that makes you nervous, call the cops right away. Better to overreact than have something bad happen."

With assurances that they would be careful, I said goodnight and returned to my Jeep. I left my cell phone in the cup holder, and once I stopped at a light, I checked for messages. Four were from Betz.

I slipped on my earphones and called him back. "Everyone's safe," I said. "Marjorie's tucked away at an old client's house, and I'm on my way home. I sent you a text."

Betz cleared his throat. I just knew he was rubbing the back of his neck, a habit he had when he was worried about me. "I was actually calling to schedule our next session at the range. Want you comfortable with that gun."

I was ambivalent. Recent developments told me I needed to adjust my thinking about my hatred of guns. As much as I enjoyed spending time with Betz, doing so messed with my resolve to move on. With today practically in the books, Marcus was a day closer. That thought sent a shiver to my toes.

But I needed to devote some time to the range. "Don't have my calendar handy," I said.

"It's okay. I'm on my way to your place. I want to see that you're safe with my own eyes."

I rolled mine. "Not necessary."

"Not taking no for an answer. Plus, there's something I want to talk to you about."

He hung up before I could protest. I spent the rest of the drive trying not to panic every time I saw a black car. It would be almost impossible for whoever it was to find me in transit, and I doubted they knew where I lived. They were after Marjorie, not me. Still, it was a relief when I turned down my street and saw Betz's vehicle parked in front of my house.

I pressed the garage door opener and pulled into my spot, watching Betz exit his SUV and walk up the driveway from my rearview mirror.

He greeted Felony and then followed me through the garage and into the kitchen. The house was dark. No sign of Joy, and since my father's car was gone, I assumed he and Millie had gone home. I flipped on the light and went straight to the refrigerator, where I got us both a beer. I laid my phone on the countertop, and we stood with the counter between us.

Betz looked tired. There was stubble on his chin, and he was overdue for a haircut. Just the way I liked him. He took a tug of beer, then put his bottle down, and cleared his throat.

"You're scaring me," I said.

He laughed. "Your life was just in danger, and I'm scaring you?"

"You look so serious."

Betz rubbed his neck. "I don't know how to say this without freaking you out, so I'm just gonna spill my guts."

I took a gulp of beer. "Okay?"

"I miss you. I've never gotten over us…. You make me crazy, but I don't know…. Makes zero sense, but I'm happier when you're driving me nuts than when you're not around. Without you, there's a huge void in my life."

The lump in my throat almost choked me. "Betz—"

He held up a hand. "Let me finish. I don't need an answer right now. Don't even want one tonight because I want you to think about it…. Really think, like I've been doing for months—not that I want you to take months…. And don't say you don't have feelings for me because I can tell that you do. I can't stop thinking about you. I don't sleep. I've lost fifteen pounds because I have no appetite."

My heart dropped to my shoes. "That's what I do to you, and you want more of that in your life?"

He laughed. "Nuts, huh?"

Felony's bark from the other room startled me, and I seized the opportunity to escape the conversation for a minute. "Hold that thought. Felony needs to go out."

And I needed a moment to digest what Betz had just said. I headed to the back of the house and flipped the patio light on before sliding the back door open and stepping outside.

While Felony did his business, my heart galloped. Conflicting feelings bounced around my brain. Betz was the best thing that ever happened to me. Our divorce, only second to my mom's death, ranked in the "worst thing" category.

When Betz came back into my life a few months ago, his sister Jasmine had insisted that I stay away. That Betz's heart couldn't take me breaking it again—which was the only ending she could fathom. Kate had also voiced her opinion that we weren't a good match.

But this wasn't about them. This was about me and Betz. He was right. I had to think long and hard about rekindling what we once had. Rushing back into things wouldn't be fair to either of us.

Felony scratched at the door. I needed another minute—a month maybe—to even process what Betz had said. But he was waiting in the other room.

Back inside, Betz stood where I left him, but he held my phone in his hand. "Marcus?" he said. "I didn't realize…."

My heart tugged as I took my cell from him, glancing at the message. *Getting close. Excited to see you!*

Good God. Talk about timing. I held eyes with Betz. "It's nothing."

"Doesn't sound like nothing." He finished his beer and tossed the bottle in the recycle bin under the sink.

Suddenly chilled, I crossed my arms. "You can't be mad. We're divorced. I didn't know how you felt until just now. I was only exploring my options."

He raised an eyebrow. "He's from Jersey, right? Seems like a long trip to explore options. You have feelings for him?"

"I...I..."

Betz's face hardened, but he shook it off. "Never mind. I said what I came here to say. Think about it."

I followed him to the door. I wanted to touch him. To have him hold me in his arms. But Marcus' text had broken the mood. Seeing Betz defeated, the fight sucked out of him, was more than I could handle.

"Lock up," he said.

And he was gone.

I threw myself onto the sofa and rubbed my eyes. Felony settled beside me, and I mindlessly stroked his head. Exhausted as I was, I'd never be able to sleep—not with Betz so miserable. All because of me.

Responding to Marcus felt wrong, but so did leaving him hanging. *Ride safe*, I texted back. Innocuous.

That would show him. I was no player; this was getting out of hand.

Chapter Twenty

After a sleepless night, I dressed in court clothes and made my way downtown for Henry Coffman's probation violation hearing. Betz's words from last night drowned out any other thoughts in my head. His forlorn expression tugged at my heart, and I couldn't shake it. Thankfully, I'd written a probation violation report that listed Henry's non-compliant behavior. I wouldn't have to rely on my memory.

Last night and into the early morning hours, I'd tossed around the idea of Betz and I getting back together. No one got me the way Betz did. We connected on so many levels. I could completely be myself with him and let my guard down. And until Marcus, I'd never felt such an attraction to anyone else.

Would reviving things be the easy way out? Lazy? Going back to the familiar? Falling back into our old routine would be simple. Getting to know someone new, not so much. Betz and I were in sync in and out of the bedroom. Being vulnerable in a new relationship scared the crap out of me.

As time went by, the reasons Betz and I divorced had become hazy in my mind. Kind of like when someone died, and you only remembered the good things about them. In reality, we were both hard-headed and sometimes our differences screamed at us louder than our compatibility. When it came right down to it, our marriage had needed work. I'd been willing, but before I could bring myself to admit it out loud, Betz said he was exhausted. That he couldn't take it anymore. I'd gotten defensive and went off alone to lick my wounds. I thought that was what he'd wanted.

But now…. Now he said he missed us as a couple.

Over three years had passed since we'd ended things. A long time for him to come around. I knew from his sister that he hadn't dated much since we'd split. Maybe us getting back together would take the fastest detour from loneliness for him, too.

Not the best reason to get back together.

When I had a break in my schedule, I'd run it by Kate. If anyone would give me a dose of reality, it was her.

But for now, I had to focus on Coffman's hearing. I pulled into the parking garage with plenty of time to get to court.

After bypassing security by showing my work ID, I checked the docket hanging outside the courtroom door. The hearing for Coffman was scheduled for 9 a.m. A peek inside the courtroom told me the lawyers had yet to arrive.

I settled on a bench across from the double doors. Placing my phone on silent, I sent a quick message to Marjorie. *How was your night?*

She got back to me right away. *Perfect. Slept like the dead. Pie for breakfast. Love Ms. Cody!*

Everybody does. Have a good day.

I dropped my phone into my bag and took out Coffman's file. Laying it on my lap, I reviewed my report. Footsteps sounded in the hall. I looked up, hoping it was Sylvia Martin, the DA, but it was Tony.

I closed the file and got to my feet. "What are you doing here?"

Hands in pockets, he rocked back on his heels. "I'm curious."

"Not a good idea."

He shrugged. "Hearings are public. Anyway, I knew I'd find you here, and I wanted to talk to you."

"Not a good idea, either. I can't help you. You're not getting your job back."

He stared at the ground. "I understand you were instrumental in me losing my job. That said, you have integrity. I trust you."

"I'm not sure where you're going with this."

Tony cleared his throat. "What if I had some information that might blow things up at the office?"

Throwing somebody else under the bus would not help his case. "I'm not sure what you're talking about, but leave me out of it."

"And you wonder why nobody likes you."

He turned and entered the courtroom before I could say anything more. The slamming of the heavy wooden door signaled an end to our conversation.

What was that about?

Having him in the courtroom wouldn't go well, but like he said, hearings were public, and there wasn't anything I could do about it. Gathering my things, I was about to follow him in when Sylvia came down the hall.

"Casey," she said. "Let's talk."

There was no one else around, so we didn't need to find a private place to discuss the case. "This looks open and shut to me," she said, adjusting the jacket of her sharp black suit. "He wasn't reporting to you, and you made a fair recommendation of two months in jail with early release to treatment. How soon do you think a bed will become available?"

I'd have to check with Marta. "Could be a few weeks. But we have bigger problems." I gave her a quick telling of how Tony violated policy when he took Henry into custody. "And Tony's here."

"You said he was fired," Sylvia stated, wrinkling her brow.

"He was. But as a member of the community, he has a right to attend the hearing."

Sylvia sighed and checked her watch. "With him in the audience…. Well, there's a delicate matter we need to address. Come with me. I'm going to ask the judge if we can meet in chambers."

I followed her through the courtroom and into the inner sanctuary of the judge's suite. A judicial assistant sat at a desk, but the door to the judge's chambers remained closed. She was the first line of defense.

"Hi, Lori," Sylvia said. "Does the judge have a few minutes to chat?"

Lori got to her feet. "Let me find out." She opened the door behind her and disappeared inside.

Sylvia pulled out her cell and typed something before slipping her phone back in her suit pocket.

Lori came back and motioned us forward. "Judge Dunn will see you."

I followed Sylvia inside. The space was cozy, with lots of plants and shelves of law books. Photos of a cute kid hugging a Golden Retriever sat next to the computer on the desk. Judge Dunn painted her lips a deep red, then dropped the lipstick into a drawer before folding her hands on the desk and giving us her full attention. "Have a seat."

"Thanks, Judge," Sylvia said. "This is Casey Carson with probation. The defense is on her way."

After an uncomfortable moment of silence, the door behind us opened, and a woman I recognized from other hearings, Melissa Brooks, entered the room. Dressed in a frumpy suit that was a size too big, she smiled at us as she took the last chair, laying a worn briefcase on her lap.

"What's this about?" Judge Dunn asked.

Sylvia leaned forward. "Ms. Brooks and I've been talking about things. Mr. Coffman's a suspect in a major drug case. Fentanyl overdoses are up. In fact, there were eight known deaths last week alone. We want the big fish and are prepared to offer Mr. Coffman a deal where he becomes an informant. That doesn't really affect his probation violation, but since his exposure is much worse on the drug case, we want to use this hearing as leverage to convince him to cooperate."

I cleared my throat. "I should add that he was in possession of a significant amount of cash during his arrest. I suspect he's been dealing. That said, becoming an informant is tricky. It's hard for us to supervise people who are allowed to associate with drug users. It's against the conditions of his probation. In fact, the department has a policy against our clients acting as informants, but there are always exceptions." Although uncommon, I'd heard of it happening before.

The judge nodded. "Ms. Brooks, have you approached your client about this?"

"He's thinking about it, but he's scared. Retribution can be more frightening than prison time."

The judge looked back to me. "Ms. Carson, can you speak to your manager and see if it's even possible for Mr. Coffman to act as an informant?"

"I can do that."

Sylvia pursed her lips. "I want to warn you that a civilian spectator is in the courtroom, so don't mention this."

"Make sure your client knows that," the judge said to Melissa. "Are we ready to proceed today?"

Melissa ran a hand over her briefcase. "Last we spoke, my client was ready to admit to the violation of failure to report. I'll make sure nothing's changed before we begin."

The three of us stood and filed back into the courtroom. Sylvia and I settled at the table across and to the left of the bench. Melissa sat alone at the other table. A few minutes later, a side door opened, and a deputy led Henry Coffman into the room. He wore jail stripes, with pink socks stuffed into orange slides, and his hands were cuffed in front. His gaze narrowed when he spotted Tony in the back of the room. Anger radiated off him. Oh no, this wasn't good.

After his shackles were removed, he joined his attorney at the defense table.

Heads bent, they conferred in hushed tones. Although I couldn't hear them, I knew the conversation was heated.

I snuck a look over my shoulder. Tony remained the only spectator in the room.

"All rise," the bailiff said in a booming voice.

We stood. Henry chanced a look over his shoulder at the back of the room. Tony crossed his arms and met the challenge with a hard stare.

The judge entered the room, her robe swinging as she climbed the podium to the bench. Purple-framed glasses set off her flaming red hair that matched her lipstick. "You may be seated."

"State vs. Coffman," the clerk proclaimed. She read the case number.

Melissa remained standing, checking the buttons on her blazer. "My client just informed me he wishes to contest the allegations made by the probation department."

What? Why? Admitting to the violation would get him at most a few weeks in jail, followed by much-needed treatment. If he had a hearing, the judge could impose anything up to and including revocation of his probation to prison. It was a big chance to take. Did Tony's presence anger Henry that much? Or did he really think he could beat the allegations, given Tony's rogue apprehension of him?

The judge cocked her head. "Okay, let's proceed."

The attorneys identified themselves, and I was called to the stand.

Sylvia spoke first. "State your name and occupation, please."

I leaned into the mic. "Casey Carson. I'm a probation officer."

"How long have you held that position?"

"Seven years."

She motioned to Coffman. "Do you recognize the defendant?"

I nodded. "Henry Coffman. I supervise him."

"For how long?"

I checked my report. "He was placed on probation in November of last year. They assigned him to my caseload from the start.

"And how has Mr. Coffman done on supervision?"

"At first, he did well. He reported as directed and lived at an approved residence. He addressed his addiction issues in treatment."

"But then he stopped reporting, didn't he?"

I cleared my throat. "About two months ago, he started struggling. He didn't admit to relapsing but failed to submit to urinalysis testing as directed. He lost his job and was terminated from housing. Then he stopped reporting."

"Were attempts made to locate the defendant?"

"Yes. I contacted his grandmother, but she hadn't heard from him. He hadn't provided a new address, so I didn't know where to look for him. I knew he played basketball at a local park, and I drove by whenever I was in the area, but I never found him."

"And you requested a warrant, didn't you?"

"I did. It's been active about six weeks."

"Nothing further." Sylvia reclaimed her seat.

The defense attorney stood and glanced at the legal pad where she'd been taking notes. "Good morning, Ms. Carson."

She sounded friendly, but I'd testified enough times to know she'd try her hardest to ruin my day. "Good morning."

"Let's talk about the arrest of Mr. Coffman. First off, he admits he has addiction issues, but is he a threat to the community? Any violent offenses in his past?"

Dealing Fentanyl made him a danger to the community, but because he had not yet been convicted of it, I knew I couldn't mention it. Plus, the judge already knew my concerns. "Nothing on his record that I'm aware of," I said.

"A probation officer tackled him and then forced him into a car," she said flatly,

Here we go. "I wasn't there when they took him into custody."

"But the police officer told you what had occurred once you arrived on scene."

"She relayed Mr. Coffman's telling of events." The door to the courtroom opened, and Suzy Vega squeezed her way into the room. I swallowed hard and fought to keep my voice level. "The officer didn't seem convinced it was entirely true and didn't file charges for that."

The attorney crossed her arms. "You were the field training officer assigned to his rogue probation officer?" She checked the legal pad on the table. "A Mr. Tony Romero?"

"Yes."

"So, you were responsible for Mr. Romero's actions?"

I needed to phrase my answer without sounding defensive or hanging Tony. "He was off duty when it happened."

"But you had trained him on how to act in such a situation?"

I looked to Sylvia, and she got to her feet. "We aren't here to address Ms. Carson's competence as a trainer."

That was helpful. I stopped my eyes from rolling, but it wasn't easy.

"Get to the point," Judge Dunn said.

"No further questions," Melissa said.

The judge looked over her glasses at me. "The witness may step down."

Relief flooded my body, but anger stopped it from taking hold as I moved off the witness stand and rejoined Sylvia at the plaintiff's table. I didn't like my competence called into question or the fact that no one defended me.

"The defense calls Tony Romero," Melissa said.

Necks turned, looking to the back of the room. Tony stood, a stupid smile plastered on his face. He was getting his fifteen minutes of fame, although why he'd want it, I didn't know.

The clerk swore Tony in, and he settled in the chair I'd just vacated. He sat up straight, his chest puffed out.

"State your name and occupation," Melissa said.

"Tony Romero," he said, his voice strong. He didn't need the mic. "I was a probation officer. Currently, I'm unemployed."

Melissa looked sympathetic. "Sorry to hear that. What made you leave?"

Tony raised his arm and pointed a finger at me. "She got me fired, but it was all a misunderstanding."

I didn't turn around, but I could feel Suzy Vega behind me, scribbling notes she'd use to prove her point that I wasn't fit to be a PO.

"Please explain," Melissa said.

A buzzing in my head had me missing some of Tony's testimony, but he threw around words like perp and subdue. He insinuated I was unresponsive and unavailable. He had no choice but to take matters into his own hands. Maybe I was jealous of him for executing the arrest on his own. He deserved another chance.

Give me a break.

Sylvia stood. "Objection. What does this have to do with Mr. Coffman's violations of the conditions of his probation?"

Melissa looked our way. "I'm trying to paint a picture of the chaotic environment at the probation office. Of the differing agendas. Both Ms. Carson and Mr. Romero were supervising the defendant. This shows how confusing the process was for my client. No wonder he stopped reporting."

The judge took off her glasses and massaged her temples. "Any other witnesses?"

"I need to contact the responding police officer. If we can continue this, I'd like to call her to the stand," Melissa said, "She can testify that the defendant, a pedestrian, was hit by Mr. Romero's car, denting it."

"Your honor," Sylvia said. "This is very unorthodox."

"I agree," Judge Dunn said. "But I can see why Mr. Coffman was confused. And that he might even have reason to file a grievance. I assume that's where this is going."

"At the very least," Melissa said.

The judge slid her glasses back into place. "This is complicated. I'd like to take it under advisement. Let's continue this hearing to next month."

Melissa cleared her throat. "Thank you, Judge. I ask that the court release Mr. Coffman on his own recognizance. I spoke to his grandmother. She's willing to have her grandson live with her as long as he's attending treatment."

Something he couldn't do if he was acting as an informant and actively dealing drugs, but I knew I couldn't bring that up.

The judge nodded. "So ordered. Anything else?"

I cleared my throat and stood. "It would be helpful if the court could give Mr. Coffman reporting instructions. My office tomorrow at one o'clock."

"Did you hear that, Mr. Coffman?"

"Yes, ma'am."

"Court is adjourned." The judge stood and exited the room.

Tony walked past me and out into the hall, followed by Suzy Vega.

"That was a mess," Sylvia said, closing Henry's file and hugging it to her chest.

"Tell me about it." I rose and followed her out of the courtroom.

In the hallway, I saw no sign of Tony. Suzy Vega paced with her cell glued to her ear. As I walked past her, I heard part of the conversation. Whoever she was talking to was getting an earful. "Why aren't you returning my calls? I thought I meant something to you. Call me!"

As she lowered her phone to her side, she made eye contact with me. The look she gave me sent a message—loud and clear. The hearing was going to make the news. I hurried to the parking garage, where I placed yet another call to Alma with more information she wouldn't want to hear.

Chapter Twenty-One

The county owed me some time since I'd worked the night before driving Marjorie to safety. I sent Kate a message asking if she was home. She was, so after stopping by my house to change into jeans and running shoes and rescuing Felony from his crate, I swung by.

I collapsed onto a wicker chair on her patio. "I don't even know where to begin."

Ashley and Ethan played in the yard, barely acknowledging my presence, but welcoming Felony into their shenanigans.

"Let's start with Dad," Kate said. "I hear he and Millie are actually hitting it off."

I'd forgotten about that. "Yeah. They were pretty cozy last night at my house, and she's getting him to drink less. I had to leave and didn't really get the scoop. But the vibe was strong that he was into her."

"Feels weird," Kate said. "I want him to be happy, but Mom was just here."

"I was thinking the same thing."

"So, what's up with you? More work problems?"

I didn't want to get into that. "Nothing I want to talk about on that front. Betz paid me a visit last night."

She raised an eyebrow. "Seems like he's around a lot again."

"It's not the frequency. It's more what he said."

She leaned forward. "Spill it."

I told her about our conversation. One-sided as it was.

Kate sighed and leaned back in her seat. "You want advice, or do you just want me to be supportive?"

I laughed. "Like you won't tell me what to do." I knew she wasn't capable of keeping her thoughts on the matter to herself. She'd had her nose in my business since the day I was born, but since our mother died, she was even more protective of me.

After some thought, she said. "I don't know. I mean, I didn't like that you split up. But once done, it seemed important that you put it behind you. Move on with your life. But you haven't met anyone else."

I pushed thoughts of Marcus from my mind. Kate would never approve of a relationship with him. She was too much of a straight arrow.

"I'm still young," I said. "Not like I couldn't meet somebody."

"I didn't mean it like that."

"And I'm perfectly happy by myself. I like living alone." Was I trying to convince Kate or myself?

Kate pressed her lips together, taking a moment. "You've always liked male attention. Even as a kid, you always had a crush on someone."

She had me there. "But I've only been in love, true love, once."

"With Betz. You still love him, don't you?"

I dropped my head into my hands. "I don't know. I mean, yes. But is that enough?"

"Marriage is hard work," Kate said. "There are days I want to strangle Kevin. Then there are days I'd do anything to make him happy. You guys were so young. And you rushed into things."

She was right. Our relationship became intense fast. When I remembered our time together—the good times—they rushed by in a blur. But I could invoke the pain of splitting up in an instant. It still sat heavy in my heart. "Anyway," I said. "He told me to think about it. In the meantime, I don't think I should be around him."

"That's probably wise," she said. "Give his proposal time to sink in. I've heard of divorced couples getting back together and making it work the second time. It can happen. Not like you ever hated each other."

Her phone buzzed on the table at her side. She reached for it and blocked the sun with her hand so she could read the screen. "Uh oh." She scrolled on her phone. "Kevin just sent me something." She held her phone out so we could both see the video.

A promo for the five o'clock local news. Suzy Vega stood in front of the courthouse. While she spoke, footage of me leaving the building played. "A judge discussed the possibility of a lawsuit against the probation department at this morning's hearing. We at Channel 6 care about abuse of power. I'll continue to look out for the vulnerable and stay on this story until justice is served. More at five."

Kate lowered her phone and looked up at me.

"Crap. Vega's photographer must have been lurking outside when I left court." I'd been so deep in thought, I hadn't noticed him. Couple that with the video at the Harrisons, and I was becoming the face of problems with the department. I had to wonder if Vega's involvement with Diablo was fanning the fire.

Chapter Twenty-Two

Back at work, I headed to Alma's office. Felony was with me, and I didn't care much about the office policy of not allowing dogs in the building—not with all that was going on. My coworkers slowed me down, gushing over how adorable my sidekick was.

When I shut the door, Alma looked up from the file on her desk. "Who do we have here?" She put her glasses on for a better look.

"This is Felony. Felony, sit," I said.

Felony planted his butt on the floor. Alma came around her desk and petted him. "He's beautiful. When did you get a dog?"

"He's not really mine. I'm looking after him for a while." Although the more time I spent with him, the less I looked forward to saying goodbye.

"Well, he's adorable. Did he get his name based on his behavior?"

It did fit, given the mess he made in my bathroom. "He came with it, wasn't my idea. Anyway, did you see Suzy Vega's latest promo?"

Alma straightened and crossed her arms. "Goodness, no. What now?"

I brought up the video Kate had sent me and played it for her. "This isn't good," Alma said. "I haven't heard of a lawsuit yet, but I wouldn't be surprised if Coffman files one. This makes me super glad we let Tony go. I can't believe he showed up in court."

"Me either. It doesn't make sense. They were talking about how he'd gone rogue, and he seemed to enjoy it. Like he was proud of what he did."

"You'd think the psychological testing we do at hiring would have caught that."

Unfortunately, he wasn't the only PO to fly under the radar. I sometimes wondered how Jerski got his job.

Alma settled back at her desk. "Anyway, thanks for looping me in on this. What else is going on?"

I gave her the details about Marjorie. "Brian Johnson also thought he was being followed. Don't know if it's a coincidence, or if someone was really after them, but Marjorie should be safe at Ms. Cody's."

"God bless that woman," Alma said. "She's a genuine success story. And a testament to how much your clients appreciate you."

"Thanks for that." A little ego-stroking was welcome after recent events. "I just hope that bringing Marjorie there didn't bring trouble to Ms. Cody's door. And there's something else." I told her about the detectives wanting Henry Coffman to become an informant.

"I'll check with Roxy," she said. "Maybe we can make an exception given how big a problem Fentanyl is in the community. In the meanwhile, do the best you can."

Story of my life.

Back at my cubicle, I updated my case notes. Tomorrow was Tony's scheduled office day. I read the latest Chronos on everyone coming in and wrote directives for each person, including my contact information, because they would report to me until Alma resolved Tony's caseload.

Next, I cleared his voicemail. Mundane things: requests for travel permits for clients wanting to visit family out of state, a treatment provider alerting us to a client's relapse and then an interesting one from Lilian Harrison. "You've been so helpful," her quivering voice said. "So nice of you to visit me in the hospital, Tony. I hope you can get my boy out of jail like you said. He doesn't belong in that horrible place. He just didn't want to be arrested. It's not like he shot anyone."

I slouched in my chair and massaged my temples. Tony had gone to see Lillian in the hospital. Did this happen before or after they fired him? Either way, it was inappropriate. I checked the time stamp on the message. Yesterday afternoon. So, after. And why would he promise to get Eric out of jail—something he had no power to do even if he hadn't been fired. Did he just not get it, or did he have some nefarious agenda?

Sick of delivering bad news to Alma, I simply forwarded the message to her. Let her deal with it. Tony wasn't my problem anymore.

After a few more hours at my desk, I took Felony for a walk before driving downtown for Brian Johnson's vigil.

A small crowd had gathered in the corner of the downtown city park. People laid flowers and swayed, holding candles while a beautiful voice belted out "Amazing Grace." Marta stood at a table, offering coffee and cookies to anyone who wanted them.

Leash in hand, I guided Felony over to her. "This is quite the turnout," I said. "Brian would be touched by this."

Her face lit up when she saw me. "Casey, so glad you could make it." She wrapped me in a tight hug. "And who do we have here?"

"Felony."

She laughed and patted him on his head. "Love it!"

I accepted a slim white candle and held it against the flame on Marta's lighter. "Anything I can do to help?"

"Got it covered, but thanks."

Someone behind me cleared their throat. I turned to see Detective Ramsey. "Nice to see you here," he said. "That's some guard dog you've got."

I leaned down and fluffed Felony's ears. "He's tougher than he looks."

Ramsey laughed. "Got a feeling it's the same with you."

When I raised my eyebrows, Ramsey looked suddenly uncomfortable. He added, "thought this might be a good place to talk to people, see if anyone knows anything that can help with the case. If you come across someone with something to contribute, let me know."

I nodded and took Ramsey's suggestion as an assignment to work the crowd. Once Ramsey disappeared into the gathering, I headed in the opposite direction, thinking, at the very least, I'd encounter someone on my caseload and get a field contact.

I estimated about a hundred people were in attendance. I squeezed past a few small groups and toward the front, where people's heads were bowed in a moment of silence.

I tried to concentrate on the Brian I'd known and not think about what had transpired since his murder. The evening was about him, and I wanted to honor his memory.

Toward the side of the swelling crowd, I spotted a client of mine standing in a circle of people mostly dressed in black.

I picked my way over to him. When he saw me, he dropped a cigarette to the ground and snuffed it out with the toe of his work boot. Still out of earshot, he made a comment to his friends, and they all moved away. I guessed he said something like, "Oh shit, it's my PO." That would break up any party.

"Sorry," I said, as if that was exactly what he'd said. "How you doing, Rick?"

He shrugged. "Better than Brian Johnson. You got details about what happened?"

"Not really. Hoping you might know something. You know, the word on the street."

Rick exhaled, and I caught a whiff of cigarette breath. He was doing well on supervision—well entrenched in the recovery community and working closely with his sponsor. I'd like to think he'd kicked his habit, but I knew sobriety was fragile and took a while. Still, Rick was miles ahead of most of my charges.

"Last I heard, Brian was struggling," he said. "I kicked him out of a meeting about a month ago because he was strung out. Now I feel bad."

So, he was using. "You had to protect the program."

"Still," he said. "I could have tried harder to help him. I was hot under the collar because someone was dealing at the meetings. Not sure if it was Brian or not, but I'm protective of my people."

"Nothing wrong with that."

He kicked at the ground. "Yeah, I guess."

"Hey," I said. "Don't beat yourself up. Helping people isn't easy. They have to want it."

"Yeah," he said. "Anyone knows that it'd be you."

Nice that he recognized that. "Did the dealing stop once Brian quit attending meetings?"

"For a few weeks. Then it started up again but stopped a few days ago."

I thought of Henry Coffman and his unexplained wad of cash. A few days ago, he went to jail. "Does Henry Coffman attend those meetings?"

Rick looked at his shoes. "I'd love to tell you, but meetings are supposed to be anonymous."

"Yeah, sorry. Shouldn't have asked. Just trying to put some things together."

"I get it. And selling to addicts in recovery is about as low as you can go, so I wouldn't protect anyone I knew who did that. But, truth is, I don't know who the culprit is."

"Well, if you find out and you're comfortable sharing the info, I'll do what I can to help."

"I'll keep that in mind. See you later," he said and walked away.

I had to keep a tight leash on Henry until I could determine his connection to Brian Johnson and whether they were working for the same drug lord. A scream interrupted my thoughts. The crowd pulsated as people pushed into each other, retreating from the area with shrieks. I scooped the shivering dog into my arms to prevent him from being trampled. Dropping the candle, I ground the flame out with my shoe, then pushed my way to the outskirts of the group.

People scattered like a box of dropped marbles. I got turned around and couldn't determine which way was which.

Marta ran up to me. "What's happening?" She pointed to the scattering mob.

"Don't know."

"Stay safe." She patted my arm and then moved away.

The screaming died down. Still holding the clinging dog, I picked my way over abandoned belongings toward the small cluster of people who remained. Chatter was hushed and sharp.

I peered over shoulders to see a man prone on the ground. Ramsey was on his knees in front of him, blocking the person's face. "What happened?"

I asked the man next to me.

"Stabbing," he said, without taking his eyes off the man lying before us.

Paramedics rushed in, and people moved to allow them access to the victim. Ramsey got to his feet, letting me get a good look at the guy on the grass.

Henry Coffman. With his head tilted back and eyes skyward, he clutched his hand to his belly wound.

I was in a vacuum. Everything disappeared as I tried to digest the scene before me. Another one of my probationers had been targeted. My stomach churned.

"Everyone stays put," Ramsey said. "Officers are on their way, and we need statements from everybody." His eyes met mine. "You, too, Ms. Carson."

I tightened my hold on Felony and followed Ramsey's gaze to a business card lying on the ground. Ramsey couldn't know that Henry was a client of mine, but as he picked up the card with a gloved hand and looked up at me, I knew I wouldn't have to break the news myself.

Chapter Twenty-Three

At the precinct, Ramsey placed a can of Diet Coke on the desk and slid it my way. He remembered. Kind of late for a dose of caffeine, but I imagined we were in for a long night. I popped the tab and took a drink.

Felony curled up at my feet. Ramsey settled in his swivel desk chair and spun it to face me. He laid the evidence bag with my business card in it on the desk. "Care to explain this?"

The soda settled in my stomach like a bowl of acid. "I was as surprised to see it as you were."

"Why do you think I was surprised?" Ramsey took a drink from a to-go coffee cup.

Really? "You were kneeling by Henry before I even got there. I was on the other side of the park when it happened. It wasn't until I saw others running for cover that I made my way over to see if I could help."

Ramsey scratched his head. "Okay, tell me about Henry Coffman."

I wasn't sure if Ramsey was privy to the fact that Coffman might be an informant. I'd let Alma figure that out.

"Before we get started, do you know his condition? Is he going to make it?"

Ramsey tapped the cell phone sitting on his desk. "Last I checked, he was critical and in surgery. Nurse promised to keep me updated."

I nodded. "Coffman has been on my caseload about two years. Like many of my clients, he's an addict, so he struggled with sobriety. He'd have good periods, and then he'd relapse, which is typical. We got along okay until a few days ago when my trainee arrested him, allegedly hitting him with his car to accomplish the task."

Ramsey cringed. "Wow. Guessing they don't teach that maneuver in the academy."

"Tony got fired over the incident and some other behavior that suggested he was a liability to the department. He surprised me by coming to Coffman's probation violation hearing, even though he'd already been fired."

"That is strange. Did you see Tony at the vigil?"

"No. But I wasn't there long when the stabbing occurred. I wouldn't put it past him to be there. He doesn't respect boundaries."

"Did Tony know Coffman? Brian Johnson?"

I nodded. "We did field work together, and before he got his own caseload, he helped me with office visits, too. So, he'd met most of my clients."

Ramsey took notes as I told him what I knew about Tony. When we finished, he dropped his pen on the desk and rubbed his eyes. "So, you think Tony is behind this?"

He was as good a suspect as any, but I couldn't imagine him having the skill to commit crimes and slip away. He wasn't exactly a smooth operator. "No. Not really. Just letting you know there was a connection between them. I have no idea who's going after my clients."

I checked the clock behind Ramsey. Just after eleven.

"What we have to figure out," he said, "is why *your* clients are being targeted. I plan to pay Tony a visit. If you have any further contact with him, I want to hear about it."

"There's something else. Not sure if it's connected." Hopefully, if I was transparent, Ramsey would stop eyeing me with such suspicion. I told him about Marjorie and the black sedan. Ramsey took more notes, then he stretched. It was almost midnight now.

He stood. "I'll walk you out."

I grabbed Felony's leash, and we headed toward the door. "Let me know when Coffman's out of surgery."

Ramsey nodded and closed the door behind me.

Even though I parked my Jeep in front of a police station, I didn't feel

106

safe until I checked the back seat, and Felony and I were well on our way home. At this late hour, the streets were mostly deserted, and I made it home without seeing a black sedan. I felt like I was being watched just the same.

Chapter Twenty-Four

My street was dark. Exhaustion had set in, and all I could think about was collapsing into bed. Felony snored softly on the seat beside me as I pulled into the driveway. I hit the garage door remote, but it didn't budge. In my sleep-deprived state, I figured I hadn't pressed it right. I tried again, still nothing.

I didn't see Joy's car parked out front, so I assumed she was spending the night at Jerski's. For once, I wished she was home. Even Jerski. Not a night I wanted to be alone.

Turning off the ignition, I sat in the car, listening for anything out of the ordinary. Quiet. Felony stretched and stood.

Something didn't feel right. I checked my neighbors' houses. No signs of life, but the porch light was lit on the house across the street. Not a neighborhood power outage.

I checked my phone. The small amount of light it provided felt like a spotlight in the darkness, making me a big fat target. After checking the time, I held it against my thigh, blocking the light.

Power went out for various reasons. Perhaps a breaker needed to be reset, or my garage door had crapped out. I hadn't left the porch light on because I hadn't expected to be out so late.

Maybe Diablo had upped their game. Could be that I was overreacting, but my nerves were raw.

My finger hovered over the contacts button on my phone, itching to call Betz. But that wasn't fair. He didn't live all that close, and it was the middle of the night. I could handle this.

Since my near-death experience several months ago, I'd been on a heightened sense of alert, keeping my baton stashed in the space between the driver's seat and the door. I reached down and wrapped my fingers around the weapon, wishing it was the gun that was locked away inside instead. The baton required close combat. Not something I had an interest in.

Taking Felony by the leash, I quietly opened the car door. Sneakers soft on the driveway, I coaxed the dog out after me, grabbed my bag, and fished out keys for the front door. Soundlessly, I eased the Jeep's door shut, then made my way up the front walkway.

The air was still, not even the slightest breeze. It felt like bird wings flapped in my stomach; I was so unnerved.

My front door looked normal, shut, secure. I slipped my key in the lock as quietly as I could.

Stepping inside, I quickly closed the door and locked it behind me. Flicking on the light switch brought no light. I activated the flashlight on my phone and swept the room.

Nothing out of place. But when the beam hit the back patio door, it illuminated a shadow outside.

My heart thudded. I tightened my grip on the baton and shut the flashlight off.

Eight careful steps, and I was at the back door. *It's nothing.... It's nothing.... It's nothing....*

On the patio, my two Adirondack chairs were undisturbed. In front of them, a dormant firepit and some planters housing dead plants. No matter how hard I tried, I couldn't keep foliage alive.

The chairs faced away from me, so when I sat in them, I had a view of the yard, as uninteresting as it was. A dark shape was in one of them. I swallowed hard. Squinted. Strained to see in the dim light the cloud-covered moon provided. Afraid to shine my flashlight toward it and alert whoever was out there to my presence, I held my breath.

Something moved, fluttered. I jumped back. Felony let out a low growl.

Busted. My stomach took a nosedive as I braced for battle.

But the lump didn't move. I risked a quick burst of light from my phone. The grill cover lay wadded up on the chair. I'd forgotten to put it back after I'd grilled chicken the other day.

I exhaled.

Just my over-active imagination.

Felony scratched at the door. Not a bad idea to take him out one last time before we went to bed.

I popped the lock and slid the door open. Felony leapt through the space, and I stepped out behind him, baton still in hand, just in case.

Felony darted to the other chair, got on his hind legs, and wagged his tail.

"Hey, there," a deep voice said.

I froze. Snapped the baton open. At the ready, I braced myself for a fight. Memories from my last encounter with Diablo that had occurred in front of my house flashed through my mind. That time, I'd had a baseball bat. Since then, I'd rehearsed better moves. Jabs and strikes at the most vulnerable spots on a man. Hopefully, muscle memory would kick in, and I stood a chance at disabling whoever was here to hurt me.

I'd prepared.

I was ready.

The figure got to his feet.

I took a step back.

"Hey, Sunshine. Don't shoot. It's me."

Sunshine?

"Marcus?"

I pointed my flashlight at his face.

There he stood.

His Hotness.

In my backyard.

I almost wished it was Diablo. I was even less prepared for this.

"How?" I said. "How did you get here so fast?"

He took a step toward me. "Energy drinks. Didn't take many breaks."

That should have occurred to me. Marcus had superpowers. Or so it seemed.

110

"Thought I'd get a better greeting," he said, coming closer. "When did you get a dog?"

My nervous energy drained and pooled at my feet. He stood there like an offering. Hair pulled back, a hint of a beard, a twinkle in his bedroom brown eyes. He wore his usual white T-shirt, worn jeans, and pull-on boots. Who could resist that?

Not me.

We were toe-to-toe now. I dropped my baton to my side.

His hands gripped my waist, and he held me at arm's length, his gaze locking on mine. "Sunshine, it's so good to see you."

A tingle rippled through my body.

Marcus leaned forward, lightly brushing his lips over mine. Teasing me. I closed my eyes.

My resolve to take things slowly evaporated as his hands moved up my back and pulled me against him. Our bodies molded together, and I welcomed his kiss. But Felony had other ideas. Felony was team Betz.

The dog pushed his way between us, one paw on my thigh, one on Marcus's, as if he were trying to separate us. I took a quick step back, breaking the connection. "Did you turn off my power?"

Marcus ran a hand over his chin and gave an exasperated sigh. "Why would I do that?"

"How long have you been here?"

"You gonna interrogate me again? Like when we first met?"

"If you weren't so evasive, I wouldn't have to…. My power's out. I'm just wondering how long since it happened." I remembered now how much he infuriated me sometimes.

Marcus laughed. "You really know how to ruin a mood."

"I'm sorry. But Diablo has shown interest in me again, and it's freaking me out." He, of all people, should understand. He was even higher on Diablo's shit list than I was.

"Oh," he said. "Gotcha. I've been here a few hours. House was dark the entire time. I figured it was because you weren't home."

"Why didn't you call me?"

"Phone's dead. Bike's old. No charger."

"I didn't see your bike."

"Parked it on the side of the house. Didn't want to block your driveway for when you came home."

I re-activated my flashlight. "Gonna check the breaker."

He followed me inside, through the house, and into the garage, where the main electric panel was. The switches were in their normal position, none tripped. For the heck of it, I flipped them back and forth. Nothing happened.

"Think you need to call an electrician," Marcus said.

I looked at him over my shoulder. "You think?"

Marcus laughed. "Why did I miss you?"

"I'm sorry. I'm tired. It's been a day." I shouldn't bite his head off. I was glad I wasn't alone. And well…. I had my reasons for calling him His Hotness….

But I had no idea what Marcus expected of me…. Well, maybe I did. He probably expected to spend the night. But after what Betz told me…. I wasn't ready. Why couldn't I be like Joy? Play the field? I was as loyal as the dog beside me.

Still, I didn't want to be alone. And it was good to see him. My body still tingled from the moment his lips touched mine.

We went back inside, through the house, room by room. Nothing out of the ordinary. All windows were locked. No sign of a break-in. I checked the website for the power company on my phone. I saw no outages reported.

When I laid my phone on the counter, I turned around and smacked into Marcus. "We don't need lights," he said. "All the electricity we need is between us."

"We're not having sex," I blurted. Tempting as it was, I owed it to Betz to figure things out before I did anything drastic. Plus, I hadn't shaved my legs. Was it presumptuous of me to think Marcus wanted anything more than a roll in the hay? That he even wanted the same thing as Betz?

Marcus held up his hands. "Point taken."

That took the sass out of me. Maybe he could have argued, just a little….

CHAPTER TWENTY-FOUR

"Do you have candles?" he asked.

I felt my way to the cabinet where I kept those kinds of things, grabbed the first two I found, and brought them to the living room. Marcus had a lighter. He was a smoker. A strike against him. Score one for Betz.

Placing the candles on the coffee table, I collapsed onto the living room couch, inviting Felony to sit on my lap—an excellent barrier. Marcus seemed to get the message, and he sat at the other end of the sofa, sideways and facing me, his arm draped over the back of the couch.

We talked about his trip, Diablo, and why I thought they were back in my life, and how I'd come by Felony. I wanted to tell him about Betz's confession. About how I couldn't make any decisions about whatever this was between us, not yet, but it didn't fit into the conversation.

Sometime during the night, I brought out Ms. Cody's pie, and we devoured it.

By now, we were sitting on the floor, cross-legged and opposite each other. Marcus tossed his fork into the empty pie container on the coffee table and got on his knees in front of me, settling back on his heels. "I still dream about when you kicked the shit out of me," he said with a twinkle in his eye. "Going for the jewels was a nice touch, but you didn't follow through."

"I'm not sure how to take that."

He gave a sly grin. "Get your mind out of the gutter, Sunshine. I meant you didn't keep fighting."

"What do you mean? If I remember correctly, you quickly became my bitch."

"Well, the pepper spray you doused me with helped, but mostly, I didn't want to hurt you. If you ever get in a situation like that again, you can't stop fighting. Ever. Not if Diablo comes for you again."

"I attend defensive tactics training every year. I got moves."

Marcus laughed. "I'm sure you do. But don't they mostly teach you how to create space between you and your attacker? How to get away?"

I'd never thought about it like that before, but he was right. "Sometimes that's all you need. A little space and time to get to a safe spot and call for help."

"What if he keeps coming at you?"

"Let me guess. You have some advice about how I should handle that."

Marcus sprang at me like a lizard catching a fly on its tongue. Before I knew what hit me, I was flat on my back, and he was on top of me. His fingers caught my wrists, and he pinned my hands over my head as he straddled me.

I squirmed beneath him, but he was stronger than me, and he didn't let up. Slightly out of breath, I said, "Now what, ninja?"

"Thrust your hips."

"You wish."

"Do you want to learn how to get out of this, or what?"

I dug my heels into the ground and shot my hips toward the ceiling, knocking Marcus off balance so his chest was now over my face. His hands automatically let go of my wrists, and he used them to stop himself from face-planting on the ground.

Marcus sat back and then lay on the ground beside me. "Now, do it to me, and I'll show you the next move."

"You just want me on top of you."

A sparkle lit his eyes. "True. But this is serious. We can get to the fun stuff later. Come on, hold me down."

I was tempted to move right to the "fun stuff," but I followed his advice and straddled him.

"Pretend you're choking me," he said.

"This is getting kinky."

"When it gets kinky, you'll know it."

"Promises, promises." I placed my hands on his neck.

Marcus did the same thing I'd done a few minutes before, thrusting his hips and throwing me off balance. Even though I knew it was coming, my hands automatically shot out to break my fall. Marcus used his knee to push my chest away and then rolled out from under me before scooting out of reach.

I lay on the floor, looking up at him. "Is the lesson over?"

He shook his head. "Now I have the advantage. Higher ground. I'm not

114

gonna do it, because I don't actually want to kill you, but I could stomp on your windpipe. You wouldn't survive that."

I swallowed hard. "Well, thanks for not killing me."

He reached down and took my hand, bringing me to my feet. "I'd never hurt you, Sunshine. But if you're fighting Diablo, it will be a fight for your life. Don't forget that."

I remembered the last time. They weren't playing, that was for sure.

"You're exhausted," Marcus said after I let out a yawn. "Go to bed. I'll stay on the couch in case Diablo pays you a visit."

I checked my watch. It was after four. My bedroom seemed seven miles away. "Nope. Here's fine." I lay down on the couch and rested my feet on his lap. Felony walked in circles, then wormed his way into the crook of my arm.

Marcus' thumb kneading the arch of my foot was the last thing I remembered before I drifted off to sleep.

Chapter Twenty-Five

I woke to something tickling my ear. I squirmed and flicked at a tongue with my fingers. I was still half-asleep when it occurred to me that Marcus might be getting friendly. A paw to my face brought me back to my senses. Felony.

Bolting upright, I took in the room. In the early morning light, I could see clearly. Candles on the coffee table had burned down to stubs. Next to them, the empty container from Ms. Cody and two forks. Marcus had been here. It wasn't a dream.

Felony stretched by my side.

Standing, a blanket dropped to the floor. Marcus must have draped it over me. But I didn't hear him leave. Was he still here?

"Marcus?"

Felony and I exchanged a look. I checked the kitchen. Empty. Same with the other rooms. I let Felony out back, taking my baton just in case. After he did his duty, we returned to the kitchen, where I fed him and got myself a lukewarm Diet Coke.

My phone was down to ten percent battery. There was one message from Detective Ramsey. With dread, I opened it.

Coffman made it through surgery. Touch and go, but he should make it.

Thanks, I responded.

I spent the next half hour tossing slowly thawing food out of the refrigerator before getting ready for work, shaving my legs this time—keeping possibilities open. I didn't have enough battery to call the power company or an electrician. That would have to wait until I made it to the office.

Every time I heard the slightest noise, I jumped. Diablo could stop by at any time. They wouldn't wait for an invitation.

My house wasn't safe, and I didn't feel right leaving Felony alone, so I took him with me.

At the office, Felony and I went straight to see Alma. She was meeting with one of my peers, but when she saw the look on my face, she ushered him out of the room and closed the door. "What now?"

I collapsed on the sofa and encouraged Felony to jump on my lap. I ran a hand over his back. "Someone stabbed Henry Coffman last night at the vigil for Brian Johnson."

Alma's hand shot up and covered her mouth. "Oh, no. Is he dead?"

"Last I heard, he's alive, but not in great condition. He should make it."

"Did they catch the guy?"

I shook my head. "There was a sizable crowd. Whoever did it probably blended in. Ramsey took me to the station for questioning last night. I would have called you, but it was so late, and there was nothing you could do. Not sure if Ramsey knows Henry was considering being an informant."

Alma sat back in her chair. "No reason for us to share that with Tempe PD. Not until now, anyway. But we were going to allow it. What I'm worried about is that this is tied to you. Is this client number three who has been threatened, hurt, or killed?"

She didn't have to remind me. It was taking up a lot of real estate in my brain. "If you count Marjorie. I've thought this through, and I can't think of a reason I'd be the common denominator. I mean, Diablo hates me, but why go after my clients?"

"I don't know."

"I guess it could be a client, or a former client. Someone whose probation got revoked, and they went to prison, maybe? I've thought about it, and no one comes to mind. I keep coming back to Tony. He's the only one I can think of who might want revenge. I told Ramsey about him."

"What did he say?"

"He'll talk to him."

Alma stood and paced the room, Felony following her every move. "I listened to the message from Lilian Harrison you forwarded to me. Roxy's going to call Tony and ask him to back off, but legally, our hands are tied. We've already fired him; not much else we can do."

"Have you talked to his dad?"

"Luigi?"

"Maybe he can rein Tony in." Although, when we talked, he seemed to put the blame for his son's behavior solely on me.

Alma nodded. "I think Roxy plans to do that."

"If that doesn't work, maybe Ramsey paying Tony a visit will scare him away."

"Let's hope." Alma sat next to me and gave Felony a scratch under his chin. "I'm worried about you."

"Me? I'm fine. No one has threatened me."

"Still, you're the common denominator."

"I'm being careful," I said. "And I'm interested in becoming armed. Can you okay that so I can sign up for training and start the process?"

Alma nodded enthusiastically. "Absolutely. Can't believe you're finally coming around."

"Yeah, well…." I placed Felony on the floor and got to my feet. "It's not something I wanted to do, but it's time."

No one said anything about the rule against having dogs in the building, so I pressed my luck for as long as I could. Lugging my stuff downstairs to an interview room, I tied Felony to the desk, set up my laptop, and stacked my paperwork in alphabetical order. Tony planned his office day to have a section of the alphabet report between nine and five. Clients usually trickled in all day, with a rush at the end—if anyone came at all.

Coworkers who also had office days or even a client or two due to come in occupied the interview rooms around me. The rooms were semi-private with three floor-to-ceiling walls, but no door. If something went horribly wrong, other officers could hear and rush in to help get the situation under control. That had happened, but most times, just letting the offender know other POs were listening was enough to keep things civilized.

While it was slow, I polled my coworkers who lived near me for a referral for an electrician. Once my phone had charged, I called around, but no one could fit me in for a few days. I sent Joy a message, warning her we didn't have power, and checked my phone every few minutes, hoping Marcus would be in touch.

I met with a client who was doing well, working, and had just completed his community service hours. I congratulated him and rewarded him with a gift card we kept on hand for such milestones. Positive reinforcement.

After he left, Ms. Cody's number flashed on my phone. I took the call. "Good morning."

"Not so sure about that." There was an edge to her voice.

"Uh, oh, what's wrong?"

"Marjorie's gone."

I closed my eyes. "Did she say where she was going?"

"She got a call. Took it in the bedroom. When she came out, she had her backpack. She thanked me for letting her crash here, then left without telling me why."

"Do you know who called her?"

"I heard a male voice on the line when she first took the call. Guessing it was her ex."

"Who she uses with. That's a shame. I don't think she's safe out there."

Ms. Cody took a moment. "I told her that. Didn't stop her from leaving."

I ran a hand through my hair. Why was it so hard to help people? "Well, I appreciate you putting her up for as long as you did. We can't force people to make wise choices."

"They have to be ready. I often remind myself of that."

Last night, I'd resisted temptation with Marcus. He was as addictive as any drug out there. If I hadn't been so tired, things might have escalated despite my resolve. "Happens to the best of us."

After ending the call, I tried to reach Marjorie, but it went straight to voicemail. I left a message, then texted her, asking her to get back to me

ASAP. Nothing.

I didn't like thinking of her out there... God knew where. Vulnerable. Especially with what had happened to my other clients.

I saw three more clients before I had time to get back to the problem of my lack of electricity. I called the power company, wondering if there was anything they could do. After being on hold for several minutes, a woman came on the line. She took my name and address. After another brief hold, she got back to me. "Sorry, ma'am, but you cancelled your service. Said you were moving."

"What? That's a mistake. I didn't do that."

Her voice went soft, talking to me like I was a dementia patient. "Well, ma'am, you had to have made the call. We ask for your account number and your social security number. Not just anyone can call it in."

"I assure you," I said through gritted teeth. "It wasn't me. When did the cancellation request occur?"

Her keyboard clacked. "A week ago. We have your moving date listed as yesterday. You said you didn't need to transfer the service because you planned to stay with family until you got back on your feet."

"Back on my feet?"

"That's what the notes say. You gave a forwarding address."

"What address?"

"I'll need your account number and social security number to share that information."

I suppressed a scream and gave her the numbers.

"On Morning Star in Phoenix." She rattled off the numbers. I took quick breaths, and my fingers became so clammy, my pen almost slid out of my hand.

My sister's address. Whoever got my social security number also knew where my sister lived. Someone was messing with me. But why? And more importantly, who?

"Can you please re-establish service?" I said. "I'm the only one on the account, and I didn't cancel it."

Her sigh was audible. "There's a reconnect fee."

And so it went. Back and forth until my head pounded. Her supervisor was even less accommodating, suggesting that although I didn't remember canceling, it was obvious that I did. In the end, my service would be restored by the end of the day, but it would cost me.

A break was in order. I told the receptionist to hold my clients and took Felony for a walk.

The office was in an okay neighborhood. Not that Diablo cared about that. The pepper spray clamped to my belt gave me a smidgen of comfort. Felony wouldn't scare off anyone.

I circled the block, picking up after Felony as we went. One of the worst parts of dog ownership was carting around used waste bags. It was hard to look cool with a bag of poop in your hand, but it was the civic-minded thing to do.

When I got back to the office parking lot, I spied a motorcycle pulling into a space. My hackles went up and I kept an eye on the driver as I made my way to the employee entrance. Tossing the bag in the trash, I had my hand on the door as a burly man dismounted the bike and headed around front to the main door.

Dressed in a dark T-shirt and black pants, a pitchfork tattoo peeked out from under the short sleeve stretched across his bicep. Diablo.

Crap.

Chapter Twenty-Six

I ushered Felony back to the cubicle I was using, fastened his leash to the desk, and then hurried down the hall to the reception area. Our receptionist, Tracy, sat behind bulletproof glass that gave her a view of the lobby. Clients checked in with her before she alerted the PO to their arrival.

I hovered behind her, getting a good view of the lobby. Several people waited, sitting on plastic chairs arranged in rows. Behind them, the security guard and metal detector visitors had to pass through before gaining entry was visible.

The Diablo guy unloaded his pockets and placed the contents in a bin before passing through the magnetometer. I'd never seen him before, but I didn't know all the gang members, just the ones I'd helped send to prison. And they got new recruits all the time.

After making it through security, the man put his belt back on and shoved his belongings into his pockets before sauntering up to the counter like he didn't have a care in the world.

"Who are you here to see?" Tracy asked.

"Tony Romero," the man said in a gruff voice.

My already thundering heart threatened to explode.

Tracy looked at me. "Since you're seeing Tony's clients, he's here for you."

The name on the sign-in sheet wasn't one I recognized from Tony's caseload.

"Looks like he's newly sentenced," Tracy said, checking her computer.

From over her shoulder, I read the demographics for Rocky McManus.

Six-two, two-hundred-and-fifty pounds. Lots of tattoos. "Scroll down," I said.

The computer file told me he was on probation for intimidation. At the PO mailboxes, I retrieved the hard file for Mr. McManus. Flipping through the pre-sentence report, I scanned the summary of the offense. McManus had threatened to beat a rival gang member with a shovel.

"Tell him to take a seat," I told Tracy.

Back at my desk, I slipped Felony a treat as I placed a call to Frank Miley, one of our gang officers. "I don't know why they didn't assign this to you," I said. "This guy's Diablo."

Frank sounded distracted. "Our caseloads are full. We're only taking the worst of the worst."

With Diablo hating my guts and all, me supervising him would be a huge conflict of interest. "Can we make an exception?"

"Let me look," Frank said. "Looks like he has priors for domestic violence. Maybe DV can take him."

I thanked him for his time and called Molly Lewis, the supervisor for the domestic violence unit. "I was wondering if you'd take a case," I said. "Name is Rocky McManus. He has a history of DV. He's not on for that kind of offense, but I'm not supposed to supervise any Diablo gang members."

"I heard about that. I'll assign him to Don Altman. Do you feel comfortable seeing Mr. McManus just this once, so you can direct him to report to Don?"

I felt relatively safe in the office, and I assumed this guy didn't know who I was. It wasn't like we were in a post office with my wanted photo on the wall. "Sure. And thanks." I jotted down reporting instructions for Don on a directive and ended the call.

Opening the door to the lobby, I called McManus back.

He slowly got to his feet and lumbered toward me. I held the door and directed him down the hallway. "Second door on the right."

McManus looked me up and down and licked his lips. I couldn't help but roll my eyes. Well deserved. A freebie. Not putting money in the jar. Two minutes, and he'd be someone else's problem.

"Have a seat," I said.

Felony stayed unseen under the desk. I mouthed "good boy" and slid into my chair. McManus perched himself on the plastic chair opposite me, so flimsy, I feared it would collapse under his bulk. "They've assigned you another PO." I laid the directive on the table. "This tells you where and when to report to him. You need to do so within twenty-four hours." My signature was illegible, so I didn't worry about him having my name.

McManus studied the paper, then looked up at me. "You don't need to be afraid of me."

I held his gaze and my ground. "I'm not. You were mis-assigned from the start. Now, please sign."

He picked up the pen that was chained to the desk and toyed with it. "I know you got balls. And I know you need to watch your back."

So much for him not knowing who I was. I almost flinched, but managed to keep my composure. Not a good tactic to let him know he got to me. But I saw an opportunity to find out just how serious Diablo was about seeking revenge. "Is that a threat?"

He shrugged.

"Given the charge you're on supervision for, do you think it's wise to try to intimidate me?"

"Is that what I'm doing?"

"You're trying. It's not working." I tapped the table. "Now, sign the directive."

He gave a gap-toothed grin. "They were right about you. You got spunk. Just don't know if spunk is enough to keep you above ground, if you know what I mean." He signed the paper, then pushed it across the desk to me.

I tore off his copy, laid it in front of him, and stood. "I'll show you out."

He pushed to his feet. "It's been nice meeting you, Ms. Carson."

I motioned for him to walk in front of me and followed him to the door.

"Until we meet again," he said, tipping an imaginary hat.

I pulled the door shut behind him and collapsed against it. Thoughts of McManus and his goon buddies driving me out to the desert to dispose of my body flashed through my mind like a premonition.

I'd fill Alma in on what had occurred and put notes in the file so Don would know what he was dealing with, but only I could keep myself safe.

Damn Betz and his firearms training. I couldn't wait until he thought I was ready. I was going to start carrying the gun he'd given me. It might be my only way to survive.

Chapter Twenty-Seven

I dropped McManus' file in the transfer bin, relieved I'd never have to see him again. A check of my messages told me Henry Coffman wanted to see me. A surprise since he'd threatened to sue me.

At least he was well enough to ask for me. I called Alma to run it by her.

She hesitated before saying, "Well, technically, he's still on supervision and you're his PO. It might earn us points if you remain an advocate. But don't discuss his arrest at the hands of Tony. If he's still upset, suggest he file a grievance. I'm just glad he's pulling through."

"Me too." I filled her in on my encounter with McManus.

"You did the right thing. Maybe you should talk to someone in the gang unit. Find out how active Diablo is these days."

"Will do." I disconnected and ended the call.

The rest of Tony's office day went smoothly. Less than half of his clients showed up, which wasn't unusual, but left me with a lot of following up to do.

I left a message for Frank in the gang unit, dropped Felony at Kate's, then made the drive down McDowell to the county hospital.

After signing the visitor's log, I stopped in the gift shop and bought a box of candy. I found Henry's room on the third floor across from the nurses' station.

The door was ajar. I rapped on it and waited.

"Come in," came a female voice.

I entered, finding Henry's grandmother standing at the foot of her

126

grandson's bed, wringing her hands with worry. Henry's eyes were closed. He had tubes up his nose and dripping fluids into his arm.

I placed the box of chocolates on the side table and offered Henry's grandmother, Edna, a smile. "How is he?"

She shrugged. "In a lot of pain. On a lot of morphine. But he's expected to make a full recovery."

"Well, that's good. The recovery part."

Edna nodded and settled on a visitor's chair. "Have a seat."

I perched on the chair across from her. "Henry wanted to see me?"

"Yes. I admit we weren't happy with you after your trainee hit Henry with his car. That was uncalled for. But we understand he's no longer employed with your agency. Is that true?"

I had to be careful. Admitting Tony's firing resulted from the incident would be admitting guilt if they sued the department. That was for Alma to sort out. "He doesn't work with me anymore, that's true."

"Henry and I talked, and we both agree that you've always been good to him. You held him accountable, but you've been more than fair. He doesn't want a new PO."

I smiled. "I'm happy to keep working with him. He's mostly been straight with me, and I appreciate that." Although not about dealing, but I would not share that with his grandma.

A groan stopped our conversation. Edna jumped up and went to Henry's bedside. She ran a hand over his head lovingly. "Casey's here, Darling."

Henry opened one eye and looked at me. He cleared his throat and struggled to sit up.

I jumped to my feet. "Take it easy."

Henry waved me away. "I'm okay. Glad you're here."

Edna hit the bed control and raised Henry's head, so he was sitting up.

"How are you feeling?" I asked.

He blew out a long breath. "Hurts like a mother, but doc says I'll be okay."

I stepped closer to the bed. "I'm glad to hear that. Any idea who did this?"

Henry shrugged. "It all happened so fast."

"Has anyone threatened you? Followed you?"

"The detective asked the same thing," Edna said.

And Ramsey wouldn't like me meddling in his investigation, I was sure.

Henry winced as he reached for the container of water on his tray table. Edna rushed forward and held the cup, while Henry drank from the straw. "I only got out of jail a few hours before the vigil." He leaned back against the table. "I met up with some of my peeps from NA, and they told me about Brian."

"You knew him?"

He nodded. "Haven't seen him for a few weeks. Now I know why."

He hadn't seen Brian because he was rotting away in the canal, but I didn't want to bring that up. "Did he tell you anything before he disappeared?"

Henry's already ashen complexion paled as he played with a fold in the sheet. "He wanted to meet. Something scared him. Thought I should watch my back, too."

"Do you know why?"

Henry wouldn't look at me but shook his head.

"Did you tell this to Detective Ramsey?"

Henry's eyes darted to mine. "The guy's an asshole."

I got the same vibe. "Any idea why he thought you were both in danger? What connected you?" Time to address the elephant in the room. "Could it be related to your dealing?"

He exchanged a worried look with his grandmother. This was getting dicey. I didn't want to interfere with an investigation, but if I could get Henry to trust me, I could pass whatever he told me on to Ramsey. And if I didn't ask too many questions... if Henry told me on his own... I wouldn't be sticking my nose where it didn't belong. I waited him out.

"I ain't gonna be no snitch. Snitches get stitches and I already got enough of those. Ain't gonna be me to bring the truth to light. But I can tell you this. There's a guy who's ready to talk. Maybe he has a death wish, I don't know. Don't know his real name, but people call him The Kid. He has proof, but he doesn't know what to do with it."

"Proof of what?"

"You'll have to ask him that. I've said too much already. But some advice, don't bring cops. You'll scare him off if you do."

Chapter Twenty-Eight

Confusion clouded my mind as I left the hospital. Henry didn't deny he was dealing drugs, which was a good reason for him not to trust cops. And he gave me a tangible lead. "The Kid" sounded like a gang nickname. Maybe Henry giving him up was the morphine talking, but I had to check it out.

After Henry's warning, I wouldn't go to Ramsey, but Frank at our gang unit might be a good source of information. He'd yet to call me back. Back at my office, I found his number in my recent call list and pressed send.

"This is Frank."

"Hey, Frank, it's Casey Carson again. Got a couple of questions for you."

"Go ahead."

"What can you tell me about a guy called 'The Kid?'"

Frank cleared his throat. "He's a new Diablo recruit. Got jumped in when he was in prison last year."

So, this circled back to Diablo. "Speaking of Diablo, what are they up to these days?"

"I heard you're on their shit list. Three of the lead members are in prison. You know about Ramirez since you used to supervise him. They're busy collecting new recruits. The members who are still in the community floundered for a while, but they're getting organized. More reckless than the OG's. Seem to have steered away from human trafficking and are back to the easier venture of dealing."

"Dealing what?"

"Fentanyl-laced pills they're selling as Oxy. Whatever they can move."

That meant Henry had a link to Diablo, too. Did he know they had it in for me? Was he sending me into a trap?

"'The Kid.' What's his real name?"

"Justin Ackerman. Just got sentenced for a new possession charge. He's a user. On probation, but not with me."

"Another gang officer? Or is he not badass enough to meet the criteria?"

Frank laughed. "Like I told you, our caseloads are full. He's assigned to a standard caseload."

I scribbled down a note to look him up and contact his PO.

"Anyway," Frank said. "You might want to wear a vest for a while. I had to do that when there was a hit out on me."

"A hit? I don't think there's a hit out on me." My voice squeaked and I cleared my throat to talk normally. "And I'm not wearing a vest. It's ninety degrees."

"Don't know how you live your life, but I figure it's hotter in hell."

Huh. Didn't think I was going there, but good to know he thought I might. I had to work on my reputation. "I'll think about it."

My personal cell vibrated on my desk. I turned it over and checked the message. Marcus. About time.

I ended my call with Frank and read Marcus' message. *You free for lunch?*

I checked my watch. Almost noon, and at the thought of food, my stomach growled. At the thought of Marcus, my heart fluttered. My whole body vibrated. *What part of town you in?*

Central Phoenix.

Meet me at George's Deli. Corner off Central & Camelback.

Be there in 15.

That gave me a few minutes to look up Justin Ackerman. A quick search of our system showed me that he was on supervision to Pete Pajerski. Small world. I'd wait to call him until after lunch. I didn't want to ruin my appetite.

As usual, the line at George's spilled onto the sidewalk. Marcus stood a few feet from the door. A respectable distance for a smoke break. When he saw me, he ground out his cigarette with his boot and flicked the butt into a nearby trash can.

"This place must be good," he said, motioning to the line with a tilt of his head.

"Would I steer you wrong?"

We got in line. Women ahead of us shamelessly batted their eyes at Marcus. If he noticed, he didn't let on.

"Where did you disappear to this morning?"

Hands in pockets, he rocked back on his heels. "Had a job interview. Construction starts early here."

"Because of the heat. You get the job?"

"Nothing sexy, but it'll pay the bills."

"Speaking of bills, where are you staying?" If he thought he was staying with me, I needed to give him a dose of reality. I wasn't ready for that kind of commitment. And with Joy around, my two-bedroom house was full.

"Since you made it clear I'm not welcome in your bed, I'll have to find a place," he said quietly and with a frown.

A flush ran up my face. "I just want to take things slowly." A job. A place. Marcus was serious.

"Yeah, I got that."

The line moved forward, and we took two steps ahead. "When do you start working?"

"Tomorrow. Building houses in a subdivision close to your place. The foreman's looking for a roommate, so I'll check out his place this afternoon."

I didn't know a lot about Marcus. He'd been vague about his past when we'd met. I could attribute most of that to his undercover status at the time, but he didn't seem overly willing to share a lot now that sleuthing was behind him. I knew he loved his family; he'd put his life on the line to protect them. As I saw it, that was a decent reason to give his shortcomings, like smoking and being evasive, a pass. I looked at his profile, his perfect face, the way his clothes clung to his hard, lean body…. Guess there were other reasons, too.

Sandwiches in hand, we found a picnic table to the side of the restaurant.

He pulled a tomato off his sandwich and put it aside. "There's something you should know."

"You don't like tomatoes?"

He smiled. "That *is* important. But also, I saw a Diablo guy on your street when I left this morning. I would have alerted you, but they followed me, so I thought you were safe. They stayed with me for a few hours, and then I guess they got bored and gave up. Now that they know I'm in town, maybe they'll come after me and leave you alone."

"Don't like either scenario," I said. "Did you get a license plate number? I can ask Betz to look into it."

"It was still dark. So, no."

I finished half of my sandwich and wrapped the other part for later. "So, what, they just stood around watching you?"

"After my interview, I ran some errands. Went to the bank, bought a few changes of clothes, new work boots. Every time I returned to my motorcycle, I spotted a guy parked a few spots back. I even waved to him, so he knew I was onto him. After my last stop, he was gone. I drove around a bit to make sure he wasn't just doing a better job of tailing me before I met you. But I figure they know where you work and live, so I don't know if that was necessary."

I glanced over my shoulder.

Marcus nudged my foot with his. "Don't worry, I've got your back. No one is watching us now."

I turned my attention back to him. "Not true. That table of women over there has been drooling over you since we got here."

He laughed. "Thought they were looking at you, jealous of your flair for style."

"Too funny."

"Anyway, I didn't ride across the country to meet women. I came to see you. But back to something you said earlier."

"What?"

"Your ex. You said you'd ask him to run the plate. That he brought you the dog. You two still tight?"

I looked down, playing with the wrapper on my sandwich. "We're friends."

Marcus raised an eyebrow. "Forgive me if I'm not a fan. The guy arrested me. He wasn't exactly gentle with the cuffs."

"You had a warrant, and you were armed," I said. "He was just doing his job."

"Seems like his job is to look after you."

"I don't need anyone to look after me."

"If you say so."

I didn't like the direction this conversation had taken. I looked at my watch. One-thirty. Time to get back to work. I tucked the rest of my sandwich into my bag, grabbed what was left of my Diet Coke, and stood. "I gotta go."

Marcus stayed seated. "I'm gonna finish my lunch. When can I see you again?"

"I'll call you later," I said. And I hurried back to my Jeep.

Chapter Twenty-Nine

Back at the office, I found Jerski sitting in my cubicle. Like an ad on social media for something you only thought about, he showed up in that creepy way of his. "What are you doing here?"

Too comfortable in my seat, he clasped his hands behind his head and rocked back so he could look me in the eye. "Nice to see you, too."

I took the leftover sandwich out of my bag and stuffed it in the small refrigerator I kept under my desk. "I wasn't expecting you, is all."

"Why not? I sent you an invite. We have a date to do fieldwork."

If I'd seen it, I would have declined. "Didn't get one."

"Well, I came all this way. And I have a list of people to see. We can squeeze your folks in along the way."

Not the way I wanted to spend my afternoon, but since he was here…. "I wanted to ask you about a client. You supervise Justin Ackerman?"

Jerski picked a piece of paper off my desk and waved it at me. "He's on the list. Why? What about him?"

"He's Diablo. Or at least an associate." Jerski knew about Diablo. He'd witnessed their handiwork firsthand.

"The only reason he joined was for protection in prison. He's quite the pretty boy, and he needed to align himself with Diablo to make his stay bearable. But he wants out. I referred him for tattoo removal."

It would take more than erasing their markings to leave a prison gang, but I appreciated the effort. "Where does he live?"

Jerski stood. He was only an inch taller than me, and that was with his chunky-heeled boots. His tac vest, army fatigues, and the gun on his hip were a bit much for my taste. "He's staying with his aunt. We can start there."

I picked up my gear bag and threw it over my shoulder. My client list was inside, but I pretty much knew where my probationers lived by heart. If Jerski could introduce me to Justin, I might learn something that would keep my clients safe.

Knowing Jerski drove a tiny hybrid car, I was surprised when he led me to an old black hearse. "Ewe," I said. "Is that what I think it is?"

Jerski beamed. "It's a Cadillac."

"That's used to transport dead people."

"Used to be. It's my fieldwork car. It's comfortable and makes a statement."

"The last ride?"

He laughed. "Her name is La Bamba. She's a bit of a gas guzzler, but since the county reimburses mileage, it's better than putting miles on my other car."

I slid into the passenger's seat. I had to admit, the interior was luxurious—plush black leather seats with lots of legroom. I glanced in back: roomy enough for two caskets. But I didn't want to think about that. I mean, who buys a used hearse, if you're not in the business? Who even thinks of doing that? Plus, there was an odor I couldn't place. I tried not to imagine the source.

Jerski handed me his field list and pulled onto the main road. "Joy loves this car."

Plenty of room for them to do what they do. Double ewe. I rubbed my temples and tried to erase the thought from my mind.

I got on the radio and put us in service, then concentrated on Jerski's driving, which was just short of terrifying. He didn't seem to be aware of how much space La Bamba required as he drifted into the other lanes. I felt pretty safe in this boat of a haunted car—it was the other people on the road I worried about.

We headed to Tempe, which was part of Jerski's territory and close to my house. He turned into an older, upscale neighborhood. The houses dated back about twenty years, but most of them looked well cared for.

Jerski parked in front of a rambling ranch. I wondered if the neighbors thought we were about to roll out a dead body. There'd be no sneaking up on anyone in this car. I called in the address on the radio and followed Jerski up the walkway. He banged on the door with his fist even though the doorbell was clearly visible.

"Probation!" he announced.

I caught my eyes mid-roll. All we needed was a helicopter circling above us to be any more conspicuous.

The door popped open, and a young guy, early twenties, stood before us, scratching a mop of silky black hair. Navy sweatpants were slung low on narrow hips. No shirt. He sported a crude pitchfork tattoo on his left bicep. Blurred lines. No doubt a prison tat. I couldn't tell from the distance between us, but given his history, I bet his veiny arms were ripe with track marks. Long-lashed bedroom eyes would make any woman jealous if they weren't too busy swooning over this perfect specimen of a boy becoming a man. A few good meals and some sober time, and he'd be too good to be true. But drugs had begun to take their toll, and if he didn't turn things around soon, he'd waste the gift that God had given him.

"What's up, boss?" He stepped back to allow us entry.

"Verifying your address," Jerski said, standing in the interview stance we'd been trained to do. But instead of having his hands up and ready, he rested one on the butt of his gun. Not threatening at all. Mental eye roll.

Justin seemed relaxed regardless. Probably high. "This is it." He waved at the living room behind him.

Someone nicely decorated the room in neutral gray tones. Everything in its place, like a model home. His aunt had money and good taste.

"Anyone else here?" I asked.

"Nope." He gave me the once over. "My aunt's at work."

"Show us where you sleep," Jerski said.

Justin led us through a modern kitchen that had obviously been updated and down the hall to the rooms at the back of the house. I brought up the rear, flicking on the hall light so there'd be no surprises. Photos lined the wall. I stopped to get a good look. My mouth dropped open, and I took a deep breath. "Ah, who's your aunt?"

Justin backtracked and pointed to a familiar face in the photo. "Suzy Vega. She's kind of famous."

I hadn't seen that one coming. Was that why his aunt had a connection to Diablo? Was she trying to pressure them into letting her nephew leave the gang? Regardless, I was glad she was at work, and I wouldn't run into her.

Justin opened the door to a room halfway down the hallway. This one looked lived in and more like the rooms I was used to seeing during home visits. Sheets and a comforter lay wadded up at the bottom of the unmade daybed. Clothes lay strewn across the floor, and food-crusted plates covered several surfaces. I doubted Suzy was happy with the condition of the room, given how she kept the rest of the house.

"Any weapons in the home?" Jerski asked.

"No, sir." Justin scratched his belly.

Charming.

"You looking for work?" Jerski said.

While Justin gave excuses, I gave the room a closer look. A little black makeup bag sat on the desk. I knew from experience why drug addicts had such things. "Mind if I look inside?" I nudged it with my knuckle.

Justin hung his head. In Arizona, we didn't need a warrant to search a probationer's belongings. If Jerski had gone over the conditions of probation with him, as he should have, Justin would know that.

I withdrew a pair of disposable gloves from my pocket and pulled them on. Unzipping the bag, I exposed two syringes, a crusty spoon, and a small vial. "When did you last use?" I asked.

Justin ran a hand through his hair. "Yesterday."

"You know that violates your probation," Jerski said, stating the obvious.

Thing is, we had options. Not every violation needed to result in jail time. But it was Jerski's decision, and I knew he was more law and order than a social worker. Detoxing in jail was one way to go, but it wasn't the most humane or successful avenue. Jail wasn't intended for that, although it was frequently used in that manner.

"Let's talk in the living room," I suggested, taking the heroin kit with me.

138

Jerski grabbed a wrinkled T-shirt off a pile of clothes on the floor and handed it to Justin. "Might want to grab some shoes, too," he said.

Justin scooped up a pair of running shoes, and we walked back down the hall, single file.

In the living room, Justin sat down to put his shoes on. I motioned for Jerski to join me in the entryway so we could keep an eye on Justin but talk out of earshot. "I know Valley View has beds," I said. "I'd be glad to call and see if they can take him."

"Rehab? The jail also has beds." Jerski cast a look back at Justin.

"But the medically assisted detox at Valley View will be easier on him. Aren't you going to recommend treatment, anyway?"

Jerski crossed his arms. "You telling me how to do my job?"

I held up my hands. "Just a suggestion."

A noise sounded from the side of the house. It took me a moment to figure out it was the garage door going up. Uh oh, things were about to get ugly.

"I think Suzy Vega's home," I said in a hushed voice.

If everything wasn't by the book—hell, even if it was—she'd be talking about it on the news.

Suzy came through the kitchen and stopped in the living room, where she took in the scene. Shoes on, Justin got to his feet. "This is my aunt," he said.

Suzy pointed at me. "You've got to be kidding me. You're his PO? And you drive a hearse?"

I shook my head, and with my thumb, I motioned to Jerski. "Nope. Just his partner today."

"And I'm going to jail," Justin said.

Suzy whipped her phone out and started recording. *Uh, oh, here we go.*

"What are the charges?"

Jerski took the kit out of my hands and held it up. "Right now, just a probation violation. Did you know your nephew has drugs in your house? He's lucky I haven't called the police and asked them to file new possession charges."

"How do you know it's his?" she said. "Didn't your friend leave that here, Justin?"

Justin looked at his shoes and shrugged. He wasn't as quick with a comeback as his aunt. Or maybe he was a terrible liar. Whichever, it made me want to help him even more.

"Well," Jerski said. "Even if that were true, Justin admitted to using yesterday. That alone is enough for me to arrest him."

"Why don't we go outside," I said. Get this show on the road. The longer Suzy had her camera rolling, the greater the potential for disaster.

Justin moved toward the door. I opened it, and we stepped outside. Suzy and her camera followed. "This is personal," Suzy said. "This is payback for my reporting on the Harrison and Coffman fiascos, isn't it?"

Oh boy, I dreaded telling Alma about this.

Jerski got on the radio and asked dispatch to send us a patrol officer to transport Justin to jail. I was running out of time to convince him to do otherwise.

Justin and I moved toward La Bamba. "Oh, wow," Justin said. "Is that a hearse?"

"It is," I said.

While Jerski dealt with Suzy, I took the opportunity to talk to Justin. "Look," I said, glancing over my shoulder and then back at Justin as he ran his hand over the shiny back door. "I talked to Henry Coffman. He told me you might have information about his stabbing. About the death of Brian Johnson."

Justin froze, straightened, and crossed his arms. "You Henry's PO?"

I nodded. Behind him, Suzy and Jerski were really getting into it. I didn't have much time. "What do you know?"

Justin's eyes darted from side to side. "Will you talk my PO into not taking me to jail?"

I sighed. "Not my decision. But Henry and Brian were both attacked. Brian's dead, and Henry's in the hospital. You seem like a decent guy. I heard you don't want to be part of Diablo. I just want to make sure more of my clients don't get hurt."

Justin held his ground. "I really don't want to go to jail. Stop that from happening, and maybe I have something to tell you."

CHAPTER TWENTY-NINE

"Give me a minute."

"Pete," I called. "Can we talk?"

Jerski threw up his hands at Suzy and walked my way. She got on her phone and moved away from us, but I could still hear her end of the conversation. "Why aren't you taking my calls? I need your input. Please, call me." She sounded desperate.

Diablo? Or a lover? Maybe the detective she was rumored to be sleeping with?

I stepped a distance from the hearse so we could talk without Justin or his aunt overhearing. "Look," I said. "I don't have time to explain, but Justin has information I need. He won't tell me if you arrest him. Can't we just get him into treatment?"

"Why do you want him to go to rehab so badly?"

"It's where he needs to be. Plus, like I said, it's the only way he's gonna talk. I'll fill you in later, but for now, I need you to trust me on this."

"Vega's gonna think she won if I do that."

"We got bigger problems than Vega," I said. "My clients are being targeted. Please, Pete, treatment will be less paperwork for you, too."

That got his attention. Jerski didn't look happy, but he called dispatch and had them call off Justin's ride to jail. Then we walked over to Justin, who was talking to his aunt and gave him the news.

The four of us stood in a huddle. I cleared my throat. "While you and Ms. Vega talk about treatment, Pete, I'll head inside with Justin and watch him pack."

Jerski looked even less happy, but he got on the phone and let Valley View know they were coming. Suzy seemed satisfied and stopped recording our every move. I followed Justin back inside.

In his bedroom, Justin grabbed a duffel bag out of the closet and started stuffing clothes inside.

"What do you know?" I said.

He dropped the bag on his bed and picked a paperback up off the desk. "What makes you think I know anything?"

"Come on... Henry said you have proof. Proof of what?"

141

"I don't know why he told you that. I don't know nothing."

"Oh, come on…. One of my clients died, and someone attacked Coffman. I'm afraid it won't stop there."

"Sorry, can't help you."

"Thought we had a deal. Or maybe you should go to jail."

Justin kicked an empty soda can across the floor. "I get my stash from Coffman, okay?"

If that was the case, why would Coffman want me to talk to him? There had to be more to it. "Did his stabbing have something to do with dealing drugs?"

He blinked. "What do you think?"

"Do you know who he works for?"

Justin zipped his bag shut and slung it over his shoulder. "I have a theory, but don't want to say anything until I know for sure. Coming forward could be bad for my health."

"And it would dry up your supply."

He laughed. "There's plenty of that out there."

"Is Diablo running things?"

His gaze darted to the ground. "I've said all I can for now."

Not exactly a "no."

I took a business card from my pocket and handed it to him. "This is important. Don't take too long."

Justin shoved my card in his pocket but made no promises.

Chapter Thirty

With Justin on his way to treatment, Jerski and I set off toward South Phoenix to see a few of my people.

Rodney Hill lived with his parents in a cute little two-bedroom house that stood out like a beacon of hope in an otherwise neglected neighborhood. Rodney had a head injury that affected his long-term memory. He lived in the here and now, which made him impossible to supervise. I'd asked the court to grant him an early termination of his supervision, but the judge held fast to the belief that my keeping tabs on him somehow made the community safer. I was no miracle worker, which was what it would take to keep Rodney in line. His parents could not control him and frequently called me worried because he had the habit of climbing out of his window at night and gravitating back to the streets where he'd gotten into trouble in the first place.

I only saw him in the field because Rodney couldn't remember to come to the office.

I knocked on the door and waited with Jerski at my side.

Rodney's father ushered us inside. "He's watching cartoons," he said.

We followed him through the orderly house. The aroma of baking bread had me longing for the half-a-sandwich I'd left at the office.

Rodney sat on a floral couch that must have been from the seventies, his feet propped on the coffee table in front of him. A lit cigarette rested between grubby fingers and overcame the mouth-watering scent of baking bread.

"Hey, Rodney." I stood before him, waving smoke from my face. "How are you?"

His eyes narrowed with suspicion. "Who are you?"

"Casey, your probation officer."

His eyes grew wide. "I'm on probation? What'd I do?"

And so it went. Every damn time.

There was no point in telling him he had quite the criminal record and had been a force to be reckoned with before he was nearly beaten to death by his lover's husband. Now, it was like talking to a two-year-old with a nicotine addiction.

"Don't worry about it," I said. "Just stopped by to say hi."

"Hi," he said.

"What a waste of time," Jerski said once we were back in the hearse.

"True." But I didn't make the rules.

My cell vibrated, and I wiggled it out of my back pocket while using the radio to tell dispatch that our home visit was complete. The message was from Betz. My heart kicked like a ninja in my chest. If he wanted an answer, I didn't have one.

Got good news for you

What?

Found a home for Felony. I can come over and get him tonight.

My throat closed. I'd gotten used to the little bugger. I didn't know how sweet he'd be when I'd asked Betz to find him a new owner.

In the field. Won't be home for a while.

Okay. Wasn't going to be for a bit, anyway.

Crap. I dropped the phone onto my lap.

"Where next?" Jerski wanted to know.

With a sick feeling in my stomach, I checked Jerski's list. "You have one on the way back to the office. Let's do that and call it a day." I wanted some time to say goodbye to Felony before Betz came to get him. Give him a special treat before he left.

"If you say so." Jerski headed up Central Avenue, still cranky about giving in to Suzy Vega.

My cell buzzed again. A call from an unknown number. "This is Casey." Cringing, I slammed on imaginary brakes when Jerski almost rear-ended the car, stopping at a light in front of us.

"Casey," came a whisper. "I'm in trouble."

"Marjorie? Where are you?"

"At my boyfriend's. I know I screwed up." She caught a sob. "I'm sorry. I didn't know who else to call."

"It's okay. What's going on?"

"I'm stuck."

"How are you stuck?"

"I think my ankle's broken. I don't have a car. I have to get out of here before he comes back. I shouldn't have left Ms. Cody's. I'm sorry."

"What's the address?"

She rattled it off. It was back the way we'd come. "Okay. We should be there in about ten minutes. Will you be okay until then, or should you call the cops?"

"I'll be okay. Hurry."

She hung up. I glanced at Jerski, who was eyeing me with irritation. "What now?"

"Need you to turn around. Head south. One of my clients needs help."

Jerski's lips pinched into a fine line. "Thought we were going to see my guy."

"After," I said. "Please."

At the next street, Jerski pulled a U-turn that caused us to fishtail. We hit every light, and I used the drive to fill Jerski in on Marjorie's situation. I knew little about her boyfriend, but I could hear the fear in Marjorie's voice, and I knew he contributed to her making poor choices. I had to get her out of there. Hopefully, Ms. Cody would take her back.

We arrived at the house, drove by it, and parked on the other side of the street. I called in the address to dispatch and asked that they check on us every fifteen minutes instead of the hour they usually allowed. It should only take a few minutes to get Marjorie out of there, and if we weren't back on the road in fifteen minutes, it would mean things had turned to crap.

The house was a normal Arizona stucco two-story with desert landscaping and no car in the driveway. I knocked on the door.

It opened an inch, and Marjorie's eye came into view. "Casey," she said with relief.

The door creaked open another foot, and she stepped back to let us inside. All of her weight was on one foot, with the other hovering a few inches off the floor. Poor lighting prevented me from being sure, but I thought Marjorie's face was bruised.

"You ready?" I asked.

"My bag is in the bedroom upstairs." She pointed to her foot. "I can't make it up there. Can you get it?"

"Your boyfriend isn't here?"

"No."

I headed up the stairs while Jerski stayed with Marjorie. I found a backpack I recognized on an end table in what I assumed was the primary bedroom. I grabbed it, knocking a framed photo to the floor. Bending to pick it up, I sucked in a deep breath when the photo came into view. Rocky McManus stood with his arm draped over Marjorie's shoulder.

She was running from Diablo. We had to get out of the house before her boyfriend returned. Jerski had a weapon, but I didn't want to test his abilities.

Before I could retreat, the garage door opened below me. I crossed to the window and looked down at the driveway as a black sedan disappeared inside. *Crap.* I ran for the stairs.

"He's back!" I skidded to a stop in the foyer. "Go!"

Jerski pulled the front door open, and we stumbled into the sunlight. Marjorie hopped on one foot, and I wrapped my arm around her, letting her lean on me for support. We'd almost made it to the hearse when McManus appeared behind us in the front doorway.

I wrenched the passenger door open and shoved Marjorie inside. Jerski ran around to the driver's side.

No room for me.

I chanced a glance over my shoulder.

McManus looked like the Incredible Hulk, shoulders shifting as he advanced down the walkway. I opened the back door, tossed Marjorie's backpack inside, and dove in after it. The space was for caskets, so there was only room for me to sit cross-legged. My head hit the ceiling, and I had to bend my neck to fit. I tried not to dwell on the previous occupants as I pulled the door shut just as McManus made it to the car.

"Step on it," I yelled.

McManus' fist pounded on the window, shattering the glass. Jerski punched the gas pedal, and the vehicle lurched forward as Marjorie screamed while ducking out of Rocky's reach. Holding onto the seat back, I struggled not to topple over as we took off down the street.

I managed a look over my shoulder, glimpsing McManus standing in the middle of the road, watching us drive out of sight.

"Son of a bitch broke my window," Jerski huffed, slightly out of breath.

Relief flooded through me as we left Rocky behind. I was thankful Jerski hadn't stayed and initiated a fight. It was becoming apparent that he wasn't as macho as he pretended to be. I thanked God he wasn't as crazy as I'd suspected, then I called dispatch to relay what had happened. The dispatcher agreed to call the police so they could deal with Rocky and meet us to take a report.

Once we put some distance between us, Jerski pulled into a convenience store parking lot, where we waited for the officer to arrive.

Keeping my eyes peeled for a black sedan, I sat on the open back hatch of the car. In the bright light of day, I verified my previous assessment. Marjorie had a black eye. "Did he do that to you?"

I slid over, and she sat in the space next to me. Hanging her head, she nodded.

"And your ankle?"

"He pushed me down the stairs."

"I hope you're going to make a report."

She wouldn't look at me. Her silence told me that filing a report was the last thing she intended to do. She seemed to shrink further inside of herself when the police car pulled into the lot.

A female officer exited the car and walked over to us. "Went by the house," she said after checking my ID. "No one was home. Saw broken glass on the road from where he smashed the hearse window. I can take a report for criminal damage."

Jerski ran a hand over his face. "Is that all? That's only a misdemeanor."

The cop shrugged. "Unless you've got something else."

I nudged Marjorie with my elbow. "Tell her."

The cop leaned in so she could get a good look at Marjorie's face. "He do that to you?"

Marjorie shook her head. "I fell down the stairs."

Her denial wasn't a surprise. Arrests and restraining orders sometimes made things worse in domestic violence situations. No one who hadn't been in her shoes could understand her fear. The best thing for Marjorie was to put some distance between herself and the bozo she probably once loved.

When the cop finished taking our statements, Jerski walked back with her to the cruiser, trying to get her to up the charges against McManus.

I patted Marjorie's knee. "We'll take you to the hospital. Get your ankle looked at. I can ask Ms. Cody if you can spend the night, but we need to find something more permanent and far away. You got somewhere else to go?"

Marjorie shrugged bony shoulders. "My grandma's in Idaho. She has a farm."

"Would she take you in?"

"If I can afford the bus ticket."

"Don't worry about that." Victim Services would probably foot the bill. I'd pay out of pocket if I had to.

A rush of emotion streamed down Marjorie's face. "Thanks, Casey."

Sometimes, that was all it took to make my job worthwhile.

Chapter Thirty-One

After the emergency room, with Marjorie's foot in a boot, we dropped her off at Ms. Cody's. On the way back to the office, Jerski complained nonstop that my clients had consumed his entire day and that he'd barely completed any of his work. He was ape-shit mad about La Bamba's window being shattered as well. Bright side? Hopefully, he'd never invite me to do fieldwork again.

By the time I drove home, it was almost seven. I found Joy in the living room watching a cooking show. When Felony noticed me standing there, he ran to greet me, his stub of a tail wagging with gusto.

I plopped onto the sofa and encouraged him to join me. He laid on his back, inviting belly rubs. I complied. No man could replace this level of unconditional love. Emotions I couldn't explain came out of nowhere and choked me as I thought about saying goodbye.

Joy gave me the stink eye. "Pete said you kept him working late. Ruined our dinner plans."

So, this was about her. Good to know. "I had a client in need."

Joy waved my words away. "Anyway, he's on his way over."

"Oh, good." I didn't mention that I'd had enough of Jerski for the day.

A knock on the door got Felony's attention. He leapt off the sofa and ran to it. Guess I wasn't the most exciting thing in the room anymore.

Joy jumped to her feet and went to answer. I prepared myself for another dose of Jerski, but it was Betz.

"Barry!" Joy shrieked. Didn't matter who the man was if one came around, she poured on the charm. "What a pleasant surprise." She wrapped her arms

149

around him.

"Why is there a hearse parked out front?" Betz said once Joy released him.

Joy giggled. "It's my boyfriend's car. He must have just pulled up."

"Interesting." Betz leaned down and petted Felony.

Jerski came in behind them, giving Joy a dutiful peck on the cheek. His face was still tight with anger.

"How about we order pizza?" Joy said.

"I could eat," I said.

"Good idea," Jerski added. "I'm starving since hotshot here kept us tied up all afternoon."

I was too tired to defend myself and let his comment slide. While Joy got on her phone to place the order, Betz followed me into the kitchen. I took two beers from the refrigerator and handed him one. "Who did you find to take Felony?"

"A friend."

"Old? Young? Man? Woman? I want details."

Betz rubbed the back of his neck and took a drink. "Woman. She's around our age."

"Oh?" I raised an eyebrow. The neck rub set my radar off. He was holding something back. "How well do you know her?"

"Thought you trusted me. I wouldn't give Felony to just anyone."

I scooped the dog into my arms and held him like a baby. "It's just that.... He's growing on me. I like having him around."

"Thought you didn't have time for a dog."

"I can make coming home earlier a priority."

Betz flashed me a questioning look. "I used to live with you. You've never had a schedule."

"I thought you wanted me to get a dog. Now you're acting like I'm not capable of taking care of one."

"I wanted you to get a gun. How's that going, by the way?"

"It's locked up in my room."

"That's useful."

I let that slide. "Speaking of guns. Diablo's been around." I didn't want to bring Marcus into the conversation, so I left the part about them following him out.

"Again?"

I nodded. "Rocky McManus is abusing one of my clients. We had a run-in with him today."

"We?"

"Me and Jerski. McManus broke a window in the hearse."

"You did fieldwork in a hearse?"

"Wasn't my idea."

Betz put his beer on the counter, reached across, and rubbed Felony's head. "Why would you go near McManus?"

"I didn't mean to. I didn't know *he* was the boyfriend." Felony squirmed, so I put him down.

Betz rubbed his neck again. "We should shoot again this weekend. I want you proficient with that gun."

I raised my hands in surrender. "I'm on board. Trust me."

Betz nodded. "I promised myself I wouldn't bring this up, but did you think about what I said the other day?"

I took a drink. "Constantly."

"And?"

Saved by the bell. The doorbell. "Pizza's here," I said. "And I don't want to have this conversation with Joy and Jerski around."

Betz picked up his beer bottle and followed me out of the room. "Probably wise."

In the living room, Joy and Jerski sat on the sofa, the pizza box open on the coffee table in front of them. Betz and I settled in armchairs across from each other. My stomach fluttered. Not with hunger. With indecision. About Felony and my future with Betz. I finished my beer.

Betz picked at his food. I was really getting to him. I needed to put him out of his misery.

As if he had some kind of mad ESP skills, Marcus sent a text. *You free tonight?*

I dropped my half-eaten slice of pizza onto the box lid and typed a reply.

Sorry, been a long day. How about tomorrow?

Sure.... Dinner?

Sounds good.

I put my phone on vibrate mode and slid it back into my pocket.

The TV was on, but someone had muted the sound. A news promo played, and Suzy Vega's face filled the screen. I lost the rest of my appetite. She stood in front of my office. I didn't know what she was saying, but I didn't need to be a lip reader to know it was personal.

I reached for the remote and upped the volume.

"It isn't just the police who abuse their power. Probation officers need to be held accountable, too. I will continue to investigate this story until the truth is revealed."

Betz dropped his crust next to mine. "Shit," he said. "She's really going after you."

And I thought getting her nephew into treatment instead of jail would have bought me some points.

"Well," Joy said. "You broke that old lady's hip."

I shot her a look, and she made a gesture of buttoning her lip. "Sorry."

Betz hung his head. "This may have something to do with me."

"You?" Joy and I said in unison.

Betz wiped his hands on his thighs and avoided eye contact with me. "I went out with her a few times a few months back. I soon realized she was a live wire. When I called things off, she didn't take it well."

My mouth dropped open. I remembered the cop at the Harrison house saying Vega had been sleeping with a detective. I never imagined that the detective would be my ex-husband. "You're kidding, right? You slept with Suzy Vega?"

"Once," he said. "Okay, twice. It was obviously a mistake."

"So, that's why she has a vendetta against me? How does she even know I exist?"

Betz sat back and rubbed his temples. "I may have mentioned that I still had feelings for my ex-wife.... Used it as a reason not to continue things...."

Joy sat up straighter, her gaze darting from me to Betz. "Oh," she said, squirming in her seat. "This is good. I so want you two to get back together."

"Shut up," I snapped. Springing to my feet, I stormed to the back door. Felony followed.

Outside, I paced the small patio. I'd held Marcus at arm's length because of Betz. Because it didn't feel right to pursue things, knowing we still stood a chance. And he was banging Suzy Vega? The nut bag?

Anger bubbled in my chest. Not so much because he slept with her, but because I'd been targeted, unaware.

The sliding door opened, and Betz came out, holding two more beers. After closing the door behind him, he held one out for me. I refused to take it, crossing my arms.

"Look," he said. "I'm sorry. We were over, you and me. Not like you didn't have any boyfriends after our divorce."

"One," I said. "One boyfriend, and that ended a long time ago. And there's been no one since you hinted you had feelings for me a few months ago." Marcus didn't count. Nothing but a few kisses. The only relationship—Vincent—had been a mistake. Something I realized before we tied the knot.

"Well, you didn't say it back," Betz said.

"But you knew how I felt. You said so the other day."

Betz placed one bottle on the table and took a long drink from the other. "Sorry."

I snatched the other bottle off the table and resumed pacing. "Why did it have to be Suzy Vega?"

He sighed. "I know. Stupid."

"You're not taking Felony," I said. "That dog's the only one I can count on."

"That's a bit dramatic."

"Screw you," I said. "Dog love is pure. They don't keep secrets."

"It wasn't a secret. Just didn't come up."

I sat down hard on the wingback chair and looked out at the dark yard. "Were there others?"

"No."

I gulped my beer and went silent for a minute, waiting for my blood pressure to come down. Betz perched on the other chair. We sat in silence, a river of regret between us. "I need to live with this for a bit," I finally said. "I had a long day, and I'm exhausted."

"So, maybe over-reacting?"

Next thing, he was going to tell me to calm down. Not wise. "Over-reacting? She's been on the news, trashing me for days. You should have told me sooner."

"I thought I could handle it."

"So, you've been talking to her?"

"This is a good reminder of why we divorced," he said, running a hand through his hair. "You're impossible to please. I was trying to get her to back off."

"Oh. My. God. It's her. You were going to give Felony to Vega?"

Betz looked away.

I sprang to my feet and shook my beer bottle at him. Liquid sloshed over the rim and spotted his pant leg. "You should leave. I need to calm down…. This is only getting worse."

Betz got to his feet. "Just put it in perspective. I love you. That hasn't changed."

We stared at each other for what felt like an eternity. I wasn't about to validate his feelings. Not now.

With a sigh, he opened the slider and disappeared into the house, leaving me standing on the patio, exhausted. Rage ran like a current through my veins.

I took my phone out and pulled up the last text to Marcus. My hands shook as I typed a new message. *Changed my mind. Can you come over?*

Give me half an hour, came the reply.

My heart skipped a beat. What had I set in motion?

Chapter Thirty-Two

By the time I went back inside, Betz had gone. Jerski and Joy snuggled on the sofa, watching a movie. The pizza box sat open with two uneaten pieces. I no longer had an appetite. The two beers I'd downed on an almost empty stomach had gone straight to my head.

I needed to lie down, but then I remembered my invitation to Marcus.

"You okay?" Joy asked, pausing Julia Roberts mid-sentence on the screen.

"I don't want to talk about it," I said. "But sorry I told you to shut up."

"That's okay, Sweetie. Sometimes, my mouth works faster than my brain."

Wasn't that the truth? "I'm going for a walk." I clipped the leash on Felony, and we slipped out the front door. I didn't want to have to explain Marcus' arrival. Especially since I'd just kicked Betz out the door. I sat on the curb and waited. The temperature had dropped into the high seventies, but it felt cooler when a gentle breeze tickled my skin. I was a desert girl, a wimp. I wished I'd brought a sweater, but I didn't want to go back inside and face Joy and Jerski again.

The night was quiet, and I almost forgot to scan the area for McManus or one of his buddies. I should have brought the gun with me. I needed to make that a habit.

Almost thirty minutes passed before I spotted a motorcycle coming up the street. For a moment, I feared it was Diablo, but as it got closer, I recognized Marcus.

I swallowed hard and got to my feet.

He pulled into the driveway and parked next to the hearse. Swinging his leg over the bike seat, he swaggered over to me.

"Who died?" He motioned to the car.

I leaned into him, kissing him so deeply, he stumbled back a few steps, before rummaging his fingers through my hair and gripping the back of my head, as if he was afraid I'd come to my senses and pull away. That would not happen. I was hungry for him.

When I finally came up for air, he laughed. "So, you do like me."

I held a finger to his lips. "Shush."

Slipping my hand into his, we interlocked fingers, and I led him through the back gate and into the backyard. We came to a stop outside my bedroom window. "Stay here."

I let go of his hand and took the few steps to the patio door, where I peered inside. Joy and Jerski still sat on the couch. "Be right back," I called to Marcus in a stage whisper. I led Felony inside, ignored the looks of confusion on Joy and Jerski's faces, and went directly to my bedroom, closing us inside.

Sliding the window open, I pushed out the screen. "Come in," I said.

"What? Your parents home?"

"Worse," I said. "Joy. You coming in or not?"

He laughed, but gripped the windowsill on either side and scooted inside like he'd done it a thousand times before.

"Commit many burglaries?" I said.

"I'll never tell." His eyes sparkled with amusement as he advanced on me, backing me toward the bed. I lowered my butt to the mattress and scooted back, welcoming him on top of me. We tore at each other's clothing, tossing items aside like we'd never need them again. Desire drowned everything else out of my mind. Marcus had a knack for this.

Although I never doubted him, some things are as good as you dreamed they'd be.

Chapter Thirty-Three

Revenge sex was everything I wanted it to be. Intense, hungry, and liberating.

Spent, we lay back on the sheets and caught our breath. I almost asked Marcus for a cigarette. If what we just did didn't call for it, I don't know what would.

He took my hand and held it against his thudding heart. "Glad you finally came to your senses."

I rolled toward him, resting my head on his shoulder. "This is nice."

"I never thought it would really happen," he said. "You and me. It was a crap shoot coming out here. I know you're out of my league."

I turned so I could look him in the eye. A tinge of fear pooled there before he blinked it away. "What do you mean?" I said.

He looked directly at me. "I don't have a decent job. No college education. I've been to jail."

"But that was all cleared up. And I don't care about status. I don't have a league."

A slow smile spread over his lips as he pulled me tighter to him. "You've stolen my heart, you know that?"

Likewise, but I couldn't force the words out. Instead, I kissed his chest. I didn't want to ruin the moment by updating him on Rocky McManus, but his life might depend on having all the information. "I hate to bring this up," I said. "But Rocky McManus, hell, all of Diablo, they're fuming mad, and they know where I live. Probably not safe for you to be here."

He squeezed my shoulder. "Yeah, I know. Not safe for you, either."

"But I live here. They will not drive me out of my home."

"I'm not leaving you to deal with them on your own."

I thought about the gun locked in its safe in my nightstand drawer. "I can take care of myself."

He kissed my forehead. "I know. You beat the crap out of me once. But remember our talk the other night?"

I flushed, remembering him on top of me. "I still think I would have won that fight if you'd fought back."

Marcus gave a heavy sigh. "I want you to realize your limitations. You're scrappy as hell, but few people can outmatch Diablo. They had nothing to do but bulk up in prison, and they don't care who they take down to get what they want."

"Anyway," I said. "I don't want to ruin tonight. I just wanted you to be aware." I'd already torpedoed the mood, and we deserved this night. It was a long time coming. Felony seemed to know his place, which had been on the floor, but now he jumped up and curled into a ball in the crook of Marcus' arm. He absently petted the dog as he held onto me with his other arm. A dog guy. My heart melted a little more.

Thoughts of Betz threatened to invade my mind, but I pushed them away and fell asleep, more at ease than I'd been in days.

The next morning came too soon. Marcus pulled away from me just before dawn, kissing my forehead and whispering, "Keep sleeping, Sunshine," before he slipped out of bed. Although I craved the warmth of his body, fatigue won out, and I fell back into a hard sleep.

When my alarm sounded at six-thirty, it pulled me out of a sweet dream that evaporated before I could remember what it was about. But the warm spot it left in my heart made me think it had been about Marcus.

Or was it Betz?

I didn't want to give Betz the satisfaction that I'd dream about him, even if he'd never know. Not after his revelation about Suzy Vega.

Ugh. Nope, not going there. Not now.

I felt for my phone on the nightstand but came up empty. Sitting up,

I rubbed tired eyes and found the glowing device in the middle of the floor, buzzing and encouraging me to silence the alarm. Beside me, Felony stretched.

Around the room were pieces of clothing I'd worn the day before. A flush of remembrance of the intense time on the sheets with Marcus replayed in my mind, forcing a smile. Leaving the bed, I silenced my phone and gathered my clothes, floating to the bathroom, where I got ready to face the day.

The remnants of my blissful mood lingered as I left my room. Joy's bedroom door was shut. Looking out the window, I confirmed that the hearse remained parked outside—Jerski had spent the night. I looked closer and saw that someone had smashed every window of the car, and glass littered the driveway. Whoever had done it was long gone. I'd bet my last dollar that Rocky McManus had gotten his revenge.

Returning to my bedroom, I retrieved the gun from my nightstand. I slid the holster onto my belt and looked in the mirror. The weapon stuck out like an unwanted growth, reminding me what my life had come to—living in fear. Finding a light hoodie in my closet, I pulled it on and left it unzipped. Not that it made the appendage at my side any less obvious. Only Betz could pull off the look.

Betz.

Unfinished business.

My good mood deflated as I went to Joy's room and rapped on the door.

"In a minute," Joy called.

Whatever they were doing, I didn't want to know about it. I walked to the kitchen, phone in hand, and called the police non-emergency line. I'd reported the damage to the hearse by the time Jerski entered the room.

"About your car," I said, sliding my cell into my back pocket. "Seems Rocky McManus stopped by this morning to finish the job."

Jerski stomped toward the door. A crazed look pinched his face. Outside, he stood, scratching his head. "Guess I should have known better than to do field work with you. Trouble follows you around like a private investigator."

"I called it in," I said. "You're welcome."

159

Jerski spent the time waiting for the police by taking pictures of the damage and calling his insurance company. Joy came out and strutted around, arms flying in the air. "So, they're never gonna leave us alone. Is that why you're carrying a gun?"

I nodded.

"How come when I wanted one, you didn't let me keep it?"

"Believe it or not," I said, "there's some skill involved. Betz has been giving me lessons."

Joy's face softened. "You still mad at him? I mean, the guy's in love with you."

I regretted airing our differences with an audience last night. But things had gotten even worse on the patio. At least Joy and Jerski hadn't been privy to that.

"I understand being jealous," she went on. "But I don't think Suzy Vega is his type."

"I'm not jealous." I hated that word. Jealousy was a wasted emotion.

Joy shrugged. "If you say so."

I might have strangled her if the police car hadn't pulled up.

I texted Marcus while the police officer wrote the report, inquiring whether the hearse's windows had been damaged when he left that morning. He assured me they weren't, which meant McManus had come by within the last few hours. I shared that information with the cop.

It shouldn't be hard to track McManus down, knowing his address and that he hung out at the dive bar with the rest of Diablo. But I knew that criminal damage wasn't the crime of the century, and looking for him wouldn't be a priority.

Normally, I would have asked Betz to step in, but I wasn't ready for that.

I wondered if Diablo was more intent on sending us a message than actually harming us. McManus and his buddies could have barged their way inside and silenced us for good, but they took their anger out on the hearse. Maybe it was because there were too many of us—safety in numbers.

Just in case, I told Joy to find somewhere else to be. She assured me she had plans with Millie and wouldn't be at home. With Felony by my side, I headed to the office.

At my desk, with Felony tucked at my feet, I placed a call to Victim Services. They had funds to pay for Marjorie's bus ticket out of town. I verified her grandmother's address and that Marjorie was welcome there, then gave Ms. Cody a call.

"Please tell me Marjorie's still there," I said.

"She is. We just finished breakfast."

"Well, tell her to get ready. I've got money for her ticket out of town. I'll pick her up in a few minutes."

I notified the probation office in Idaho that Marjorie would come their way and got emergency reporting instructions. I'd complete the formal application for Interstate Compact later.

The drive to Ms. Cody's was uneventful, but I kept my eye out for McManus' black sedan just in case.

With snacks from Ms. Cody packed in Marjorie's knapsack, I drove us downtown to the bus station. Felony and I waited with Marjorie while she purchased a ticket for the ten-a.m. bus. That gave us a few minutes. I found a bench away from the hustle and bustle, and we sat down.

"So, tell me about Rocky," I said. "How long have you been together?"

Marjorie bit her thumbnail, and the bright blue polish flaked onto her shirt. "I've known him for years. I know, dumb, but I keep taking him back."

"What's his status with Diablo?"

She squirmed in her seat. "Since some of them went to prison, he's been stepping up. Kind of like an acting president, though I don't know if it's official."

"Did you ever hear him talk about me?"

Marjorie dropped her hand into her lap. "When he found out you were my PO, he seemed interested. Said you were a nuisance."

Like a gnat? Insulting. "Did he have plans to get rid of me?"

She glanced at me, then around the room. "Not that I know of, but he didn't share much Diablo stuff with me."

An announcement for boarding the bus to Boise came over the loudspeaker. Marjorie stood and grabbed her bag, hugging it like an infant. I walked with her to the door, where she got in line with a handful of people.

"There's one thing," she said, turning to me. She leaned in close and whispered in my ear. "I overheard him saying your boyfriend has to go. He thought if he took care of him, it would earn him big points."

Marcus. My stomach dropped to my shoes. I knew he was on their shit list, but hearing Marjorie confirm it made me shiver. "Any details on how that's supposed to happen?"

She shook her head. "I just know Rocky's mean enough to do it. Please be careful."

Marjorie hugged me, then boarded the bus. I stood looking after her as the bus pulled away, knowing I'd done all I could to keep her safe. Now I had to find a way to protect Marcus. I only knew of one person who could help me with that.

Chapter Thirty-Four

J asmine's number was in my phone, although I could count on one finger the number of times I'd used it. There was good reason for Jasmine to act as a mama bear to her younger brother. Their mother had a substance abuse problem. And although they had different fathers, they were both deadbeats and not around. Five years Betz's senior, Jasmine had stepped up to help raise him as their mother fell deeper and deeper into her addiction. Jasmine ran a tight ship, hoping to squash the dysfunction that was in their genes. The result? Betz was a straight arrow. Law and order down to his skivvies, as I liked to say.

At first, I thought it was funny that Jasmine didn't trust me. I was known to bend some rules, but basically followed the law. After all, I passed the psych eval and polygraph during the hiring process for my job—I had morals. As I got to know Jasmine better, I started to fear her. She had a lot of pull with Betz. She was watching me. Waiting for me to slip up.

And slip up, I did. I'd committed the greatest sin—I'd broken her brother's heart.

I had no idea how much he shared with her. Did she know he wanted me back? Even if he didn't tell her, she was an astute judge of character and could read people like a clairvoyant. I assumed she knew.

Unfortunately, I needed someone with her clout to protect Marcus. If that was even possible. Or if he'd go along with it.

I was unsure if Marcus was armed, although he definitely didn't have a gun on him last night. I blushed, remembering how I'd ripped his clothes off like he was a box under the Christmas tree, and I was expecting there to be a puppy inside. I shook my head. I couldn't let what happened between us distract me from what I had to do.

I placed the call.

I was startled when she answered the phone. I was half-hoping to get her voicemail.

"Casey?"

"Hey, Jasmine. How are you?"

"Fine," she said, skepticism dripping from her voice.

She would not make this easy. No surprise there. "Look," I said. "I need your help. Any chance we could meet up?"

Silence. I pictured her running scenarios of how she could avoid me through her mind. She was in the middle of a root canal, or maybe she'd moved to Bangkok. "Can't you tell me over the phone?"

"It's a lot," I said. "I'd really appreciate it if we could do this in person."

"Oh, all right... I've got a meeting in a few. Come by the precinct at one-thirty. I'll squeeze you in."

Her turf. Great. Like she wasn't imposing enough. "I'll be there. And, Jasmine, could you not share this with Betz?"

"I make no promises," she said, then disconnected the call.

Next, I sent Marcus a text. *Got confirmation that Diablo has it in for you. Please lay low.*

A few minutes passed without a response. Hopefully, he was busy pounding nails and not being pounded by Rocky McManus.

From my cubicle, I could see the hallway to Alma's office. Detective Ramsey walked my way. He had a phone pressed to his ear and a manila folder tucked under his arm. Deep in thought, he didn't see me. I waited for him to turn toward the stairs, then got up and took Felony to Alma's office.

Settled at her desk, Alma's fingers flew across her keyboard. I let Felony loose and shut the door behind me.

"I hate to be a killjoy, but we don't allow dogs in the building," Alma said. "Someone complained."

164

One of the rules I chose to bend. "It's dangerous at home. I can't leave him."

Alma patted her lap and invited Felony up. He complied and once he settled, she scratched him behind his ears. I appreciated her half-hearted attempt to enforce the rules, but she was putty in Felony's paws.

"Dangerous? Have things gotten worse?"

I told her about the windows of Jerski's hearse.

"Jerski...I mean, Pete, is spending time at your house?"

"Ewe!" I collapsed onto the loveseat. "Not for me. He's dating my cousin."

"I wondered."

" Anyway, what brought Detective Ramsey around? Any leads on the Brian Johnson case?" I asked.

Alma cleared her throat and placed Felony on the floor. "Actually, he was here about you."

"Me?" I squeaked.

"Your clients are being killed or injured. I'm not surprised he's looking into you."

"Looking into me, how?"

"He asked for a list of your clients. It's public information, so I gave it to him. I believe he intends to ask you some questions."

Felony seemed to sense my unease, and he jumped into my lap. I'd read studies that suggested animals reduced stress, and I needed Felony to do his job. "Well, I guess that makes sense." I thought most of my clients liked me. They knew me holding them accountable was part of being on supervision. Still, some took it personally.

"What else did he want to know?"

"Your background. What I thought of you as an officer. Funny thing is, I can't find your personal file."

"What's in that file?"

"Your personal info, your performance reviews. Any notes kept by a supervisor. You know I'm your biggest fan, so nothing bad is in there from me."

But there was information that might be useful to someone wanting to turn off my electricity. "Is my social security number in the file?"

Alma nodded. "Probably the most troubling part."

"When did you see it last?"

Alma frowned. "I had it on my desk the day we let Tony go. I'm sorry. I should have locked it up if my eyes weren't on it."

I shifted in my seat. "Signs point to Diablo messing with me and attacking my clients. But the whole Tony angle bothers me."

"Me too," Alma said. "The guy's just not right."

Chapter Thirty-Five

I dropped Felony off at Kate's and headed back downtown.

Even though I'd finished the half sandwich I'd saved from yesterday, an empty feeling engulfed the pit of my stomach when I parked outside the police headquarters where Jasmine worked. I hoped I wouldn't run into Betz, as he was in the same building. I was still miffed he'd even considered giving my dog to Suzy Vega. Yes, *my dog*.

I locked my gun in the glove box and went inside. After identifying myself at the front desk, I signed in and took the elevator to the third floor, where Jasmine had an office.

The support staff person sat behind bulletproof glass, even though you had to go through security to get that far. With so many armed people in the building, there was always the threat that one of their own could become an active shooter, a sad reality in today's society and something we considered at our own agency. Drills were now part of our ongoing training. As an unarmed officer, my job was to hide under my desk while some disturbed gunman tried to hunt me down, hoping one of my armed coworkers would disable the threat before they got to me. Another reason to become armed. I didn't like leaving my fate in someone else's hands.

At the desk, I gave my name and took a seat in the waiting room as directed. The walls were full of portraits of high-up officials in uniform. Jasmine was among them. In it, her short, spiky hair stood at attention, thick with product. She stared directly at the camera, challenging anyone who looked at the photo to question her abilities. I'd seen that look before. As always, it unnerved me.

The smell of burnt popcorn permeated the air, adding to my nausea. Seventeen minutes of waiting was, I was sure, designed to remind me she was "squeezing me in" and had better things to do.

I considered trying another tactic. Go to Betz instead. But he was already jealous of Marcus. And I didn't want to give him ammunition to justify his sleeping with Suzy Vega. Remembering their romp on the sheets still had me buzzing with resentment.

I was pretty far down the jealousy rabbit hole when Jasmine breezed through the door from the hallway. Dressed in a sharp black suit, with I'm-in-command heels and a power red shirt—she darted a look my way as she held the ID hanging from her neck to the sensor at the side of the door. A buzz got me to my feet, and I followed her inside.

She moved so quickly down the hall, I had to jog to keep up with her. She rounded the corner into an office with a floor-to-ceiling view of South Mountain.

"Sit." She motioned to a well-worn leather chair meant for guests and slid onto the swivel chair behind her desk. A wall-to-wall bookshelf housed photos of Jasmine with important city officials. Nothing personal.

Before I could form a thought, I complied, dropping onto the seat across from her.

"What can I do for you?" she said, booting up her computer. Checking her watch, she added, "I only have a few minutes."

I sucked in a breath. "Sorry to bother you. I know you're aware of the whole Diablo debacle a few months ago—"

"Yes, yes, of course. Are they after you again?"

"Well...yes, but that's not why I'm here." I gave a succinct version of what had transpired with Marjorie and Rocky, adding that Marcus was a target.

"Marcus is the guy from New Jersey involved in that mess last time?" she said, arching well-manicured eyebrows.

I nodded.

"And he's back in town?"

Here we go. "He is."

"Why would he be so stupid as to come back?"

I cleared my throat. "Well...he came to see me."

Jasmine smiled. "So, you're off the market?"

Who says that? Like I was a piece of real estate. "We're friends."

"Does Betz know?"

"There's nothing for him to know. It's nothing." But I was pretty sure the flush burning my cheeks gave me away.

"You usually go to Betz for help. Coming to me is...well, surprising."

And probably a mistake. I swallowed hard—difficult as it was with my mouth bone dry. "Is there anything you can do to protect Marcus?"

"Does he know he's in danger?"

"Yes."

"Ask him to file a police report about being followed. I'll talk to the sergeant in the gang unit. See what the intel is on Rocky McManus. Put it on their radar. What are you doing to protect yourself?"

"I have a gun."

Jasmine's eyes went wide. "Thought you hated guns."

"I do. Just hate the thought of dying more."

She nodded. "I suppose you get self-defense training at work."

"Yearly defensive tactics classes, yeah."

She checked the time. "Is there anything else?"

I shook my head and got to my feet. "Thanks for your time."

"Good luck with your new romance," she said as I walked out the door.

God, I hoped the visit to her was worth it.

Chapter Thirty-Six

Back at my Jeep, I checked my phone. Still no response from Marcus. I resisted the urge to drive back to the east valley and check on him at the construction site. I was half-worried for his safety and half-afraid he was ghosting me. Maybe last night didn't meet his expectations. I could still feel the imprint of his lips on my cheek when he'd left that morning. Not a sign of someone who wasn't into me. But stranger things had happened.

I needed to get out of my head. I was already in Phoenix and close to my office, so I drove there.

Since I lacked clearance to carry a firearm at work, I locked the gun in my Jeep's glove box. I stopped by the training unit on the first floor and signed up for the next firearms academy, still months away. I half-hoped that by the time the date rolled around, I'd no longer feel the need to carry, and I could cancel.

At my cubicle, I checked my messages. One was from the restaurant where Brian Johnson had last worked. I'd called them before I knew he was dead in an effort to locate him before I requested a warrant. That was weeks ago. Since today's caller asked me to get back to them, I obliged.

"Is Alex in?" I said.

"Hold on."

Restaurant sounds came over the line—muffled voices, clanking plates, background music. I brought up my email as I waited.

"This is Alex," came a voice on the line.

"Alex, this is Casey Carson returning your call."

"Thanks for getting back to me. Brian Johnson used to work here. I understand he's deceased. He listed you as his emergency contact. Wondering if you know anything about his uniform. He didn't return it, and we want it back."

"Wasn't he a dancing chicken?"

"Yeah. That chicken suit was expensive."

"Sorry. Don't know why he listed me. I have no idea where his stuff is."

"Thought I'd give it a shot. I know he was staying at the homeless camp by the Salt River."

"He was?"

"Yeah. Said he shared a tent with a woman named Irene."

"Irene Goss?"

Alex hesitated. "Maybe. Not sure of her last name. If you know her, can you see if she knows where the suit is?"

Irene Goss was on Claire's caseload. She was one of her problem people. I'd see if she owed her a visit.

After further assuring Alex that I didn't possess the chicken suit, I hung up and turned to Claire, who was at her desk next to mine. I liked Claire, but she had her nose in everything. I wasn't surprised that she'd overheard my call.

"What about Irene?" she asked.

"Seems she was living with Brian Johnson."

"The guy who was just murdered?" She leaned forward, practically drooling at the thought of drama.

"That's the one. Feel like paying her a visit?"

Claire shut her laptop. "This warrant will not write itself, but it can wait a bit. Let me gear up."

Claire, like most of my peers, was armed. Gearing up meant a lot more than me clipping my pepper spray, radio, and handcuffs to my belt. While I waited for her, I switched out my running shoes for thick-soled hiking boots. Because of Diablo, I put my body armor on, too. They recommended we always wear our vests in the field, but Arizona was just too damn hot. Plus, it was stiff and confining. Wearing one equaled what I imagined it would feel like to be suffocated by a boa constrictor. But if there were any indication the shit might hit the fan, I sucked it up and wore the damn thing.

"You drive," Claire said. "My car's low on gas."

We got in the Jeep and started toward the river. Although it sometimes did in winter, water rarely ran through the usually dry riverbed. The underpass provided some protection from the sun and was a popular spot for houseless individuals.

We parked just north of the camp and called in our approximate location before exiting the Jeep and walking toward the encampment.

One benefit of being a PO for as long as I had was that I usually knew someone in the areas we frequented. This place was no different. Grant McAvoy greeted me with a meth-induced, decaying-toothed smile as we ducked under the bridge. His weathered face belied his forty-something years, making him look much older. Drugs and the resulting lifestyle did that.

"Hey, Ms. Casey. What brings you to my neck of the woods?"

Funny because there wasn't a tree in sight. Just some dried-up sage bushes.

At least a dozen tents filled the area, haphazardly placed on either side of the dry waterbed. In the rare occurrence of rain, a river would appear, and the residents would have to pack up and seek higher ground. They'd be safe for at least another month or two when the rainy season started and snow melting from up north made its way to the valley.

It wasn't the tents that bothered me about encampments. It was the trash. My hiking boots protected my feet from the used needles littering the ground, but it still creeped me out to hear them snapping under my weight. "Hey, Grant. How you doing?"

"I'm off paper."

"Yeah? Congrats. You still seeing your provider? Taking your meds?"

Grant spat on the ground. "Naw. I don't need that shit."

With that attitude, he wouldn't be off supervision long. One of probation's many benefits was keeping people like Grant linked to the services they desperately needed. Without a team in place, people tended to drift back to old habits. And those habits were usually at odds with the law.

"That's too bad, Grant. It was nice to see you doing so well last time I saw you."

Unaffected by my disappointment, he shrugged.

I had no power over him, so I moved on. "You know Irene?"

"Doesn't everyone?"

"Which tent is hers?" Claire asked.

He pointed to a tattered light blue one with an expensive bicycle leaning against it. I'd bet my paycheck the bike was stolen. Crushed beer cans littered the ground. The air was ripe with the scent of discarded, rotting food. I tried to keep my breathing shallow.

Claire and I navigated the terrain over to the tent, and she bent down at the open flap. "Irene?"

A middle-aged woman dressed in shorts and a tank top emerged from the tent. Bony limbs and a gaunt face, her cheekbones stuck out like razors on her face. She couldn't weigh more than a ten-year-old. Another gift from meth.

"Oh, hi," she said. Fidgeting, she scratched scarred arms with broken fingernails.

Claire got right to the point. "You want to admit to using or go through the rigamarole of taking the bus to drop a UA?"

Irene hung her head. "I'll sign."

"I appreciate that," Claire said. "I have an admission form in the car. Walk with us."

We walked single file back to the Jeep, ignoring the other residents watching us with interest.

While Claire stuck her head in the car, searching her bag for the form, I introduced myself. "I'm Casey. I understand you knew Brian Johnson."

She stopped scratching and bit her lip. "Yeah."

"So, you know what happened to him?"

"He's dead."

"Any idea who killed him?"

She glanced over her shoulder and then up and down the street.

"No one can hear us," I said.

Tossing matted hair over her shoulder, she said, "There's speculation."

"Yeah? What are the theories?"

"Brian thought his PO was after him. Said he didn't trust you guys."

I tried to keep my expression neutral. She obviously didn't know I was his PO. "You actually think his PO killed him?"

"Maybe not directly. But they could have had it done. There are bad POs out there."

I crossed my arms, realized it was a defensive move, and dropped my hands to my sides. "Were you at the vigil?"

Irene leaned down and scratched her leg. "Until the chaos."

"Did you see Henry get stabbed?"

"No. But I heard about it." She leaned forward, eager to share a detail. "And guess what? Henry and Brian had the same PO. Henry came over one night, and I heard him and Brian talking. They were both afraid their PO was going to come after them if they didn't do something they didn't want to do."

"You know what that was?"

"No. Just glad I'm not on that caseload."

"I bet."

Claire emerged from the Jeep, paper in hand. She fastened it to a clipboard and clicked her pen open. "So, I listed meth. You use anything else?"

"Better add weed."

Claire shook her head, added the drug, and held out the clipboard.

Irene scribbled her name. "You gonna violate me?"

"Come to the office on Monday at ten, and we'll discuss it. If you can give me a clean UA by then, maybe we don't need to tell the judge." Claire turned her attention to me. "Did you get what we came for?"

That I was the primary suspect? "Guess so."

"You done with me?" Irene asked.

"Just one more question," I said. "Do you know what happened to Brian's work uniform?"

"The chicken suit?"

I nodded.

"He was on his way to work the last time I saw him. He had the suit with him. Haven't seen it or him since." With that, she turned and made her way back to camp.

Chapter Thirty-Seven

We stopped to see a few more probationers on the way back to the office. At each one, I wondered if my clients feared me. And why Brian and Henry had thought I wanted them to do something they didn't want to do. I had only asked that they engage in treatment, pay their fines, finish community service, and stay out of trouble. Nothing out of the ordinary.

On the drive between home visits, Claire and I talked about it. "Why would Brian be afraid of me?" I said. "We were cool. Until he disappeared, I didn't have a problem with him."

Claire shrugged. "You know how it is. You're riding someone hard, and they complain about you. Rumors spread. That's why I always tell my folks in jail not to listen to the other inmates. They've had a bad experience, or they wouldn't be in custody. They're not the best judge of how hard we try to help them."

I had a few clients who'd been in jail shortly before Brian had stopped reporting. I couldn't think of anyone who would think me capable of murder, even if they blamed me for their incarceration and not the poor choices they'd made. Eric Harrison wasn't my biggest fan, but I couldn't see him thinking I was going after my clients. "Being a dick PO is one thing," I said. "But knocking off clients is a whole other level."

Claire reached over and patted my arm. "You need to relax. You're strangling the steering wheel."

I looked down at my white fingers and loosened my grip. "My clients aren't the only ones wondering about me." I told her about Ramsey's visit to Alma.

Claire giggled. Something she did when she was nervous. I knew sharing my plight with her was a risky move. Even the office cleaning staff would know my business by morning. But fieldwork with a partner often turned into therapy sessions. Something about sharing the experience and spending so much time in a car two feet apart led you to bare your soul. One reason I preferred to work alone. "It's his job to look into everyone," Claire said. "I wouldn't read too much into it."

I pulled the neck of my vest down half an inch; it was choking me. "Let's go back to the office. I can't wait to get this damn thing off."

"Fine by me," Claire said. "I heard what happened when you were out with Jerski. Feeling blessed nobody's chasing us today."

Like I said, Claire was president of the rumor mill. But on this, I couldn't blame her. I was the Typhoid Mary of the office. I drove the rest of the way at the speed limit, wary of causing any more drama.

Shedding my vest and leaving it on my desk, I felt lighter. Unfortunately, my shirt was drenched in sweat. I grabbed a spare out of my file cabinet and went to the ladies' room to change.

Locked in a stall, I heard two women walk in laughing. I recognized both voices.

"I hear Casey's a suspect in her own client's murder," Trashy Tracy, our snotty receptionist, said.

"You don't think she did it?" Gullible Grace asked.

Claire had wasted no time. I stepped out of the stall and glared at them. "No, I didn't do it. What's wrong with you?"

I left them speechless, which was a miracle in itself.

I headed to Kate's to pick up Felony. Why had I let my guard down? My sister was my sounding board. Sometimes Alma. I should have gone to one of them. I didn't dislike Claire. She didn't spread information to hurt me. She couldn't help herself. And I knew it. Shame on me.

With my angst misplaced, I'd forgotten about Diablo. But mid-drive, I came back to reality. I didn't want to lead anyone to Kate's house. Checking my surroundings, the traffic was thick, but nothing jumped out at me. To be certain, I checked the glove compartment to confirm that the gun was still locked inside. It was. I needed to chill.

When I neared Kate's place, I circled the block a few times, just to be sure no one had followed. She lived in an upscale, ungated neighborhood. Kevin had a good job at a bank. I never understood what he did, but he was successful enough that Kate could stay home with the kids.

After three passes, I thought it was safe and was about to turn into her driveway when a black sedan came around the corner. The car sped toward me, and I passed Kate's driveway and drove straight ahead. Daring a look at the driver, I was shocked to see the face of a chicken.

The car passed me, and I whipped my head around. No. It couldn't be.

I pulled into the next driveway and turned around. Driving down the same street, I glanced down each driveway I passed. No sedan. At the main road, I braked at the stop sign, searching for the car. Traffic was heavy and going at a good clip. I waited for a break, but there was no way I'd catch up to the sedan. It was long gone.

When a break came, I circled the block. No black sedan. No giant chicken.

Was I losing my mind?

Quite possible.

But Brian Johnson's chicken suit was missing. How many of those could there be?

And the black sedan? Rocky had one. So did millions of others. Even Luigi's car was black. Could Tony have borrowed it?

I practiced deep breathing on the way back to Kate's and debated on whether I should call the police. I could picture the dispatcher, doubled over in laughter as I reported the nondescript car driven by human-sized poultry. As far as I knew, there was no law against that as long as the chicken had a license.

Still, I was unnerved. When I got to Kate's, I called her from the driveway. "Open your garage. I'm not leaving my Jeep outside."

"Why?"

"Just do it!"

"Okay, okay," she said. "Hang on."

When the door rolled open, I pulled into Kevin's spot and shut the engine off. I didn't breathe until the door closed behind me. I checked my messages, several from Kate, which she could fill me in on in person. Still nothing from Marcus.

Kate stood by the kitchen door. She crossed her arms and tapped her foot. "What now?"

I walked past her and into the house. "I need a minute." In the kitchen, I went straight to the cabinet, removed a glass, and filled it with water. I downed it in one gulp, then refilled it.

"You want something stronger?" she asked.

What I wouldn't give to dull my senses. But I had to stay sharp, and it was only mid-afternoon, so I declined. "Where are the kids?"

"Out back playing with Felony."

I lowered my glass to the counter and buried my head in my hands.

"What's wrong? You're scaring me."

I looked up at her. "Would you believe me if I told you I just saw a chicken driving a car?"

Kate stepped forward and held her hand against my forehead. "Do you have a fever?"

I swatted her hand away. "Maybe I'm losing my mind, but hear me out. I had a client who had a chicken costume. I've seen it. Now he's dead, and the suit is missing."

"You're serious?"

"And I just saw a giant feathered thing driving down your street."

She looked at me like I said I saw a UFO or a ghost. She wasn't buying it. "Don't tell me Bigfoot was in the passenger seat."

I glared at her.

"You need a vacation," she said. "You've been under a lot of stress with that reporter talking bad about you and Betz wanting to rekindle things."

She didn't know the half of it. She didn't know about Marcus. "I think someone's trying to drive me nuts. Someone pretended to be me and had my power turned off."

"Who would do that?"

"I don't know."

"Let's go outside," Kate said. "I don't want to leave the kids unattended. Not with you bringing the crazies out."

I took my glass and followed Kate to the backyard. Felony bounded over and greeted me with a wagging tail, doing his job of reducing my stress. I could feel my blood pressure drop.

After checking in with the kids, Kate and I settled on the patio. I rested my head against the cushion and closed my eyes.

"Anyway," Kate said. "Did you see my message?"

I patted my pocket. No phone. Must have left it in the car. "No."

"I wanted to talk about Dad's new friend."

"Millie?"

She nodded and pursed her lips. "Kevin had a work dinner last night. Our regular sitter had the flu, so I asked Dad to fill in."

"That was brave."

"On the one hand, Millie's been good for him. He's not drinking as much."

"And on the other hand?"

Kate sighed. "He brought her with him. When we came home, they didn't hear us come in. They were getting cozy on the couch."

"Ewe."

"I'm scarred for life."

"Like making out...?"

"Let's just say I saw more of Millie and Dad than I'm comfortable with."

"Yuck. I've got the Joy and Jerski show at my house. It's that time of year. Hormones are running amuck."

"You and Betz?" she said with a wink.

"Nope." I told her about Suzy Vega. "So, that's not happening. Not now, anyway."

"His holding a torch for you isn't enough? You expect him to be celibate while you decide what to do?"

Ouch. "It was Suzy Vega!"

"Like you haven't made your share of poor choices." Which she would think was the case if she knew about Marcus.

I rubbed my eyes so hard, I thought they'd pop out. "Why are you attacking me?"

"I'm not attacking you. I'm playing devil's advocate. I gotta say, I was happy when you told me Betz wanted to get back together. I don't like you being alone. At least with Betz around, someone is looking out for you."

"You're looking out for me," I said. "I don't need a man."

Kate laughed. "You've always needed a man. That doesn't take away your independence or your strength. You like male companionship. Nothing wrong with that."

"Unless it's Dad and Millie."

Now we were both laughing. "Not the same thing at all," she said.

I left feeling somewhat better. But I made Kate promise to lock her doors. "And watch out for giant driving chickens," she added.

"Yeah, that too."

Chapter Thirty-Eight

By the time I got home, I was exhausted. To stay alert, I shook myself like a wet dog and drove around my neighborhood three times before I was satisfied there were no angry gangsters or wayward fowl afoot. Parking in the garage next to Joy's car, I sat in the Jeep for a minute, preparing myself to face her. I never knew what I'd walk into, since she'd come back into my life. She kept me on my toes. But my toes were tired.

My phone showed several missed messages. I knew about the ones from Kate, but there was also one from Betz, one from Marcus, and three from Joy. I checked Marcus' first, glad to see that he was letting me know everything was fine. Cross one worry off my list. I didn't check the ones from Betz or Joy. I didn't have the energy.

I let Felony out of the backseat, and we entered the house through the kitchen door.

Joy was at the counter seasoning a pork tenderloin. "There you are," she said. "I've been trying to reach you."

"Just saw that. Sorry. I was busy."

She placed the saltshaker on the counter and reached for the pepper. "You had a visitor."

My stomach clenched. "You let someone in?"

"He was the nicest young man. Said you used to work together."

"Who?" Although I was afraid to know. My hands balled into fists.

"His name was Tony. When I came home, he was at the door. Said he was about to leave a note."

"Jesus, Joy. You let him in?"

"He was harmless," Joy said, blinking fake eyelashes at me. "You know I'm psychic. I'd know if something was off."

I had a thousand arguments to prove she didn't have psychic abilities. I could cite her poor choices in men, or the fact that she was once kidnapped. But I knew proving her wrong would be impossible—like reasoning with a fit-throwing toddler—so I swallowed my comeback. "What did he want?"

"Advice, I think. We got to talking and he never said about what."

"What did he drive?"

"A car."

I tapped my fingers on the counter. "What kind?"

She shrugged. "I don't know. A regular car."

I wanted to shake her. Prove my clients right. I was unhinged and dangerous. I counted to ten in an effort to calm down while Joy popped dinner in the oven.

"What time was he here?"

"You just missed him. He left not ten minutes ago."

"How long was he here?"

"About half an hour."

So, he could have been in Kate's neighborhood when I saw the black sedan with the chicken. He knew where my sister lived, because I'd stopped by with him once when we were in the field. Still, it seemed like a leap.

I threw up my hands and fed Felony dinner, then grabbed a beer and went out on the patio. Tony had no boundaries. He'd proven that at Eric Harrison's hearing. He blamed me for losing his job and probably came over to ask me to get it back—something I had no power or desire to do. I wouldn't put it past him.

But it could have been more than that. I hadn't ruled him out as the one targeting my clients. Something was off about him. But was he a killer?

I sat down and threw a ball for Felony while I nursed my beer. It had been a hell of a few days, and I couldn't think straight. I wasn't any closer to figuring out why my clients were being targeted. Marjorie's case seemed different from what happened to Brian Johnson and Henry Coffman. She was in a domestic violence relationship, and I reminded myself that most of my clients led tumultuous lives. It wasn't uncommon for me to deal with several crises in a day, all unrelated. Johnson and Coffman were Ramsey's problem. That he was looking into me was irritating, but there was nothing I could do about it, and in the end, he wouldn't find anything. Marcus was in danger. That outcome was something I had a chance of influencing.

And Betz. Well, he just had to cool his heels.

I opened the message from Marcus. *At work. I'm fine. Will I see you tonight?*
We need to talk for sure
Don't like the sound of that
It's about your safety
U threatening me?
Just get over here and make sure you're not followed
U want me bad, I understand
Just come over
Finishing up. Give me an hour.

Felony was pooped. He stopped bringing me the ball and laid down, panting. I finished my beer and ushered him inside. I didn't plan on doing anything with Marcus that required a shower, but I cleaned up just the same.

Chapter Thirty-Nine

I had no appetite but slipped a slice of pork off the platter Joy had set out for her and Jerski. They sat at the kitchen table holding hands around almost empty plates.

"So, you're a suspect," Jerski said.

Damn Claire. "I'm not a suspect."

"But your clients are afraid of you."

"Stuff it, Pete." I grabbed a piece of asparagus and left the room. I almost turned on the TV but knew I couldn't handle Suzy Vega reporting the same gossip Claire was spreading. I couldn't look at her without picturing her and Betz together. I plopped on the sofa, and Felony settled at my side. He had something in his mouth, and I wrestled it from him. "Give me that."

I pinched his jaw, and he gave it up, spitting a feather into my hand.

My stomach churned. I jumped to my feet, spun around, and checked the room. That day at the pet store, I'd gotten Felony a stuffed panda, a hard bone, and a ball. Nothing with feathers. I wouldn't put it past Joy to own a boa, but I'd never seen her wear one.

Dropping to my hands and knees, I looked under the couch. Nothing, except a reminder that dogs shed, and I needed to vacuum. Where did the feather come from?

I hurried to the kitchen, Felony at my heels. Joy and Jerski were doing the dishes. Both turned their attention my way. With a feather in my open palm, I held out my hand. "Where did this come from?"

They exchanged glances of concern.

"I don't know, Sweetie. A bird?" Joy said.

"Felony had it."

Joy shrugged. "Well, he goes outside. There are birds."

"You think he killed a bird?" Jerski said.

"No, I don't think he killed a bird," I snapped. "Was Tony dressed like a chicken?"

They looked back at each other, exchanging a look of concern. Joy turned off the water, wiped her hands on a towel, and walked over to me, laying a hand on my arm. "You're not yourself, Sweetie. Why don't you go lay down, and I'll fix you a plate. A nice meal and a good night's sleep will set you right."

I wrenched my arm away. "Stop treating me like I'm crazy."

"Well," Jerski said. "If it quacks like a duck."

I might have punched him if the doorbell hadn't rung. I threw up my hands, spun on my heels, and went to answer.

I checked the peephole. Marcus. I pulled the door open.

"Okay to use the door?" he asked in a whisper. "Or should I go to the back window?"

"Ha, ha." I held up my hand to stop him from entering. "Neither. We're going for a walk." I called Felony over and fastened a leash to his collar.

On the street, Marcus struggled to keep up with me. "Good to see you, too, Sunshine. Are we running? This feels like running."

Realizing I was going at a good clip, I slowed my stride. "Sorry, I'm just trying to keep it together."

Falling into step beside me, he rubbed my back. "What's wrong?"

Where to begin? "Give me a minute," I said. "Let me sort things out."

"Okay."

We walked in silence through my neighborhood and to the dog park on the other side of the main road. Once we passed through the double gates, I let Felony off-leash, and he ran across the lawn to an eagerly awaiting beagle. They sniffed each other in familiar ways and then happily chased each other in giant circles. The beagle's owner was the only other human in the park. She sat on a bench reading a book. Marcus and I found a picnic table at the other end of the space and sat on top of it.

The sun was setting, but streetlights illuminated the area. "Whenever you're ready," he said.

I dropped my head into my hands.

Marcus rubbed circles on my back. "This isn't about last night, is it? Because I feel like a million bucks."

"No."

"No second thoughts?"

"No regrets. It was perfect. I'm happy."

He snorted. "I can see that."

"It's just that things with me are complicated right now. But that's not what I want to talk about."

"Diablo?"

"Yeah. One of my clients was dating Rocky McManus. You familiar with him?"

"I've run into him a time or two. Nice guy, and by nice, I mean a total asshole."

"Well, they aren't following you because they're the paparazzi. They want to kill you. Retribution for your role in sending a chunk of Diablo to prison."

"*We* had a role in sending them to prison. They hate you, too."

I rested my head on his shoulder. "I know. But they specifically mentioned you. I'm really worried about your safety."

"I'm careful. Aware. And armed. What else can I do?"

I placed my hand on his knee. "You can speak with police. There's a gang unit. They would talk to you."

"I doubt that."

"No, they will. I have connections. I've asked about it."

"Your ex? Butz?"

"Betz." I leaned back and looked at him. "Actually, his sister. She's a lieutenant. She thinks you're nuts for being here."

He pulled me to him, kissed me, then rested his forehead against mine. "Nuts for you. And we can't live in fear."

"You'd be safer in New Jersey."

"So would you."

"I'm not moving to New Jersey."

He laughed. "It's not so bad. We have the Jersey Shore. Farms. It's the garden state."

"And snow. The Mafia."

"But no Diablo."

"Anyway, it's too soon to talk about me running away with you. I don't even know if we should date."

Marcus removed his arm from around my shoulders, settled his hands in his lap, and looked straight ahead. "You're still hooked on Betz."

I rubbed my temples. "It's complicated." Best not to go there. A change in topic was in order. I considered telling him about my clients being targeted, but I didn't know how to do that without sounding crazy. Especially the part about the chicken.

The lady with the beagle walked over to the gate and I called Felony over so he wouldn't slip out with her. It was dark now, and the three of us started back to the house. When we walked up the driveway, Marcus let go of my hand. "Shit."

"What?"

"My tires." He walked over to his bike, scratching his head. Someone slashed both tires.

"Sorry," I said. "Should have had you park in the garage since they got Jerski's hearse early this morning."

I couldn't wait for Marcus' permission. This was my home. I took out my phone and placed a call to Jasmine. "Sorry to bother you, but I think McManus struck again. Marcus is visiting, and the tires on his motorcycle have been damaged."

Jasmine sighed. "Just leaving the office. I'll swing by. Tell Marcus to sit tight." She disconnected before I could give her my address. She'd never been to my house, but cops had their way of finding things out.

"My sister-in-law, well, ex-sister-in-law, is on her way," I said.

"Slashed tire report seems under her paygrade."

"This isn't even her jurisdiction," I said. "She's helping out because of Diablo." And because I groveled.

Marcus pulled the hem of his jeans up on his right leg, exposing an ankle holster tucked into his boot. "If the cops are coming, do I need to get rid of this?"

"As long as you're not a convicted felon, you can carry concealed in Arizona without a permit."

He let his pant leg fall. "The Wild West."

"But you weren't concerned enough to learn the law."

He shrugged. "Figured the gun was necessary, given the situation."

A few minutes later, Betz's 4Runner pulled to the curb. No wonder Jasmine didn't need my address.

Jasmine exited the passenger seat while Betz got out of the driver's side. Assessing their surroundings, they walked up the driveway. Betz went to the motorcycle, squatted down, and inspected the damage. "Message from Diablo?"

I nodded. "Who else?"

Jasmine looked Marcus up and down. It was the first time they'd met.

"Marcus, this is Lieutenant Faulk."

Marcus put out his hand, and she reluctantly shook it. Then he turned to Betz. It was a challenge, and everyone knew it. Betz had no way to decline graciously, so he shook Marcus' hand.

Jasmine cleared her throat and focused on Marcus. "Casey filled me in on Diablo's quest to retaliate for you duping them a few months back. I checked with our gang squad, and it seems the intel is true. Although Diablo is less organized now, the bounty on your head will earn McManus significant points. Best thing you can do is get out of town."

Marcus crossed his arms. "What about Casey? They've got to be after her, too. And they know where she lives and works."

Betz squeezed the back of his neck. "We need to figure that out, too."

"I'm not leaving without her," Marcus said.

Betz looked at the ground. "Staying here is dangerous, Case. My guestroom is open."

"I'm not staying in your guestroom," I said. "And I have to work. I won't become a prisoner."

Jasmine held up her hands. "You came to me for help, and I'm offering it. Casey, you stay with me and Betz. Marcus, I don't see any reason for you to stay in town. You don't live here."

Marcus crossed his arms. "I do now. And, like I said, I'm not leaving without Casey."

This was awkward. "I can't leave Joy alone. Don't say go to my sister's or my dad's. I'm not bringing trouble to their doorsteps. We can't hide forever. Can't we do something about Rocky McManus? Can't we at least get him off the streets for a few days? I can try to talk his girlfriend into pressing charges for DV."

"We've tried to find him," Betz said. "He's smoke."

"Have you talked to his PO?"

Jasmine nodded. "Rocky won't report to him until next month. His PO has the same contact info that we do, but he hasn't been home."

"I'm wondering," I said. "Detective Ramsey's working a case about the murder of one of my clients and the attempted murder of another. Could those cases be connected?

"Nathan Ramsey?" Betz asked.

"Oh, yeah, you know him. I was supposed to tell you he said hi."

Betz scoffed. "He didn't ask you to do that."

I thought back to our conversation. "Maybe not. Maybe I assumed he'd want me to, given that you know each other. Please tell me there's not bad blood between you."

Betz stuffed his hands into his pockets and looked at the ground. "We went to the academy together. Not a fan."

I gritted my teeth. "Let me get this straight. There are two people who hate you, and I'm in both their crosshairs?"

"Suzy doesn't hate me."

"Oh, right, she's in love with you. She hates me."

Marcus' eyes darted back and forth between me and Betz. A smirk spread across his lips before he looked down, tried to reign it in. He was enjoying the show. And Jasmine crossed her arms—probably to keep from clapping. This was what she wanted. Me and Betz at odds, and both of us in other relationships.

Betz tapped his chest with his hand. "Anyway, let's get back to keeping you safe. Guestroom's available. This isn't the time to be hard-headed. Diablo isn't messing around."

Jasmine tapped Betz on the shoulder. "Step away with me for a minute."

He followed her back to the car, where they spoke out of our earshot.

"That was interesting," Marcus said. "I hate to hand you over to him, but they're right. You'll be safer at their house. You should go."

"And you?"

"I'll be okay."

I threw up my hands. "You're impossible."

I looked back at Jasmine and Betz, who appeared to be arguing. Every relationship here was strained, and I didn't like it one bit. If I went with them, this would be the second time Diablo pushed me out of my home. Joy could stay with Jerski. Or even Kate. They weren't after her. I just didn't want her to become collateral damage again. I started picturing the idea of going to Betz's house. Ordinarily, if it were just Betz, I'd consider it. But Jasmine didn't make me feel welcome, even though she'd extended the invitation. And I wasn't about to leave Marcus so vulnerable.

Betz and Jasmine walked back toward us. Betz looked uncomfortable. Like he'd rather be anywhere else. Jasmine cleared her throat. "Both of you can stay with us. Marcus can sleep on the sofa. Tomorrow, we can figure out something more permanent."

"You're kidding," Marcus said.

"For some reason, you're important to Casey," Jasmine said. "Don't read too much into it."

My heart softened. I knew it was Jasmine's idea, but Betz would only go along with this crazy plan because of one thing. He cared about me. He knew I wouldn't go without Marcus. If Betz kept Marcus safe, it was for me. My anger at him dissipated.

"Maybe just tonight," I said. "Let me talk to Joy."

Marcus' mouth dropped open, but he didn't object. I walked back to the house, knowing the three of them were looking after me.

Chapter Forty

With Joy on her way with Jerski to his mom's place, I felt a little better. Two people were safe and out of the way. I packed an overnight bag, hoping that would be all I'd need—enough for one night. I talked Betz and Jasmine into letting us go solo to Marcus' boss's place to get his things since Diablo probably didn't know about Marcus' new living arrangement. I promised we'd head directly to Betz's house afterward.

"This is bizarre," Marcus said from the passenger seat of my Jeep. Before we left, we'd pushed his motorcycle into the garage, where it would hopefully be safe from further vandalism.

"Bizarre is one way to describe it." I reached over to pat Felony, who was sitting on Marcus's lap. Bringing my lover to my ex-husband's house was not on my bingo card.

"Never been part of a love triangle before," he said, laughing.

I smacked his arm. "Stop it. It's not a love triangle, and you're enjoying this way too much."

"As long as I'm in the running, I'm not going anywhere."

"Even if it gets you killed? That's ridiculous."

"Says the most stubborn person I've ever met."

"Fair."

Marcus directed me to a house a few miles away. I felt silly taking the gun I'd stashed in the glove box with me, but it wasn't doing me any good locked away. Once we parked, I slid the holster onto my belt, then joined Marcus and Felony on the sidewalk.

"You're armed. Sexy," Marcus said with a wicked grin. "You think they'd notice if we took half an hour to, you know...." His eyebrows shot up.

"You need half an hour?"

"For what I want to do to you, I need a few days. I'm trying to be reasonable."

I was tempted by his good looks as he swaggered up the walkway. But then the door popped open, and a man stood there dressed in paint-splattered coveralls, ruining the moment. "Oh," he said. "I was just gonna mow the lawn."

Marcus introduced us. "This is Bill. He's the foreman on the job."

I shook his thick, calloused hand. "Nice to meet you."

While Bill went into the yard, we ducked inside, and I followed Marcus through the house to a back room. The place screamed "bachelor pad," with cheap furniture and stuff piled high on every surface. Soil and wear marred the carpet. At the end of the hall, Marcus flipped a light on in the bedroom. A single bed was against the wall, and a backpack sat on the only other piece of furniture, a wooden kitchen chair.

"It ain't the Ritz," he said. "It's temporary."

Marcus hadn't settled in. Was he still hopeful I'd extend an invitation?

He glanced at the bed. "Half-an-hour?"

"I haven't done it in a single bed since college," I said. "I'll pass."

He shrugged. "Thought you were more adventurous than that."

Maybe if Bill wasn't outside the window mowing the lawn and Betz and Jasmine weren't expecting us. But I had some standards.

Marcus grabbed his backpack, and we headed toward the door.

"Is that all your stuff?"

"I have more," he said over his shoulder. "I stored my things in my mom's basement before I left Jersey. This is all I need for now." He stopped in the bathroom and came out with a toothbrush and a razor, tucking them inside his bag. "All set."

Marcus opened the front door, and we stepped into the yard. Bill had activated a floodlight so he could see what he was doing, and it seemed like mid-afternoon outside. In the distance, an engine roared to life. Tires screeched, and two headlights came out of the darkness. "Get down," Marcus shouted, pushing me toward a truck parked in the driveway.

I ducked and pulled Felony with me. Marcus scrambled for cover behind us.

Two motorcycles raced by. Gunshots sounded, and the flash of muzzles crackled in the dark. Bullets pinged as they hit the vehicles. One round buzzed over my head. I drew my weapon but stayed behind the pickup. Marcus stayed crouched next to me, gun in hand.

I held back a scream. *Shit...shit...shit.*

It was over before I could get my bearings. The motorcycles continued down the street and out of sight. All was quiet except for the purr of the lawn mower.

"Bill!" Marcus darted from behind the truck and ran to his roommate, who lay on the grass. I followed, dragging Felony behind me—my weapon aimed toward the ground.

Marcus holstered his gun as he leaned over his friend.

"They got me," Bill said, his hand covering an oozing hole in his bicep.

I pulled my phone out of my pocket and, with shaking hands, dialed 911.

"Nine-one-one. What's your emergency?"

"Send help," I said. "There's been a shooting. We need an ambulance. Please hurry."

Chapter Forty-One

While we waited for help to arrive, I ran inside and got a towel. Passing it to Marcus, he pressed it against Bill's wound. Bill was still conscious, and I took that as a good sign. Felony, traumatized, clung to me like a small child just awakened from a nightmare. I kept watch for another round of gunfire, but only heard sirens.

Within five minutes, three patrol cars arrived on scene. "Drive-by?" the first cop said.

While we filled him in, paramedics pulled up and went to work on Bill.

"Did you get a description of the vehicle?" a second officer asked.

'Harley's," Marcus said. "Pretty sure they were Diablo."

We were in Tempe, so not Betz and Jasmine's domain, but I intended to call them anyway. Before I could, another car pulled up. Ramsey got out. *Here we go.*

"Ms. Carson," he said. "Why am I not surprised to see you here?"

"I'm not hurt, thanks for asking." I was cranky. I didn't enjoy being shot at. Nor did I like Ramsey's tone.

"Well, that's good." He deflected my demeanor, not taking the bait, his attention on Bill being loaded into the ambulance. "Anybody else hit?"

One cop shone his flashlight on my Jeep. Holes riddled the side. Good thing we weren't inside it at the time. My heart still dropped. I loved my Jeep.

"Does this take me off the suspect list?" I said, still irked at Ramsey.

He gave me a wide-eyed look. "For this shooting. I'll need to take your statements. How about while my people process the scene, we take a ride

195

downtown?" He motioned to his vehicle, idling at the curb.

"How about we meet you there," I said.

"Your Jeep is part of the crime scene."

Damn it. Marcus got in the back seat, while Ramsey gave me the courtesy of letting me sit up front with a still-shaking Felony on my lap.

"Cute dog," he said. "Is this a client's house?"

"No." I pointed with my thumb to the back seat. "Marcus stays here. Diablo is after him, and maybe me." I still didn't want to believe that. "Betz and his sister, Lieutenant Faulk, are aware of the situation. If you don't mind, I'm going to give them a call."

Ramsey gave me the side-eye. "I do mind. This is my investigation."

Great. I almost died, and he wanted to have a pissing contest with Betz. "Let me at least tell him what happened. That we're safe. He's expecting us to arrive at his house any minute. I don't want him to worry."

I didn't wait for permission. I placed the call.

"Where are you?" Betz said before I could say anything.

I told him what happened.

"I knew I shouldn't have let you go alone. I'll be right there."

I glanced at Ramsey. "Ah.... The detective handling the case doesn't want you to come."

"Ramsey?"

"Yup."

I was sure Ramsey could hear Betz sigh. It was so loud, I had to hold the phone away from my ear as he said, "I'm heading over, anyway. Once Ramsey's done with you, I'm escorting you back to my place. No arguments."

"Fine by me. I don't have my Jeep." I ended the call.

"You and Betz. I thought you two were divorced," Ramsey said.

"Doesn't mean we hate each other," I said, as much for Marcus' benefit as for Ramsey's.

"Guess I just assumed. That's usually the case."

"So, what happened between you two?" I asked.

"Me and Betz? Let's just say he undermined me."

"Details?"

Ramsey snorted. "If you're so close, ask him."

At the station, they separated me and Marcus, placing us in different interview rooms. I was no longer given respect for being in law enforcement, like when I was allowed to chat with Ramsey at his desk. Now, I was a victim. One Ramsey didn't trust. Whether it was because of my relationship with Betz or the fact that my clients were dropping like flies, I wasn't sure.

I answered every question. Almost two hours later, I was free to go. I assumed Marcus' and my stories matched enough for them to know we were the prey, not the aggressors. Although both of us were armed, neither of us had fired a shot. Thank God there wasn't time for a two-way gun battle, or the investigation might have taken a different path.

When we were done, I found Betz waiting in the lobby. I didn't care that there'd been a chasm between us. I rushed into his arms.

He held me so tightly, I couldn't breathe. "I'm sorry," he said. "I shouldn't have let you out of my sight."

And he kissed me. Eager, lingering... yet his lips were soft as butter. I drank him in and drifted back to three years ago and the last time we'd kissed. His arms felt like home.

Then, the door behind me banged open. We stepped apart. And Marcus entered the room.

I wiped my hand across my mouth, like I could inhale what had just happened. Make it part of me.

Betz cleared his throat. "My car's out front. Let's go."

We walked single file out the door. Betz's SUV was parked in a visitor's spot. My Jeep idled at the curb. A uniformed officer held out the keys, and I took them. "Processed and returned. Sign here."

He held out a form, and I scribbled my signature under the beam of his flashlight.

I handed the keys to Marcus. "You mind taking the Jeep?"

He looked skeptical, but he took the keys. "Sure."

I wondered how much he'd witnessed. I wasn't up to hiding my feelings for Betz. We had history. Marcus needed to understand that. And Betz's kiss complicated things.

We went to our respective vehicles. I slid into the passenger's seat of Betz's truck and settled Felony on my lap. Betz put on his seatbelt and checked his rearview mirror before backing out of the space. From the side mirror, I watched Marcus pull out behind us.

"So, you don't hate me anymore?" Betz said.

I snuggled Felony against my chest and stroked his head. "I never hated you."

"I could have lost...." The last word stuck in his throat.

"Me. I know."

What else was there to say? His intentions were obvious. As were Marcus'. My heart felt like a ping-pong ball. Why couldn't I make up my mind? I wouldn't make such a big decision tonight, that was for sure. Not after all that had transpired. So, I deflected. Typical Casey move. "What happened between you and Ramsey?"

Betz kept his eyes on the road, one hand on the steering wheel, his Adam's apple pulsing in his neck. "I caught him cheating in the academy. Turned him in."

"Why didn't he wash out?"

"Rumor had it his dad was tight with the class sergeant. I don't really know. Ended up backfiring on me. My ass was the one on the line."

"Obviously, you made it through."

"Not without a lot of ugliness. Anyway, it's ancient history."

"Doesn't seem that way."

Betz shrugged. "You hungry?"

End of that conversation.

"Not really. Being shot at ruins your appetite. But I should probably eat something."

"You want the low-carb crap Jasmine stocks in the house, or should we hit a drive-thru?"

"Is In-and-Out Burger open this late?"

"You don't know? You clearly have to get out more."

I laughed. "Gonna text Marcus and let him know the plan."

CHAPTER FORTY-ONE

I felt a cloud form over our heads at my mention of his name.

Betz pulled through the drive-thru, and we placed our order. My treat. I hadn't heard back from Marcus yet, but I ordered an extra burger and fries for him. "Tell me you have beer," I said.

Betz gave me a knowing look. "What do you think?"

Sacks of fast food in hand, we parked and entered the house through Betz's front door. Jasmine, dressed in shorts and a T-shirt that made her almost look mortal, stood in the kitchen drinking a cup of tea. She shut her laptop as we walked into the room.

"Glad you didn't get hurt," she said without feeling. "Guestroom is ready, and I put some bedding on the sofa for you, Marcus."

I laid the food on the counter. "Thanks."

She placed her cup in the sink. "I'm heading to bed. Good night."

"Night," we all said in unison.

Betz took three bottles of beer from the refrigerator, and I doled out the burgers and fries. Marcus perched on a stool while Betz and I stood at opposite ends of the counter. We devoured our food. Not talking but exchanging fleeting glances. I flicked Felony a couple of fries.

Finished, I wadded up my food wrapper and laid it on the counter. "What's our next step?"

All eyes were on me.

"About what?" Betz said.

"Diablo. Are we supposed to hunker down in hiding until they get arrested? I mean, I've got a life to live, a job."

"Will be hard to do those things if they succeed next time," Betz said.

"I know. But I should be safe at the office."

Betz gathered the food wrappers and threw them in the trash. "I'll drive you there in the morning. Don't leave on your own." He turned to Marcus. "You're a grown man. Not gonna tell you what to do, but I'd watch my back if I were you."

Marcus got to his feet. "Thanks for the advice. Where's the bathroom?"

Betz pointed to the hallway behind him. "On your left."

Marcus left the room. Betz crossed over to me and took my hands in his. "That kiss," he said.

My breath caught. Was he going to do it again? "Yeah," I said. "It was…"

He squeezed my hands. "Brought back a lot of memories."

"Yeah."

"You want to come upstairs? Even if I just hold you…."

I did. I wanted to snuggle in his arms. Feel safe. Go back in time. There was a pull, like we were both magnets, with no power to stand on our own. But Marcus…

"Not tonight," I said. "I need a minute."

From down the hall, I heard the bathroom door open. I pulled my hands free, dropped them by my sides.

"Life's short," Betz said. "But whatever. You know where to find me." He turned and climbed the stairs.

Alone, I felt suddenly cold. I almost ran after him. But that wasn't fair. I couldn't leave loose ends. Was that what Marcus was? No. He'd become much more than that.

Marcus entered the room. I froze until I heard Betz shut his bedroom door.

"Survived another near-death experience together," he said. "This has been one hell of a ride."

"Yeah," I said. "You want to get off the merry-go-round? Go back to Jersey?"

"Is that what you want me to do?"

I should have said yes. It would be for his own good. But my willpower wasn't that strong. I shook my head, crossed my arms, and hugged myself.

Marcus tilted his head to the side, his gaze penetrating my armor, touching my soul. He tucked a clump of hair behind his ear. The look of longing on his face was almost more than I could handle. "Unless you give me the boot, I'm not leaving. I'm in for the long haul. You really gonna make me sleep on the couch?"

It was like I was in a candy shop, but I could only pick one piece of chocolate when I wanted the whole box. I couldn't disrespect Betz, though, not in his house. "Sorry."

My back pressed against the counter; Marcus blocked me from walking away. I gently laid my hands on his chest and gave a little shove. "Try to get some sleep."

He took a step back and let me pass. "You too, Sunshine. Pleasant dreams."

I called Felony, and we moved together down the hallway, found the guestroom, and I closed us inside. A good chunk of the night had passed, yet morning still felt miles away.

Chapter Forty-Two

I was wrong. Apparently, conflicting feelings after a major adrenaline dump begot a good night's sleep. Once I hit the mattress, I forgot about the two desirable men in the other parts of the house. Forgot that Diablo was seeking revenge. Forgot that my clients were under fire, and the rumor was I was the one doing the targeting. I forgot about my job. I even forgot about the sweet little dog curled against my neck.

If Felony hadn't scratched at the door and someone opened it to let him out, I'd still be dead to the world. Maybe being trapped in Betz's guestroom wasn't the worst fate.

There was a wall of books. And the kitchen was just down the hall. I could get comfortable here.

Who was I kidding? FOMO was already setting in.

Stretching, I slowly got out of bed. My cell sat on the nightstand. Not much battery left. I'd been too lazy last night to dig my charger out of my backpack. It was almost ten. I needed to call Alma and explain why I was two hours late for work.

After a quick trip to the bathroom, I did exactly that but got her voicemail. "Call me."

I wandered out to the kitchen, passing through the family room where Marcus had spent the night. He had neatly folded and stacked the bedding on a sofa cushion.

Felony bounded across the room to greet me. I loved on him for a minute, then proceeded to the kitchen.

Jasmine sat at the counter, her laptop open in front of her. The TV was on in the background, muted. She looked at me over tortoiseshell cat-eye glasses. "I was about to check on you. Thought you died in your sleep."

Sorry to disappoint. I rubbed my eyes. "Guess I was tired. Betz here?"

"He waited as long as he could. Had to go to work."

"Do you know where Marcus went?"

"Same. He took your Jeep."

"Great." I was stuck then. "I'd like to clean up, get dressed. Think I could get a ride downtown afterward?"

"At your service."

I was about to head back to the guestroom when I spotted Suzy Vega on the television. "Can you turn that up?"

Jasmine picked up the remote.

Vega's voice filled the room. "Another unexplained death of a probationer. I did a little research, and Officer Casey Carson also supervised this person. It's the second death plus an assault on her clients that has occurred this month. The probation department has declined comment."

I gulped air, but it did little to ease the rush of lightheadedness that overcame me.

The next segment came on.

"Did you know about this?" Jasmine asked, putting the TV back on mute.

I stood, speechless. I started to sway, and grabbed the counter and held on, so I didn't topple over. "Ah.... No."

Jasmine narrowed her eyes and stared at me. I shuffled back to the bedroom and checked my phone. The battery was still in the red, and I'd missed a few calls. I scrolled down and sure enough, there was a message from Alma. I played it.

"Casey, it's Alma. Call me ASAP."

I returned the call, but once again, got her voicemail. "Alma, I just saw the news. Who died? Please call me back. I'm going crazy here."

Digging through my bag for my charger, I removed a fresh pair of jeans, a navy T-shirt, and clean underwear from my backpack, then took a shower in the guest bathroom with my phone plugged in on the counter so I could reach it if it rang. I combed out my wet hair and let it air dry, while constantly checking my cell. No return call.

Jasmine was still in the kitchen, but she'd changed into a classic black suit and white blouse. As usual, I was out dressed. I adjusted the strap on the backpack I'd slung over my shoulder and plugged my phone charger into the kitchen outlet, standing by, ready to take a call.

"I didn't think we'd be here again so soon," Jasmine said. "I thought I was clear when we talked about you staying away from Betz. Isn't that why you came to me instead of him?"

"You invited me."

"Before that."

The situation with Suzy Vega was none of Jasmine's business. Neither was my relationship with her brother. I was tired of her judgment. And I didn't want to deal with her in my panicked state. As important as Betz was to me, the death of another client was taking up most of the room in my head. "Look," I said. "I'm kind of cranky, given what happened last night and the news I just got. I don't want to say something I'll regret, but back off. Betz and I need to figure some things out. I know one thing for sure, though. We love each other. Whether or not we're together, that won't change. I know you don't like me, but that doesn't really matter to me at the moment."

Jasmine blinked, took off her glasses, folded them, and placed them in their case, then slipped them into the purse sitting on the stool next to her.

Her silence made her point. I'd struck a nerve. She wasn't used to pushback, especially from me. She packed up her laptop and a notebook, then pursed her lips before she spoke. "It's not that I don't like you, Casey. In fact, following your antics can be highly entertaining. You're just not good for my brother."

"I understand you feel that way, but like I said, not your business. I know what you were doing, inviting Marcus here last night. You hoped it would show Betz I'd moved on. Your plan backfired. That he would do that for me…. Invite Marcus into his home to stop me from worrying, only makes Betz more appealing."

Jasmine stood and picked up her bag. "You can find another ride."

Alone, I tried to calm down. Why did I let her get to me like that? Why did I care what she thought? I should have felt good for putting her in her place, but instead, I felt deflated. Betz valued his relationship with her. I didn't want to come between them. And if we ever decided to get back together, I didn't want bad blood between me and her, either.

"Damn her," I said to Felony. "What am I supposed to do now?"

Felony cocked his head like he was considering my question.

I knew they wouldn't have Diet Coke, but I searched the refrigerator, anyway. All I found was almond milk and coconut water. Jasmine was as strict with her diet as she was with me. I settled for a glass of tap water.

When my phone had enough juice, I sent a group text message to my family saying I was checking in. All assured me they were alive and well. I didn't mention the drive-by, but I recommended they avoid my house until a work issue was resolved.

Next, I privately messaged Hope. Because she used to be a PO, she was savvier than the rest of my family. *Any chance you could give me a ride?*

Sure. Where are you?

Betz's house. I'll send you the address.

K. Won't be long.

I took the glass of water and my phone and went out back with Felony, finding an outlet so my cell could continue charging. The wicker patio furniture was inviting and familiar—I'd picked it out when Betz and I were married. My heart tugged, remembering selecting the set in the store, with hopes of Betz and I sharing a bottle of wine after a long day's work. But we'd split up before the nice weather and had never fulfilled that dream. The furniture had held up better than our relationship.

I sat down and sent a message to Marcus. *Any news on Bill's condition?*

His response came in less than a minute. *Already home. Should be fine.*

Thank God

You staying safe?

Yup. You?

Yeah. Let me know where you are after work, and I'll bring your Jeep.

Sure thing.

My phone buzzed in my hand. Alma.

"What happened?" I said in greeting.

"Nelson Martz is dead. Gunshot wound to his head. His son found him when he didn't answer his calls."

"Oh, no." I lowered my head into my hands and rocked back and forth. My catatonic state must have worried Felony. He came over and licked my hand.

"Can you come in?" Alma said. "Roxy wants to talk."

"Yeah. Sorry I'm late." I told her what had transpired the night before.

"They shot at you? My God, are you alright?"

"Just a little traumatized. Gunshots are louder than they seem on TV. My ears are still ringing."

"Maybe you shouldn't come in."

"I'm waiting on my ride. The office is probably the safest place for me right now."

I promised her I'd be careful and that I'd be in as soon as I could, then ended the call.

The next text was from Hope. She was waiting out front.

Inside, I gathered my things, Jasmine's words hanging heavy in the air. They still stung.

I didn't want to push my policy breaking by bringing Felony to work. He was safe here, so I locked him in the bathroom, begging him not to be too destructive and hoping I had enough in my savings account to replace anything he damaged.

Locking the door behind me, I met Hope in her car, which idled at the curb. Her Honda was one of the few belongings she'd managed to hold onto after she'd lost her job.

It dawned on me that Hope might have information about Rocky McManus since her entanglement with Diablo led to her current situation.

Once seated, I told her what had happened the night before.

Hope hung her head. "I'm so sorry, Casey. It's my fault you got sucked into Diablo's world."

I shrugged. "You were in a tough situation. You didn't ask me to stick my

206

nose in it."

"But if you hadn't…. Well, God only knows what would have happened."

Hope had taken her arrest hard, but she was starting to come back to her old self. Naturally thin, she'd almost wasted away, but she seemed to be better accepting of her situation and was getting stronger.

"What I'm wondering," I said, "is do you know Rocky McManus?"

She nodded. "I met him a few times. Do you think he was the shooter last night?"

"I do. Any idea where he'd hang out?"

Hope drummed her fingers on the steering wheel. "I think the police raided most of the places they had, and they abandoned them. There is a bar they used to frequent. Not sure if they still do."

The one I followed Suzy Vega to? It was on the way to the office. "The one off the freeway," I said. "Can you swing by?"

Hope cringed.

"Just drive through the parking lot. See if their bikes are there."

"Okay," she said. "But a condition of my probation is that I stay away from Diablo. Not supposed to be in bars, either."

"I understand. Just want to check out the parking lot." After a beat, I said, "How's the probation thing going?"

Because Hope was employed as a PO when her crime occurred, her supervision was tailored to make it more comfortable and fairer for everyone. She was supervised by a neighboring county instead of being assigned to one of her former peers.

She shrugged. "Like I used to tell my clients, probation is only hard if you're trying to hide something. I report once a month and pay my fines. Still, I never thought it would come to this. Me being on the other side of the desk."

I couldn't imagine. Ramsey treated me like a criminal. Although it didn't compare, I didn't like my morals called into question. I felt for Hope.

It was just after eleven when she pulled into the bar's parking lot. I assumed they started serving food around now. Only a few cars and a handful of motorcycles were in the parking lot. They didn't look like gang bikes, mostly

BMWs. If Diablo wasn't here, it was probably the safest time to see if I could learn anything useful.

I unbuckled my seatbelt. "Gonna run inside for a minute. Wait here."

"Do you think that's a good idea?"

"Probably not. But I'm sick of waiting for them to come for me. Just being proactive."

My gun was in my bag, and I took some comfort in knowing it was accessible. While Hope idled at the curb, I jumped out and walked up to the front door with my bag slung over my shoulder.

The double dark heavy doors were closed, but a neon sign in the window flashed "Open."

Inside, I blinked at the dusty space. A bar with an assortment of liquor bottles lining the back wall took up most of the room. Most of the stools were unoccupied, but there was a cluster of older men at the far end. Four pool tables were unattended. No sign of any Diablo gang members. Too early for them was my guess.

I approached the counter. The bartender stood with his back to me, wiping down glasses he took from a crate before placing them on a shelf.

"Excuse me," I said. "Got a minute?"

The man slowly turned my way. He had greasy black hair, parted down the middle and hanging in ropes past his shoulders. Veins popped on heavily muscled arms. No one would mess with him. The glare he shot my way wasn't welcoming. "What'll you have?"

"Oh," I said, flashing a smile. "Sorry, not ordering anything. Just have a question."

"Unless it's for directions, questions ain't on the menu."

I dropped my shoulders and turned up the charm. His blank stare was unaffected. I was losing my touch.

"Just want to know if Rocky's been by recently."

After giving me a hard stare, he turned his back to me and returned to what he was doing. I looked at the old men at the end of the bar, all nursing drinks. They were studying me. My common sense screamed at me to leave. For once, I listened.

I turned to go. A voice startled me from the row of booths lining the opposite wall. It was so dark I hadn't even noticed the tables when I'd come in. I could make out the shape of a person. "Psst, hey, come here."

I slipped my hand into my bag. Feeling the gun, I took a step closer.

"Over here, sit."

I side-stepped to the edge of the table, squinting to make out the man's face.

"Casey," he whispered. "It's Carl. Betz's friend. Sit."

I leaned on the table with one hand and patted my chest with the other. "Jeez, Carl. You scared the shit out of me."

"Sit," he said again.

I slid into the booth across from him. Carl gave a hard stare toward the men at the end of the bar. They turned away and engaged in hushed conversation.

"You shouldn't be here," Carl said in a voice slightly above a whisper. "Shouldn't be asking about Rocky."

"Well," I said. "He shot at me. You guys can't find him, and I'm sick of living in fear."

"I'm a gang detective these days," he said. "Betz clued me in on what's been going on. I'm trying to find Rocky—it's why I'm here. Wouldn't be a good idea for him to find you first. Betz would have a cow if he knew you'd come to their turf."

Carl wore all black and had a Duck Dynasty beard—a big change from the clean-cut guy who'd been at our wedding. He fit in just fine. I hugged my bag to my chest. "I know. So, probably a good idea if you don't tell him. Can I ask you something, or are questions off the menu for you, too?"

He laughed. "Go ahead."

"Any idea what Suzy Vega was doing here a few days ago? Aside from her nephew, does she have a connection to Diablo?"

He took a sip of coffee. "And how do you know she was here?"

I looked at my lap. "I followed her."

He ran a hand over his beard. "Because of her relationship with Betz?"

"Jeez, did everyone know but me?"

"Shit. I shouldn't have said anything."

"It's okay. He told me he dated her a few times. And no, I followed her because she's been sticking her nose in my business."

"I had no idea she was here, but I'll keep that in mind," he said. "You should go."

I got to my feet. "Please find Rocky and put him in jail where he belongs. And stay safe."

"You, too, Casey."

Chapter Forty-Three

Hope dropped me off at the office. I locked my bag and gun in my file cabinet and went directly to Alma's office. It was empty, but a note on the dry-erase board directed me to Roxy's office. For emergencies and for Casey. She'd underlined my name. Comforting.

I trotted down the hall, passing coworkers at their cubicles. Nervous glances darted my way, but when I made eye contact, they all turned their attention back to whatever they were doing. The rumor mill was obviously running smoothly. Thanks, Claire.

Roxy had a large corner office with a good view of Camelback Mountain. I'd only been in the room a few times. I knocked on the door and heard a muffled "Come in."

Inside, Alma, Roxy, and Detective Ramsey sat at a round table in the far corner of the room. The mood was somber. Only Alma looked happy to see me.

Roxy patted the only empty chair. "Shut the door and come sit."

My stomach dropped into my shoes as I tried to reason why Ramsey was in the room. I gave him the side-eye as I took my seat.

"How are you?" Alma asked.

I picked a piece of lint off my shirt and met Roxy's disapproving stare before I could drop it to the floor. Instead, I shoved it into the pocket of my jeans. "I'm okay. Aside from being shot at and learning, I have another dead client."

"About that," Ramsey said. "Where'd you go after we talked last night?"

I was glad to have an alibi. Perhaps it would put his suspicions to rest.

"Betz's house. Both Marcus and I stayed the night." I almost added that we slept in separate rooms, but I didn't want to overshare.

He wrote something down in the small notebook on the table in front of him. "So, Betz and Marcus can attest to that?"

"Lieutenant Faulk was there too." No shame in dropping as many names as I could.

He nodded. "What can you tell me about Nelson Martz?"

I rubbed sweaty palms on my jeans. "I'd need his file for specifics, but he was an okay guy. Early fifties. Can't remember his exact charge, but he was on probation for stealing from his employer."

Roxy turned her laptop my way. On the screen was Nelson's electronic file and my case notes. I scooted the machine closer to me and scrolled through the log. "He's been on my caseload for a few months. He was transferred to me from the Glendale office after he moved to central Phoenix. Worked as a delivery driver for one of those food service apps. He struggled to pay his restitution, given how high the payments were, but somehow, he scraped some money together and paid off the balance last month. Once he completed his community service hours, I planned to ask the judge to early terminate his probation.

"He was doing well in treatment for an alcohol problem. He got divorced. Has adult kids."

"When did you see him last?" Ramsey asked.

I looked back at my notes. "A week ago. I did a field visit at his house."

"Any reason he'd fear you?"

"Fear me? No."

Ramsey slid a clear plastic evidence bag my way. Inside was a typed note. *I can't live with the constant scrutiny. Nothing I do is good enough. Can't stand having a prison sentence hanging over my head. She never lets me forget she has the power to send me away.*

A suicide note? I read it three times, then pushed the paper back toward Ramsey. "Nelson didn't write this."

"How do you know?" Alma said.

"First off, he was looking forward to getting off probation early. Second,

English is his second language, and he was still mastering it. Can I get his hard file?"

Ramsey nodded.

I hurried back to my cubicle and rummaged through my files. Someone was trying to make it look like Nelson was afraid of me. File in hand, I returned to Roxy's office.

I opened it, laid it flat, and turned it toward Ramsey, pointing to the golden reporting forms clients filled out whenever they came in. Ramsey read the block writing. Neat, but almost every word was misspelled.

He snapped a photo with his phone.

"That's helpful, thanks. I have one other question. Did Nelson have birds, chickens, maybe?"

I swallowed hard. "No. Why?"

"We found some feathers near his body. Bright yellow."

Guess it was time to come forward about the giant driving chicken.

Chapter Forty-Four

When I finished talking about Brian Johnson's missing chicken suit, my human-sized poultry sighting, and the feather I'd found in my house, my audience collectively gasped and leaned back in their chairs—as if to distance themselves from me, the nut bag.

After an uncomfortable silence, Ramsey cleared his throat. "We've kept two things from the public, so I'd appreciate it if this conversation doesn't leave this room, but feathers have been found at all the crime scenes. So have Casey's business cards. We haven't tested the feathers found at Martz's house yet, but the others are synthetic, not real."

"So Brian's killer took the suit as a souvenir," I said.

Ramsey closed his notebook. "That's one theory. His body was moved, so he was obviously killed elsewhere. If he was killed at home, the killer could have taken the suit."

"He was living at a homeless camp with Irene Goss. She didn't seem to know anything," I said.

Ramsey tapped his pen on the table. "You working the case?"

I brushed a hair off my forehead. "Not stepping on your toes. It came up during a field visit. Didn't seem like you were looking beyond me as a suspect, so I didn't feel comfortable going to you."

"Well, if your alibi checks out, we'll cross you off the list. Not a fan of Betz, but I can't see him lying to interfere with an investigation."

Something Ramsey might do, given what Betz said, but I held that comment back.

"What camp?" he said.

I gave him the location. He jotted the information in his notebook.

"So," Alma said. "If a feather was in your house, whoever's been masquerading as a chicken has been inside?"

"Tony was there. But my cousin didn't mention him wearing a chicken suit, something even she would find odd. But other than family and Marcus, no one else has been in my house. Well, Jerski, but it couldn't be him."

"Jerski?" Ramsey said.

Alma kicked me under the table. "Pete Pajerski. He's a PO."

Ramsey repeatedly clicked his pen open and shut. "Since Marcus was out of town when Brian Johnson was killed, we eliminated him as a suspect."

I had no idea Ramsey had looked into Marcus. But knowing he was cleared was a relief. Not that I ever suspected him, but Ramsey obviously had.

"I talked to Tony," Ramsey said. "The guy's pretty scattered. Hard to pin him down on anything. Poor historian."

"One of the many reasons we let him go," Roxy said.

Ramsey checked his watch, pocketed his notebook and pen, and got to his feet. "Could be a disgruntled employee, and Tony is certainly that, but that's only a hunch. Remember, ladies. Nothing we've talked about leaves this room."

"Got it," Roxy said, and she walked him to the door.

I started to get up, but Alma held out her hand to stop me. I slouched in my seat.

Roxy came back to the table and sat down. "Let's talk about the other issue. Alma told me someone fired shots at you last night. It was on your own time, not work-related, right?"

I drew circles on the table with my finger. "Yeah, I guess. My friend was staying at the house. Someone must have followed us. They were probably after my friend, not me. The shots were fired from two motorcycles. Thinking Diablo. The gang squad is on it."

Alma gathered her hair into a bun. "You're making light of this. It's serious."

"Oh," I said. "Believe me, I know."

"Anyway," Roxy said. "These are police investigations. Up to them to figure things out. My concern is your safety and the safety of your clients. What can we do to keep you safe?"

"No fieldwork alone," Alma said. "Can you stay with family?"

I wasn't bringing them into this. And after the words exchanged between me and Jasmine that morning, getting shot might be less painful than staying with them. "Thinking of going to a motel."

"Just make sure you're not followed," Roxy said.

I nodded.

"And wearing your vest when you're not in the office wouldn't be a bad idea," she added.

I gave a mock salute. "Anything else?"

Alma and Roxy exchanged a worried look, and my nerves galloped into overdrive. "Upper management is concerned," Roxy said, laying her hands on the table. "This isn't a good look for the department. If there's anything you need to share with us, now would be the time to do it."

"Like what?" my voice squeaked.

"If you've done anything.... If you've—"

"We know you have nothing to do with this," Alma butted in.

But Roxy didn't look so sure.

I crossed my arms. "I don't know why my clients are being targeted. You have to know that."

"Of course," Roxy said. "You can go."

I wanted to convince Roxy that she had nothing to worry about, but with two clients dead and another in the hospital, anything I thought of sounded inadequate, even to me.

I stood on wobbly legs and tried to gain control of my extremities as I walked to the door. I'd probably fail a sobriety test, and I hadn't had a drink. Unfortunately, it was a little early to get the party started.

Chapter Forty-Five

Back at my desk, I put my earphones on—listening to Brandi Carlile while I checked my messages. One was from Lilian Harrison. Back to her sweet self. Had dementia erased her hatred of me? She was concerned, she said, because Eric hadn't been home for a few days.

I checked the jail roster. Eric remained in custody. She'd obviously forgotten that.

Despite her earlier pleas to have me fired, I felt bad for her. Her caller ID told me the hospital had released her, since she was calling from home. I called her back.

"Hi, Lilian, it's Casey. I'm returning your call."

"Oh, Casey. I'm so worried about Eric. He hasn't been home for days."

I didn't want to remind her of her broken hip and her hatred of me, so I only said, "Eric's safe. He's in jail."

"Oh, dear," she said. "What did he do?"

"Just a probation violation." No need to mention the new gun charges.

"Oh, I don't know what to do then…. There's someone here. They're in Eric's room, tearing it apart. They won't leave."

"A police officer?"

"I don't think so. They're dressed like a bird."

I straightened. "Excuse me?"

"Not a bird. A chicken, maybe."

"Lilian, I need you to go outside. Find a neighbor." Keeping her on the line, I used my cell to call 911.

"I can't," Lilian said. "I have a broken hip…. A walker. It hurts to get up."

The 911 operator came on the line. "What's your emergency?"

I identified myself and rattled the Harrison's address off from memory. I'd been there so many times I'd never forget it. "There's an elderly woman home alone, and I think there's an intruder in the house."

Or Lilian was out of her mind, but given what I'd seen lately, her story made sense. Still, I didn't mention anything about the chicken.

Once the operator assured me help was on the way, I focused on Lilian. "You still there?"

"Yes."

"What's the man doing now?"

"I don't know. I'm in the living room. I had to sit down. My hip hurts if I stand too long."

"They let you go home alone?"

"I'm not alone. Eric lives here."

I massaged my forehead, dizzy from the circles of our conversation. "What did the man say to you?"

"The chicken? They asked for Eric. Then said they left something in Eric's room that they needed."

The dispatcher came back on the line. "The officer's at the door."

"Lilian," I said into my cell. "Can you make it to the door? A police officer is there. I need you to let them in."

"Oh, okay." The receiver clunked against a tabletop as she put the phone down. A creaking noise came over the line. I assumed it was her walker. A moment later, the door opened, and I heard muffled voices.

I asked the dispatcher to have the officer pick up Lilian's landline. In a moment, a male voice came over the line. "This is Officer Lannister."

"Casey Carson with Adult Probation. This is going to sound crazy, but Lilian told me a man dressed as a chicken is in her son's bedroom. It's a long story, but I believe he may be armed and dangerous."

"A chicken suit?"

"I know, crazy. Please humor me and check the house."

"Okay." The phone hit the table again.

"I'm going to disconnect," the dispatcher said.

"Okay, thanks." I ended the call and pressed the receiver of my desk phone against my ear. Muffled voices were in the background,

A few minutes later, the cop came back on the line. "No chicken. No man," he said. "But the bedroom window is open, and a trail of feathers leads up to it. I checked the rest of the house, and no one is here. I'll have Mrs. Harrison lock up, and I'll drive around the neighborhood. Not sure what else I can do."

"Okay, thanks."

I hung up and hurried to Alma's office. She was at her desk.

The look on her face said, "What now?"

"I need to head to Lilian Harrison's. Something isn't right. Not sure what I'm looking for, but I'll know when I see it."

Alma gave a giant sigh. "Give me a minute to gear up. I'm coming with you."

Chapter Forty-Six

Since I didn't have my Jeep, and the two county cars had been checked out, Alma drove her ancient Volvo. I called Ramsey on our way and filled him in on the bizarre call with Lilian.

Ramsey had already parked his SUV in front of the Harrison's house when we arrived. We gathered on the sidewalk, then walked to the door and rang the doorbell.

"Might take her a while to answer," I said, reminding them of Lilian's broken hip.

And it did. Eventually, she came to the door.

"Why, Casey," she said with a smile. "What a nice surprise."

"Do you remember our phone call, Lilian?"

Her blank expression answered my question.

"This is my supervisor, Alma, and this is Detective Ramsey," I said, motioning to them. "Can we come in?"

She navigated her walker back a few feet so we could enter. I clicked my flashlight on and shone it around the dark living room. Anyone could be lurking in the shadows. Every time I entered the room, I had the urge to open the dust-covered curtains. How anyone could live in a cave was beyond me.

"Do you mind if we check Eric's bedroom?"

Lilian shrugged. "I don't think he's home."

"I know," I said. "But if we could just have a look."

"Fine by me."

I led Alma and Ramsey to the back of the house, where Eric slept. I flipped on the overhead light. Like the responding officer said, a trail of yellow feathers littered the floor and made a path to the open window.

"Stop," Ramsey said. "Don't disturb anything." He snapped a few photos.

I froze just inside the doorway and took in the room. Eric was a slob. His bedroom always looked like the aftermath of a tornado, so it was hard to tell what was out of place.

"It's hard to imagine someone walking around dressed like a chicken and not drawing attention to themselves," Alma said. "You'd think they'd be easy to spot."

"Have you heard of furries?" I said.

Alma shook her head.

"It's a subculture," Ramsey said. "Mostly teens, young adults. They dress in animal costumes."

Alma scrunched up her nose. "Why?"

"Beats me," Ramsey said.

"You'd think Phoenix would be too hot for that," I said.

"Great disguise when committing crimes, though," Ramsey said. "Question is, is it Brian Johnson's missing chicken suit or someone from the furry community?"

"That would be a big coincidence," Alma said.

"So," Ramsey said. "POs don't need permission to search, but I'd feel more comfortable getting a warrant. This could be tied to a murder or two, the probationer isn't here, and a woman with dementia is giving us permission to look around. Any decent lawyer would tear an unwarranted search apart. Give me a few." He wandered out of the room with his phone to his ear.

Back in the living room, Alma and I found Lilian dozing in the recliner. I cleared my throat, and she slowly opened her eyes. "Casey, what are you doing here?"

"I'm concerned about you," I said. "They released you from rehab thinking your son would be around to help you out."

Lilian nodded. "He's very helpful."

"Did they give you a release plan? Some sort of paperwork?"

Her gnarled hand reached for a folder on the tray table by her side. She picked up a blue file and handed it to me. Flashlight tucked under my armpit, I flipped through the papers until I found one with the heading I was looking for. "Says here you're supposed to set up physical and occupational therapy and arrange for a nurse to come out and see how you're doing. Did you do any of that?"

"I think Eric did."

"Eric's not here. Mind if I set it up for you?"

"Sure."

I spent the next twenty minutes on the phone advocating for Lilian's care. Once I had everything set up, I wrote her appointments on a calendar she kept close by.

By the time I'd finished, Ramsey had an electronic warrant for us to search Eric's bedroom. We reassembled in the room, donned disposable gloves, and started looking around. I wasn't surprised to find empty beer bottles, which I photographed as evidence for his probation violation hearing. I had no idea how long they'd been there, but I could testify that they hadn't been in the room the last time I'd checked it. So, long after he knew he wasn't supposed to drink.

On the desk was a pile of papers. On top, a credit card application with Lilian's information filled out. Maybe stealing his mom's identity had helped him in making payments on his probation fines and fees. I snapped a photo of that, too.

The next paper was from the church where Eric had been assigned to complete community service. According to the form, he'd gone the last six Saturdays, bringing him close to the completion of the hours ordered by the court. Eric had done something right. The judge would want that information, too.

"Pay dirt," Alma called, her flashlight aimed deep in the closet.

Ramsey and I walked over and peered over her shoulder, where the light illuminated an open duffel bag. Inside were pills. Piles and piles of blue pills.

"Good thing the patrol officer scared off the chicken man before he found these," Ramsey said.

Drug dealers had bosses. And bosses wouldn't want their product sitting around while their employee was in jail. Probably where Eric got the money to pay off his financial obligations. Would be faster than committing credit card fraud.

Coffman had been dealing opiates. At least that's what Justin had said. Eric and Henry obviously worked for the same people, but what about Nelson Martz?

With such a big find, Ramsey called in some of his own people and excused me and Alma from further searching the room. I promised to call Lilian the following day to see how she was doing.

"That's nice of you, dear," she said. "But Eric's looking out for me."

"Let's brainstorm this," Alma said as we drove back to the office.

"Bet those pills test for Fentanyl. Looks like several of my clients were dealing. Thinking about it, they all made big payments toward their restitution, fines, and fees recently. I wondered where they got the money."

"Which would lead to early termination of their probation grants," Alma said.

"Too bad Brian Johnson and Nelson Martz will get those early terminations for another reason. They must have done something to make their bosses, maybe Diablo, mad enough to kill them."

"Were they making payments, too?"

I nodded. "All four of them seem tied together. I'll alert the jail to keep an eye on Eric Harrison before he becomes victim number four."

"Well," Alma said. "I'll fill Ramsey in on what they have in common. It's up to him to determine who they've been working for. But why kill them if they're pushing their product?"

"Don't know." Maybe my arrest of Eric Harrison had kept him alive.

Halfway to the office, my cell rang. Jerski. What now?

Chapter Forty-Seven

I took Jerski's call. "Hey?"

"I hate to rub it in," he said. "But your brilliant idea to put Justin into treatment instead of letting me haul his ass to jail has backfired."

His tone was gleeful, in fact, rubbing it in. "Let me guess, he absconded."

"In the front door and out the back."

"Well," I said. "It happens. You calling to gloat, or do you have a point?"

"Thought you'd go with me to arrest him. You owe me that."

I rolled my eyes, calculating how much I owed the eye-roll jar. At this rate, I'd need to take out a home equity loan. "I'm limiting my fieldwork these days."

"It's just one arrest."

I glanced at Alma and blocked the speaker with my thumb. "How do you feel about me helping Jerski with an arrest?"

"Stop calling him that."

"He can't hear me."

She squeezed the steering wheel. "Still."

"So how about it?"

Alma glanced at the clock on the dashboard. "Sorry, can't join you. I have a meeting."

"Can I go? Then he can give me a ride home. Wherever that will be."

"Jerski is armed, isn't he?"

I laughed. "You called him Jerski."

"Damn you," Alma rolled her eyes. My bad habits were catching. "You can go. Just this one arrest."

I dropped my thumb and brought the phone back to my ear. "Pick me up at the office."

"What? Now I'm your chauffeur?"

"Only way I can go. Don't have my Jeep." Thoughts of my bullet-riddled Wrangler made my stomach roll.

"Okay," Jerski said. "I'll text you when I'm outside."

By the time I got downstairs, La Bamba was parked at the employee entrance. A handful of smokers were gathered a few feet from the door, and they watched with amusement as I got in the car. One more thing for the rumor mill.

I was itchy under my vest and had my bag with the gun between my feet. "You sure Justin's home?"

"No idea. But thought I'd try going there before I did a warrant and let the police find him."

He handed me a booking sheet that was filled out and ready in case we succeeded in making the arrest.

Lips a tight line, he cast a glance my way. "Four new tires cost me a fortune."

Like it was my fault. "Sorry."

"When is Joy able to go back to your place? My mom isn't thrilled about her staying with us."

"Can't believe you live with your mom."

"Don't judge. Rents are expensive. And Joy is cramping my style."

Style? A thirty-five-year-old man living with his mother was a look that drew attention. There was that. "She can come back when Diablo stops shooting at me."

"When will that be?"

I shrugged. "I'm not privy to that information."

We ran out of conversation, and I spent the rest of the time clutching the seat below my thighs, fearing we'd collide with the surrounding traffic as the hearse drifted from lane to lane. Jerski seemed oblivious to the blaring of horns around us.

When we pulled up to the house, all was quiet. No cars in the driveway, but I knew Suzy parked in the garage, so no guarantee she wasn't home. It was almost time for the four o'clock news, so I assumed she was at work.

I called in our location, and we approached the house. Jerski pounded on the metal screen door with his fist. If I were Justin, I wouldn't answer.

But Justin wasn't that bright.

The wooden door opened a few inches; the screen door stayed shut. "Open up," Jerski said.

"No."

Breaking down doors wasn't part of our protocol, so I was at a loss for our next move. I didn't think Jerski was keen on sweet-talking our way inside, which was the only approach I could see working. "Open the damn door!" Jerski made my point.

"Nope."

"Can I talk to him?" I said.

"Yeah, let *her* talk," Justin said. "I like her."

Jerski threw up his hands and stepped back. Keying his mic, he asked for a patrol car.

"Yo, Justin," I said, plastering a smile on my face. "You'll feel better after you face up to your responsibilities. Living on the run is no fun. Let us take you downtown and get a court date set up."

"That's just a nice way of saying I'm going to jail."

"Not for long if you cooperate. If you make this harder than it has to be, it might be a different story."

I could see him weighing his options, his eyes going wide when a patrol car pulled up to the curb. *We* didn't break down doors, but police could force entry for a warrantless arrest. The stakes just went up.

I didn't want that to happen. No telling what Suzy Vega would do if her house was damaged during a probation violation arrest. It would be one more nail in the coffin of my reputation. Why had I agreed to come?

"Please, Justin," I said. "Let's not have this turn ugly. You don't want to change a measly probation violation into new charges of resisting arrest."

Justin kicked at the doormat, then looked up at me through long lashes.

CHAPTER FORTY-SEVEN

"Only if you keep that cowboy away from me."

Glancing over my shoulder, I motioned for Jerski to back up. He threw up his hands and moved toward the patrol officer, who'd just gotten out of his car.

"And get rid of the cop," Justin said.

I crossed my arms. "That's not how it works. Plus, last time we had a deal, it blew up in my face."

He leaned closer to the door and lowered his voice. "Your boyfriend's in danger. If you want to save him, you'll listen to me."

"Boyfriend? I don't have a boyfriend."

"Whatever you call him, he's a target."

"You get this info from your Diablo buddies?"

Justin ran a hand through silky hair. "Indirectly. If you don't believe me, ask your client, Marjorie. She knows what's going on."

And she'd already told me. Maybe Justin wouldn't be helpful after all. "I already know my friend has a bounty on his head. Looks like you got nothing. Maybe you should go to jail."

Justin looked over my shoulder at the cop and licked his lips. "Well, there's more than that."

"You gonna tell me?"

"Would be better if you asked Marjorie."

"And how do you know her?"

"We did community service together at a church in Maryvale."

"What church? There must be a dozen churches in Maryvale."

"Well, this one is special. Remember, I told you about my dealer?"

"Henry?"

"He's connected to the church, too. Figure it out and I'll meet you there at eleven. Come alone." He shut the door in my face. I looked back at Jerski who was deep in conversation with the patrol officer.

I counted to ten. I wanted to find out what Justin knew more than I wanted him off the streets. And he wouldn't be able to meet me if he was in jail. When I thought I'd given him enough time, I walked over to the cop car. "I think Justin is heading out the back door."

"Crap," Jerski said.

The cop jumped in his patrol car, and Jerski got into the hearse. I slid into the passenger's seat, slowly closing the door. "Hurry up," Jerski said, stepping on the gas.

I buckled my seatbelt and called in our departure. We cruised the neighborhood, looking down alleyways, but the kid had gotten away. I knew where to find him at eleven, but I kept that to myself.

Chapter Forty-Eight

On our third pass through the neighborhood, Jerski finally figured out that Justin had gotten away. I sent Marcus a text. *You okay?* No response.

My insides tightened. When Justin said "my boyfriend" was in danger, did he mean Diablo had already gotten to him?

I called Marcus, figuring a phone call seemed more urgent than a text message and he might pick up. But the call went straight to voicemail.

What if they had him?

My finger hovered over Betz on my contact list. He already knew Marcus was on a hit list. I really had nothing more than further confirmation of that and a gut feeling. No reason to bring Betz into this. Not yet.

I studied Jerski's profile as he muttered under his breath. I couldn't imagine him waiting with me until eleven o'clock to walk into God knew what.

There wasn't much I could do about Marcus not answering my calls. I still had hope that there was a reasonable explanation. I had time to kill–and something I needed to check out.

After Jerski dropped me back at the office, I pulled up Marjorie's electronic file on my computer, tabbing over to the community service page. Just like Justin said, she'd been assigned to a church in Maryvale. The Worshipers. Although the name sounded familiar, I didn't know anything about them. A Google search led me to a simple website that gave its mission statement: A safe place for those in need. God doesn't judge.

Maryvale wasn't my area, so I wasn't familiar with the church, but from the testimonials on the website, I assumed lots of probationers would take advantage of their services. There were photos of the pastor, a kind-looking man named Father Luke, laughing in a sea of adoring faces.

I wanted to know more about him. Luigi Romero, the supervisor of the community service unit, would be a logical person to ask. But after what happened with Tony, he wasn't my biggest fan.

I tapped my pen on the desk. Where had I seen the name of that church before?

When I'd first met Justin, he'd mentioned my other clients, specifically Henry Coffman and Brian Johnson. I opened Brian's electronic file and tabbed over to the community service menu. Brian had also been assigned to the church, and Father Luke had signed off on his completed hours.

Next, I checked Henry Coffman's notes. Then Eric Harrison's and Nelson Martz's. Same thing.

Their completion of community service hours had struck me as odd, but I had more pressing matters on my plate at the time and I hadn't thought much about it. I was grateful when my clients started checking off the boxes of the things they needed to do for an early termination from probation. Each one on its own wasn't that surprising. But I'd been at the job long enough to conduct some informal research. I didn't have exact numbers, but I knew only a small percentage of my probationers completed their community service hours. And those were the result of constant badgering on my part.

With each of my clients in question assigned to the church, I hadn't been pressing that particular condition of probation. Making sure they were addressing their addictions came first. Yet, here they were, knocking it out of the park.

That was suspicious.

I searched the church's website for contact information for Father Luke, but all I could find was an email address. I sent him a note, identifying myself and asking for him to call me ASAP.

Now what? It was after hours, and the probation office was deserted.

My phone pinged, and I reached for it, hoping it was Marcus. But it was

Betz.

"Just making sure you're okay," he said.

"I'm fine. But I could use a ride."

"Where to?"

"Was thinking of going to church."

"Really? Guess a little prayer wouldn't hurt."

"It's a lead," I said. "How soon can you be at my office?"

Betz hesitated. "I need about an hour or so."

"Great," I said. "Hope to be home by then. Meet me there."

"No way. Not safe."

"I'm armed. I need to change."

"I'll have someone meet you. Don't want you by yourself. Especially at your house."

"Okay," I said. "If you say so."

I requested an Uber and spent my wait time printing off booking photos of Marjorie, Brian Johnson, Eric Harrison, and Henry Coffman. I wanted to make sure Father Luke recognized them as the people who'd completed the hours.

In between, I continued to reach out to Marcus. Nothing, and then a text back. *I'm fine, Sunshine. Just a little busy.*

Thank God.

I need my Jeep.

Will bring it by as soon as I can.

Good news. I hurried outside to catch my ride.

Chapter Forty-Nine

Even the sky was in a bad mood by the time I got home—dark with low-lying, angry clouds. As the driver dropped me off, I scanned the area for any signs that Diablo might be waiting for me. But all was quiet except for a dog barking in the distance, reminding me I'd left Felony in Betz's bathroom and that he must be going berserk by now, hungry and tired of being locked up alone. Once Betz got here, I'd ask him to have Jasmine check on Felony the minute she got home.

As Betz promised, a patrol car was parked out front. I stopped and checked in with the officer, who said he'd stay put until Betz arrived.

I entered through the front door. The house was empty. I turned on the nearest lamp, warming the space. Everything was how I'd left it, but I checked each room, even under the beds, to make sure.

The gun in my bag made a clunking sound when I placed it on the dining room table. I took it out and clamped the holster to my belt. Since the temperature had dropped, I pulled a loose-fitting sweatshirt over my tee. It covered the gun nicely.

I still had a little battery on my phone, but not enough to get me through the night. Plugging it into the charger, I checked for messages. None.

I placed another call to Marcus, wanting an ETA on my Jeep. I wanted to see him, but not with Betz on the way.

No response came. I tried not to let his silence freak me out. *He's working, he's fine...*

Marjorie's number was saved in my phone. I found it and hit send.

"Hey, Casey," she said.

"Hi, Marjorie. Just wanted to make sure you made it to Idaho okay."

"Yeah, it was a long bus ride, but I'm happy to be on my grandma's farm. I slept over twelve hours last night."

"You must have needed it."

"I guess."

"Listen, Marjorie, what can you tell me about the church where you did your community service?"

"With Father Luke? It was okay. I made sandwiches he hands out to the homeless."

"Nice. Were there other clients there with you?"

"Sometimes?"

"Justin Ackerman?"

"Yeah."

"He says you know something about Brian Johnson and Henry Coffman."

She was quiet for a moment. "They were supposed to be there, but they never showed up."

Interesting. "Eric Harrison?"

"Didn't show either. Saw all their names on the schedule, but don't think I ever met them."

"If I text you their photos, can you let me know if you recognize them?"

"Sure."

I laid their mugshots on the table and snapped photos, sending all three.

Marjorie gave a sharp inhale of breath. "I have seen them. But not at community service."

"Where then?"

"I was with Rocky. We met those guys in a park. I stayed in the car. Rocky took a duffle bag out of the trunk and passed it to the big guy."

I thought about the duffel bag Alma had found in Eric's closet. "Eric Harrison?"

"I don't know his name. But it's the big, goofy guy in the photo you sent me. After Rocky handed him the bag, the guy passed Rocky an envelope, which Rocky shoved in his pocket. I recognize a drug deal when I see one. I'm not stupid. But I didn't say anything. Rocky didn't like me sticking my nose in Diablo business."

"Anything else?"

"Nope. We left and never talked about it."

"Thanks, Marjorie. Glad you're safe. Call me every Monday, okay?"

"Sure thing. And thanks for helping me. I feel like I have a fresh start."

"My pleasure." I hung up, feeling hopeful for Marjorie. She'd been stuck in the cycle of abuse for a long time. Sometimes, the only path to success was leaving the past behind.

I picked up the photos. Eric Harrison's dull face stared boldly at the camera. I shuddered when I thought about him pulling a gun on me before his arrest. It was more than a probation violation for drinking that he'd been worried about. He'd been dealing Fentanyl and working with Diablo. I shoved the photos back in my bag, planning to show them to Father Luke and see what he had to say about the drug-dealing trio. I hadn't thought to print Nelson Martz's booking photo, but Betz could probably bring it up on his phone. I had a feeling he was connected to Diablo, as well.

Hearing a car door slam, I moved to the kitchen window and peered through the blinds.

Betz.

Once he'd come inside, I watched the patrol car pull away before I closed the door.

Betz glanced at the gun on my hip. "Good girl," he said.

"I hate it."

"Until you need it."

"Let's hope I never will. Have a seat." I motioned to the sofa. "I need to update you on something."

Betz sat on the couch, and I perched on the arm at the opposite end. I filled Betz in on Justin's offer to meet me at Father Luke's.

"You let him evade arrest?"

I shrugged. "There's something to this. Community service ties my clients together. So does their association with Diablo and dealing Fentanyl."

"And you think Father Luke is involved?"

"He fits in somehow. It hadn't occurred to me until now, but my clients racking up community service hours is strange. Some clients, mostly the low-risk ones, take their hours seriously. But for people like Brian Johnson, Eric Harrison, and Henry Coffman, it's rare for them to do more than a few, if any. That's if I ride them. I didn't. I was more focused on them getting clean and sober. They also made great strides toward restitution payments, another thing that rarely happens. I guess selling drugs can answer where they got the money. Add to that Justin's warning, and all signs point to the church."

Betz checked his watch. "Let's head over there. We can talk to Father Luke before Justin gets there."

Chapter Fifty

It was almost ten by the time we arrived at the church. The steepled building where worshipers gathered for services was up front—a beacon of stability and hope in an otherwise rundown neighborhood. A nondescript building sat further back. Betz drove toward it through an open gate, parking next to a truck with a trailer.

The door stood wide open. I stuck my head in and looked around the room, which was a kitchen with industrial appliances and a long counter where I imagined Marjorie had made the sandwiches Father Luke handed out to the community's houseless individuals.

A ceiling fan made a whooshing sound as it made its rounds, and under cabinet lights illuminated the gleaming metal counter and cooktop. Otherwise, the room was dark.

"Hello?" I called, rapping on the open door with my knuckles.

No response.

A sign said: COME IN. SANDWICHES IN THE COOLER. GOD HELPS THOSE WHO HELP THEMSELVES.

"Guess that's an invitation," Betz said, squeezing past me. Inside, he activated his flashlight, brightening the dark corners of the room.

No Father Luke.

Being so late, I figured he could have gone home for the night, wherever that was. He'd leave the door to the kitchen open in case someone was hungry.

And then I spotted splotches of red on the concrete floor.

I elbowed Betz.

He aimed a beam of light at the spot by his feet and then followed it, careful to step to the side.

We walked around the center island and then toward the back, where a large pantry was. Keeping his flashlight aimed at the floor, we walked single file, following the trail of what appeared to be blood. A back door was open.

We passed through it.

More property went back twenty feet. A dilapidated cottage butted against a rotting fence.

The porch light was on, as was an interior lamp.

I followed Betz to the front door, where more blood pooled on the porch. A wooden screen door wasn't latched, and when Betz knocked on it, it moved inward. He pushed it all the way open with his free hand. "Father Luke?"

Silence.

We moved inside. A neatly made bed was pushed against the side wall. The space was small. Besides the bed, there was only enough room for the loveseat and a desk. A simple place for a man who probably spent most of his time at the church helping those in need. No sign of someone prospering from dealing drugs.

There was one more door, cracked open. A bigger puddle of blood soaked into the wooden floor. I stepped over the sticky substance and pushed the door open with my sneaker.

The door only moved an inch before it got stuck on something. Far enough for me to see an open hand lying on the floor.

"Betz?"

I moved out of the way as he drew his gun and rushed forward, shoving the door with his shoulder, increasing the opening just enough to reveal a body lying on the floor.

I recognized Father Luke from the photos on the website. But unlike the vibrant man in the pictures, this man appeared lifeless.

Betz yanked his cell from his pocket and called for backup.

I took a few steps back, stopping against the desk that sat before an open window. Deep breaths helped quash the feeling that I would vomit or pass out. I concentrated on them, looking down at the ledger left open on the Kelly-green blotter.

The words "Community Service" were written in bold above a list of names. In moments, forensic technicians would block off the area while processing the crime scene. The book before me would soon be evidence, and I wouldn't be privy to the information.

I knew I couldn't touch it, but the page was open, and the listed names were there for me to see. They were all there. Marjorie, Justin Ackerman, Brian Johnson, Eric Harrison, Henry Coffman, and Nelson Martz. But only Marjorie and Justin had hours listed under their names. In the slots designated for my other clients, someone had recorded big fat zeros.

Chapter Fifty-One

While Betz did his cop thing, I gave a statement to another detective and then waited out front for Joy to pick me up. I'd seen enough dead bodies and was ready for some normalcy. Even if Joy wasn't normal.

I checked my watch. Quarter past eleven, and no sign of Justin. The police activity had probably scared him off.

When a hearse pulled up, my first thought was that it was there to collect Father Luke's body. But the coroner had a van, and I recognized the hearse as belonging to Jerski. Not someone I was in the mood to see.

I opened the door and peered inside, relieved to see Joy at the wheel. Until I noticed the tears streaking her face.

"Get in and close the door," she said.

I slid into the seat. She pulled from the curb before I could comply with demand number two. "Jeez, Joy. Give me a minute." I pulled the door shut as she careened out of the neighborhood. "What's wrong?"

She did the side-eye thing, tilting her head toward the back of the hearse. I looked behind me.

Rocky McManus had stuffed himself into the too-small space, his legs crossed and bent at the knee. The roof pushed against his head, twisting it at an odd angle that would surely lead to a stiff neck. In his hand was a gun.

My heart skipped. "Cripes." I'd walked right into the trap. "Where are we going?"

Joy cleared her throat. "If I don't do what he says, they'll hurt Pete. We're going downtown."

She took the on-ramp onto I-10 and headed east.

I looked back at Rocky. "You have Marcus, don't you?"

"Pretty boy's alive. Thought it would be fitting for you two lovebirds to go together."

I pressed my elbow against the gun on my hip. Because it was dark, I didn't think Rocky noticed it when I walked up to the vehicle, so he probably didn't know I was armed. I wished I'd practiced my quick draw and was more comfortable with the gun.

"What are you going to do to us?" I asked as Joy switched lanes.

Rocky waved his gun in the air. "You'll find out soon enough. Stop yakking and put some music on."

Joy reached for the radio and turned up the volume. A hip-hop song I didn't recognize came on. "Ooh," Rocky said. "I love this." And he started rapping along.

Rocky wasn't playing with a full deck, which probably made him more dangerous, if not unpredictable. I'd have to find a way to use that.

With hardly any traffic, it didn't take us long to get to the heart of downtown Phoenix. This wasn't the playlist I'd envisioned I'd die to. I tried to come up with a plan, but the music and my rapidly beating heart made it hard to concentrate.

My mess sucked Joy in again, and I felt a love for her I hadn't known I harbored.

Rocky stopped singing and tapped my cousin on the shoulder with the muzzle of his gun. "Exit here."

We got off the freeway and onto Buckeye Road. We were near the airport, but at this hour, the area, full of warehouses, was deserted.

"Take the next left."

Joy's shaking hand reached for the volume on the radio, and she turned the music down.

"Pull in here."

We turned into the empty parking lot.

"Drive around back."

When we rounded the corner, two motorcycles and a black sedan came into view. Joy pulled into a spot and turned off the engine. Rocky leaned forward and pressed the gun to the back of my head. "Get out, hot stuff," he said to Joy. "Come around and open my door."

Joy exited the vehicle and, on high heels, joggled around front, stopping at the door behind me.

"She has nothing to do with this," I said. "Please let her go."

"Like that's gonna happen," he said coldly.

The back door opened, and the gun was no longer aimed at my head as Rocky struggled to get out. It wasn't a move easily executed for anyone over forty pounds, and it was next to impossible for this tank of a guy. Rocky hadn't thought this through.

As he floundered, I pushed my door open and hopped out. Joy took the opportunity to slam the door on Rocky's hand that held the gun. As his fingers were crushed, he yelped and dropped the weapon. Seizing the moment, I pulled mine and aimed it at him.

Joy leaned down and scooped Rocky's gun off the ground.

Rocky grunted his way out of the hearse, cursing. Once he was standing in front of us, he held his smashed hand to his chest. I kept my weapon aimed at him.

With my other hand, I took out my phone and dialed 911. But there was no signal. The metal buildings were no doubt interfering with my service.

I handed the phone to Joy. "Run back to the road and see if you can get through to 911."

Joy kicked off her shoes, took my cell, and hurried out of sight.

"You don't move," I instructed Rocky.

My newfound control left me woozy, and the gun felt heavy in my hand. Rocky didn't know I was a firearm novice, but I did.

A gun racked behind me. "Drop it," came a voice.

Shit. I might be able to outmaneuver Rocky, but he wasn't alone.

My stomach dropped to my shoes as I slowly turned around. Another man, obviously Diablo, pointed a handgun at my chest.

"One got away," Rocky said. "Give me your gun, PO lady."

"No way."

The other goon reminded me he was in charge, waving his weapon in my face.

I couldn't bring myself to hand my gun over to him, and instead, I lowered it to the ground.

"Bitch," Rocky said as he leaned down to retrieve it. And then he took off after Joy.

Chapter Fifty-Two

Hands up, I walked ahead of the nameless gangster. Obviously, not fast enough, as he shoved me forward, his hand hitting between my shoulder blades. I could sense the gun aimed my way, as if it had a heartbeat. It was all I could think about.

The door opened, and with a push, I stumbled into the dark, empty space, a hollow belly of the warehouse where every sound echoed. The dank scent of mildew permeated my nostrils. A single bulb swung in the middle of the space, illuminating a folding chair where Marcus sat. Another gangster stood next to him—a big one who reminded me of a gorilla. The skinny one who had brought me inside was bow-legged and resembled the scarecrow in *The Wizard of OZ*.

We were screwed, and Marcus knew it. Defeat clouded his usually lively eyes.

He'd been roughed up. Dirt and dust smeared his plain white T-shirt. A bruise bled under his left eye, and a cut marked his cheek. He hadn't given up without a fight.

My stomach flipped like a pancake on a griddle. Dread rushed through my veins. The only way they could make this—our impending death—worse was to force us to watch each other die.

Which was exactly what they intended to do.

I didn't think I could bear the weight of that pain. Marcus wasn't just a distraction from Betz. Not anymore.

That one night we'd shared flashed through my mind. We'd barely scratched the surface of our relationship. I wanted more. There had to be more.

Another shove, and I staggered forward, realizing one night was all we'd ever have.

The gorilla dropped a second folding chair in front of Marcus and forced me to sit across from him. Our knees touched. From that close, I could see his hands were tied in front of him.

We locked eyes.

Marcus gave a half-hearted smirk. "Sorry, Sunshine."

I shook my head as tears pooled in my eyes. "Not your fault."

I leaned forward to touch him, but my arms were yanked in front of me before I could make contact. Zip ties circled my wrists. Pulled tight. I immediately started to lose the feeling in my hands.

There was so much I wanted to say, but Marcus knew. He knew what he'd become to me. I could feel it.

"Just want to make sure you both know what you're dying for," Scarecrow said.

The gorilla got out his phone. "Hold on. I want to record this so we can show it to Ramirez someday. It's really his revenge."

Ramirez. The gangster I'd helped send to prison. I'd tried to convince myself that he wouldn't hold a grudge. Thinking he did was too much for me to swallow. It would have immobilized me, if I let it. But a seven-year prison sentence obviously left him bitter. He hadn't let it go.

"Why did you go after my clients?" I asked. "And Father Luke? What did they have to do with this?"

The gorilla looked at the other thug and laughed. "When people know too much, when they get greedy, sometimes they gotta die."

The scarecrow waved his gun at me and Marcus. "This isn't about that. This is about settling your score with Ramirez. Who wants to go first?"

I wouldn't make it easy for them, and at this point, I had nothing left to lose. *Never quit*, Marcus had said. *Keep fighting*. Without further thought, I sprang to my feet, turned to the left, and kicked the scarecrow. My foot connected with his arm, and the gun flew out of his hand and skidded across the room. Following my lead, Marcus jumped to his feet, and his chair clattered to the floor. Dropping his head, Marcus charged the gorilla like a bull. The goon stumbled backward, and Marcus fell on top of him.

I ran to the weapon lying on the floor, kicking it like a soccer ball. It flew across the room and bounced off the wall.

Neither Marcus nor I had the use of our arms. I was quicker on my feet than the scarecrow and escaped his attempts to embrace me in a bear hug. Marcus wasn't as lucky. The gorilla pinned him to the ground with his bulk, his hands around Marcus' neck. Marcus tried the move we'd practiced, but it would take a crane to move the gorilla.

The gorilla grabbed Marcus by the shoulders and slammed him back to the floor, his head crashing into the concrete.

I had to do something.

I propelled myself forward, dropped my shoulder, and slammed into the gorilla like a wrecking ball. He fell forward, catching himself before he face-planted onto the floor. He rolled away, landing on his back.

I stood over him, remembering Marcus' suggestion. *Go for the windpipe. No one can survive that.*

I picked my foot off the ground and held it over the gorilla's throat. All I had to do was stomp down and crush his airway. His size wouldn't save him from that.

Out of the corner of my eye, I saw the scarecrow move toward me. He caught his foot on the chair Marcus had knocked to the ground and tripped. Landing hard on his arm, he cried out in pain.

Marcus slowly got to his hands and knees.

I looked down into the face of the gorilla. All I had to do was lower my foot. Hard and fast, and this would all be over. For a fraction of a second, I tried to grasp what it would feel like to take a life. But I knew what I had to do if me and Marcus were to have a chance.

It went against everything I'd been trained to do. But Diablo didn't play by the rules. Why should I?

My foot started to fall as Marcus shoved me aside with his hip and delivered a kick to the gorilla's gut.

The goon rolled over, pulling his legs into the fetal position.

"Backups here. We don't have time," Marcus said.

Breaking out of my trance, I became aware of the sound of revving engines coming from outside. More Diablo had arrived. Arms still tied in front of him, Marcus nudged me with his elbow. "Leave him, come on."

I followed him to the far side of the room, where a row of metal doors lined the back wall. Marcus shoved one with his shoulder. It didn't budge. We moved to the next one.

The sound of loud, angry voices came from the parking lot. They'd be in the building any second. And they wouldn't be happy to find the scarecrow and the gorilla lying on the floor.

Marcus shoved the last door, and it swung open. We rushed through it, letting the door slam shut behind us with a deafening clang.

"Run," he said.

We darted down a narrow hallway, up two sets of metal steps and down a catwalk two stories up. I glanced down at the room below. Heavy machines sat dusty and unused. Some sort of manufacturing plant. I couldn't tell what the product was, but it gave off an earthy essence.

Down another catwalk, we ran deeper into the building. If I tripped, I'd fall flat on my face since my arms were not only falling asleep but tied in front of me.

An alcove was to our right. Marcus ducked into it, and I followed.

Breathing hard, Marcus took the end of the zip tie between his teeth. "Pull it tight," he said.

"Tight?" That made no sense.

But Marcus wasn't about to argue with me. He inched his restraint tighter until it must have cut off all the blood flow to his hands. Then, in one fluid motion, he raised his arms above his head, opened his elbows, and forcibly brought his arms down to his sides. The bonds broke, and his hands came free.

I didn't take the time to ask him where he'd learned that. I probably didn't want to know.

I copied his move and, after a sharp pain cut across my wrists, my hands were free. The zip ties floated to the warehouse floor two stories down.

The heavy metal door we'd slipped through moments before slammed open, and three men dressed in black spilled into the room.

Marcus grabbed my hand and pulled me further down the walkway.

Gunfire erupted, and bullets pinged off the surrounding metal, ricocheting. Marcus ducked his head, and I did the same, running along the corridor behind him.

A chute at the bridge's end must have been used to carry grain down to the main floor. Under it was a giant vat.

Marcus pushed me in front of him. "Go!"

I chanced a glance behind us. One gangster had made it to the footbridge and was advancing toward us, his gun held out in front of him.

I didn't want to take the slide to nowhere, afraid the container below us would become my grave. But as another shot rang out, I knew I had no choice. I dropped to my butt and let gravity take its course. I shot down the chute, tumbling into waist-deep grain at the bottom. Marcus crashed into me and knocked me face-first into a mountain of dried and rotting corn kernels.

I struggled for air and spit out kernels as Marcus dragged me forward. Across from us was an opening.

Another shot sounded from above. I waded toward the side of the vat and dove for the hatch headfirst, ramming my shoulder on the concrete as I somersaulted onto the floor. On his stomach, Marcus skidded to a stop behind me.

That was going to leave a mark.

No time to take stock of our injuries. Marcus jumped to his feet, pulled me to mine, and we ran, dodging equipment and large containers until we came to a loading dock.

Backed up to it was a delivery truck. "Get in," Marcus said.

I raced around to the passenger's side and climbed onto the seat as Marcus got behind the wheel. He felt for the ignition, but there was no key. He pulled the visor down, but only a pair of sunglasses fell into his lap. Reaching over, he opened the glove compartment. Still no key.

"We should keep running," I said.

Marcus ignored me, reaching behind him and finding a toolbox. He flipped the lid and grabbed a screwdriver. "Keep watch behind us."

I reached out the open window and adjusted the side mirror so I could see what was happening back in the warehouse. I knew Diablo was moving toward us, but it would take a few minutes for them to maneuver around the heavy equipment. Was that enough time?

I glanced at Marcus. He pounded the ignition with the screwdriver, and the cap popped off. He pulled the wires out and separated them into three groups. With nimble fingers, he twisted them together, and in a few seconds, the engine roared to life.

He'd obviously done this before.

As he punched the stick shift into gear, the men spilled onto the loading dock.

"Go!" I yelled.

The truck lurched forward, and all three Diablo skidded to a halt on the dock, unable to make the leap onto the truck as we pulled away. I watched from the mirror as they fired at us, hitting the trailer, but not penetrating the cab as we increased the distance between us.

"Joy," I said. "She's still out there."

Chapter Fifty-Three

The truck tipped for a moment as we rounded the corner, bringing us to the front of the warehouse. A line of Harley's blocked the road. Marcus slammed on the brakes, and we sat, staring at the line of bikes and their riders. Engines revved.

We were bigger, but there were more of them. And they all pointed handguns our way.

"What now?" I asked, chancing a glance at Marcus.

He blinked repeatedly, as if he couldn't believe our next hurdle. He didn't look good.

"Marcus?" I reached over and touched his arm. "Are you okay?"

He shook me off. "Duck down."

Marcus put the truck in gear and flattened the gas pedal, careening toward the motorcycles. Shots rang out as I wedged myself between the seat and the dashboard. A round embedded itself in the back of the seat where I'd been sitting just moments ago.

Next came thuds and the sound of scraping and crushed metal as Marcus plowed through the roadblock. The impact momentarily slowed us, but Marcus powered on.

Shots continued to fire, and the windshield exploded, glass raining down on me. I automatically covered my head with my hands, and pockets of pain ran across my knuckles as the shattered glass pierced my skin.

And then we came to a stop.

"Hands up!" a voice demanded.

Marcus put the truck into neutral and held his hands up by his ears. "Cops," he said.

Thank God. I wiggled out of my spot and slowly emerged from my place on the floor, hands in the surrender position. The door flew open, and they yanked me from the truck, throwing me to the ground. I obeyed the officer's commands, lying prone until he handcuffed me and then pulled me to my feet.

Once we cleared the front of the truck, I saw them do the same to Marcus. Cops crawled all over the place.

While I was escorted toward a waiting police car, I noticed Betz in the distance.

It was over.

We were safe.

Betz rushed forward. "Let her go. She's with me," he said.

Without thinking, I leaned into him and rested my head on his shoulder. "How did you know?"

"Joy," he said. "She called."

"She okay?"

He nodded, stroking my back and kissing my hair. "She managed to hold Rocky McManus at gunpoint until we arrived. She's becoming quite the badass."

"So, it's over?"

Betz pulled back while the officer behind me unlocked my cuffs, freeing my hands. I looked down at them, bloody and shaking, and slowly looked at Marcus.

"Can I?" I asked.

Betz followed my gaze toward Marcus as a second cop freed his hands. Pain filled Betz's eyes as he nodded. "Go. It's over." I wasn't sure if he meant Diablo's revenge or my relationship with him. But the bond between me and Marcus was obvious. And the finality of Betz's words hit me like a brick in the face. Without looking back, I rushed toward Marcus.

Marcus sat on the ambulance's back bumper, a blood pressure cuff on his arm. His feet dangled, boots clicking at the heels. Loose hair hung in his face, and when he looked up at me, I gasped, taking in the bruising on his neck that I hadn't noticed in the warehouse. Just a few more minutes, seconds maybe, and he wouldn't be here.

My heart tugged.

"You sure you're okay?" he said.

"Me? I saw that gorilla bang your head against the concrete and strangle you. Are you okay?"

He rubbed his head. "I couldn't let you kill him…. To live with having taken a life. Plus, I knew we had to get out of there."

The paramedic released the blood pressure cuff. "BP is normal. Still, you should go to the hospital and get checked out."

Marcus shook his head and slid off the bumper. He swayed a little, then steadied himself against the side of the ambulance.

"Don't be an idiot," I said. "Go to the hospital."

"I'm fine."

"You're not. And a medical report will be useful if this goes to trial."

Marcus winced when he ran a hand through his hair. "Well, since you put it that way."

I gave him a hug. When I started to pull away, he held me tighter.

My voice was muffled against his hair. "If they would have—"

"Don't. They didn't. I was about to go all ninja on them, anyway."

I was an inch away from losing my composure. I didn't want to think about what-ifs. I broke our embrace and watched him climb into the ambulance, not turning away until they drove out of sight.

Joy stood across the parking lot, arms crossed and tapping a high-heeled foot on the pavement as she spoke to a young cop. I ran over and hugged her tightly. "Thank God you're okay," I said.

She squeezed me back. "You, too, Sweetie. That was quite the predicament."

As eccentric as my cousin was, she always came through in a disaster. "And Pete? Is he alright?"

Joy nodded. "This kind officer has assured me he's alive and well. They apprehended the thug who held him hostage."

Despite my feelings for Jerski, I was relieved that he was okay. He and Joy. I'd pulled them both into this and felt responsible for their safety.

Betz came up behind us, massaging the back of his neck. "God damn, Case. That was close. You sure you're okay?"

I nodded and stepped into him. At first, he was stiff, but then he melted and placed his arms around me. My adrenaline faded, and tears of relief washed down my cheeks. I rested my head on his chest.

His lips went to my ear, and his deep, shuddering breath poured through me, down to my toes. While Marcus was an exhilarating, wild ride, Betz was safety. Betz was home. Tacos or spaghetti and meatballs. Who could choose?

Just five minutes ago, I thought I'd lost him. Not because I thought I'd die, but because I knew he'd witnessed the electricity between me and Marcus. He would never forget that I went to Marcus first. Even I couldn't make sense of that.

But Betz wouldn't give up on me. Maybe romantically. But I knew he would always be in my corner. No matter how many times I trampled his heart.

Suddenly, it was clear. I knew what I had to do.

I sat in the Interceptor, trying to process what I'd just been through. Diablo wanted us dead, and they'd almost succeeded. I was at my limit for near-death experiences and looked forward to going home and going to bed. For a week.

A good chunk of Diablo was in custody and wouldn't be coming after me anytime soon. But something still nagged at me. When I'd asked about targeting my clients, about killing Father Luke, the Diablo goon said they knew too much, had gotten too greedy. My guess was it was about their drug dealing, but it could have been more than that.

My cell buzzed in my pocket, and I grabbed it.

I didn't recognize the number.

"Hello?"

"Casey?" a familiar voice said. "It's Tony."

"Tony? This isn't a good time."

"It's the perfect time. I'm here with Justin. We need to tell you something. It's important."

"How do you know Justin?"

"We went to high school together. He wants to know if Father Luke is dead."

There was a noise, like wind, and then Justin came on the line. "I went to meet you. Cops were crawling all over the church property. I saw a body wheeled out."

I activated the speaker on my phone so Betz could listen in.

"Things are out of control," he said. "Me and Tony are ready to come forward. But we only trust you."

Both of them? "Where are you?"

"Go to the Desert Foothills trailhead. Hike up to the stone hut. No cops." The call disconnected.

I stared at my phone and then glanced at Betz. "No cops."

"Well," he said. "You're not going alone."

Chapter Fifty-Four

Telegraph Pass Road weaved through South Mountain. Man-sized cactus stood in the shadows like soldiers. Clouds obscured the moon, and light raindrops sprayed the windshield, bringing a chill to the air.

"So," Betz said. "This Justin kid, Suzy Vega's nephew, you trust him?"

"Not really. Do you know him?"

"What?" Betz laughed. "No. I told you I only went out with Suzy a few times. Not long enough to meet her relatives."

I didn't want to go back down that road. Not tonight. "I can't believe Tony was friends with a felon, and he didn't mention it. The background check the department conducts on all newly hired employees should have caught it. What else was he hiding?"

"I think we're about to find out."

Close to the trail, Betz pulled off the road and parked.

"He said no cops," I said. "Can you at least try to look like a civilian?"

We got out of the SUV and Betz untucked his shirt, letting it fall and cover the sidearm holstered on his belt. The darkness would help. I had left my gun, part of the Diablo crime scene, behind.

I knew the area. From this part of the National Trail, it was just a half-mile hike to the stone hut where Justin told me to meet him. Switchbacks and loose gravel on the mountain-hugging path made the climb tricky in the black of night—the reason the park closed at dusk. The light from our cells was just enough to see a few steps in front of us. Not enough to spy rattlesnakes or other desert creatures lurking in the shadows.

I tried not to dwell on that.

The only sound was our breathing as we navigated the sometimes-steep pathway. Intermittent rain fell, dampening our clothes and hair and making our footing slick.

As the structure came into view, we stopped and looked at each other. Betz reached out, took my hand, and squeezed it before letting go. "Stay close," he said, his voice low.

Hands on hips, I took a few seconds to catch my breath, then took the last steps on flat rock, coming to a stop at the peak of the mountain. I'd done the hike a few times and knew that in daylight a breathtaking view of the valley rewarded people who'd gotten this far. Tonight, the city lights twinkled below us, while darkness shrouded the hut. Two dark figures sat on the stone wall.

When they saw us, they got to their feet.

Betz illuminated them with the flashlight on his phone.

Justin. And by his side, Tony. They didn't appear to be armed.

I gulped a fresh breath of air. "You asked me to come. What the hell's going on?"

"Who's your friend?" Justin asked.

"Barry," I said. "You didn't think I'd meet you in the middle of nowhere alone, did you?"

Justin seemed to buy it, or he was unconcerned. He cleared his throat. "You know Tony."

"Of course." I had a million questions. I wondered mostly about Tony's strange, unexplained behavior. "Let's start with the big question. Why were my clients targeted?"

Tony and Justin exchanged a glance. "Tell her," Tony said.

Justin ran a hand through damp hair. "When I got out of jail, my PO sent me to sign up for community service. I went to the office, and they brought me back to a room. I was surprised I got the big boss himself. I knew Mr. Romero because Tony and I had been friends growing up. He even coached baseball when we were in middle school. He was a mean sucker, and I didn't know if he was going to give me special treatment because he knew me or ream me a new one for fucking up like I did and having a criminal record.

"Anyway, he said he had a special assignment for me. He told me to meet this guy in a park, pick up a package, and deliver it to the church."

"Go on," Betz said.

Justin flicked rain off his shoulder. "It seemed hinky, but I did what he said. I expected to meet a stranger, but it was Rocky McManus who met me in the park. I knew him from prison when he jumped me into Diablo. I'd hoped to distance myself from the gang, yet here I was, sucked back in. Once I had the package, I delivered it to Mr. Romero at the church. In exchange, he gave me a sheet saying I'd completed eight hours of community service. But I hadn't even met Father Luke yet."

Tony nodded. "Justin told me about it, and I knew my dad was running some kind of scam. When Justin was given his next assignment, I told him to open the package."

"Sure enough," Justin chimed in. "It was pills. Lots and lots of pills."

"So," Tony said. "Next time I took one of those little recorders we use to sometimes record interviews with our clients at work. Justin stuffed it in his pocket and recorded the exchange with my dad."

"You trapped your own father?" I asked.

"My father's an abusive asshole. You don't know how bad I had it growing up. Nothing I did was good enough. And when I got fired, well, he blew a gasket."

Cold from the rain, I hugged myself. "What about Brian Johnson, Nelson Martz, Eric Harrison, and Henry Coffman?"

"All dealers. They sold drugs, and in exchange, they got credit for completing their fictitious community service hours. Then, they got greedy. They couldn't get off probation early until they paid their restitution and fines. They got together and threatened to expose my dad if he didn't pay up. Big time."

"He gave them enough to pay off what they owed the court. Problem was," Justin added. "Diablo wasn't happy with that. The drugs came through them. They're the ones holding the purse strings."

"So, who killed Brian and Nelson, your dad or Diablo?"

CHAPTER FIFTY-FOUR

"Diablo."

"Who was running around in the chicken suit?" I asked.

Tony pursed his lips. "What are you talking about?"

"Never mind. Why are you telling me this?" I asked.

"Justin doesn't trust cops," Tony said. "I have to admit, I was mad at you for getting me fired, but I knew you were a good PO. And I was sick of my dad getting away with murder. I convinced Justin that you'd know what to do."

"Why did you want us to meet you here?" Betz asked. "Why in the middle of the desert in the rain?"

"Because this is where I hid the recorder," Tony said. "But there's a problem. It's gone."

A rack of a shotgun broke the silence, and Luigi stepped out of the shadows; his weapon pointed our way.

Chapter Fifty-Five

Luigi pointed the gun at his son. "You're an idiot. Don't you know I can track your phone? Can't you do anything right?"

"Dad—"

"Don't 'Dad' me. You're a traitor. How do you think I've supported you all these years? I had to work with Diablo. You think the county pays me enough to put you through that fancy school you almost flunked out of? And what good did that degree do? You couldn't hold a job if it was in a basket."

Tony's shoulders sagged. I felt for him. It must have been hell growing up and never being able to live up to your father's expectations. And it took guts to turn his father in.

"Luigi," I said. "It's over. Don't make this worse."

He turned his gun on me. "Shut up! Don't you know I got nothing left to lose? I go to jail, and Diablo will silence me. I can't win. Now, get your hands up, both of you."

Betz and I lifted our hands in the air. His shirt still covered the gun on his hip, and the darkness helped conceal it. But with his hands held high, his gun was inaccessible. If he reached for it…. Any sudden movements would surely cause Luigi to react. Even Betz wasn't that fast.

"Here's how it's gonna go," Luigi said. "You, Ms. Carson, are already in the news. Suzy Vega has painted you as a loose cannon. Her portrayal will lead people to believe you killed these three and then committed suicide. As for me, I'll head back downtown and get back to my life."

I had to keep him talking. Give us a bit more time, and maybe something would come to me. Or Betz. "You don't have the guts. Diablo isn't here to do your dirty work."

"Shut up!" Luigi said.

And then it came to me. *Learn from your mistakes.*

"If you're going to kill us," I said, wiping a fake tear off my cheek, "at least let me say a proper goodbye to Barry."

"Oh, Jesus," Luigi said. "Be quick."

With a silent prayer, I approached Betz with my arms open. If this were going to work, I had to act fast. I had one chance. If Lilian Harrison could get to the gun and pass it to her son before I could react, I should be able to do the same thing.

Betz and I stood toe-to-toe. So much was unsaid between us. If this didn't work... "I love you," I mouthed.

Betz gave me a wink. "Love you, too."

Wrapping my arms around him, I felt for the gun on his belt. My thumb pushed the release on his holster, and I pulled it up and out, while shoving Betz in the chest with my other hand. "Get down!"

Betz broke away as I brought the sights to eye level. Memories from the make-shift range calmed me. Betz's voice in my head. *Smooth trigger pull. Steady. Watch your sights.* I focused and fired a single shot before Luigi could react.

The blast exploded in my ears. The bullet connected. Luigi stumbled back while Betz raced forward, slamming into him. Luigi lost his grip on the rifle, and it landed with a thud on the hard rock behind him.

The others scattered.

Betz scrambled for the rifle, scooped it up, and held it at his side. "Nice shot."

Not center mass—which was my intention—but through his shoulder. Enough to disable him. Good enough for me.

My hands shook as I lowered the gun and held it against my thigh. Betz came toward me and reclaimed his weapon. Handing me the rifle, he stood over Luigi and got on his phone. "Send an ambulance," he said, then gave our location.

Pocketing his cell, Betz took off his belt, dropped to his knees, and made a tourniquet on Luigi's arm. He'd live to face justice, thank God. I had enough to sort out without being responsible for someone's death.

Chapter Fifty-Six

The paramedics had a half-mile hike to get to us. Time seemed to stand still as I processed what had happened. Betz stood guard over Luigi and read him his rights, but Luigi wasn't talking.

Tony sat on the wall, his head cradled in his hands. I felt sorry for him. It took every ounce of strength I could muster to take the five steps his way. "That took a lot of guts," I said. "Turning on your father."

He blinked at me, tears rushing down his cheeks. "He would have killed me."

I believed that. But that was too heavy a burden for Tony to shoulder. "Nah," I said. "He never would have gone through with it. But I owe you." I reached out and squeezed his shoulder. "Thank you."

Justin joined us, and I left them to console each other. It would be a lot to come back from.

Even more time passed after they put Luigi on a gurney and carried him down the hill before loading him into a waiting ambulance.

A helicopter circled overhead as we made our way back down the path. Headlights from six squad cars made the area brighter than daylight. Betz stood next to his SUV. On wobbly legs, I walked over and leaned into him. His arms wrapped around me. "Thanks for saving my life," he whispered in my ear.

"Anytime," I said automatically. But I wasn't feeling brave. I got lucky. I knew it, and so did he.

I rested my head on his shoulder. "We need to head to the station," he said.

"Make statements."

"I'm sick of making statements. But it's nice to know that I wasn't the PO my clients were afraid of. Luigi was."

Betz rubbed my back. "Ties everything neatly with a bow."

So, why did I feel so unsettled? We climbed into the 4Runner and headed back to town.

When I emerged from the interview room at the police station, Betz was waiting. "You wanna spend the night at my place?"

I didn't have the stamina to face Jasmine. "Not tonight, or what's left of it. I need to sleep in my own bed."

He bit his lip, then gave a sheepish grin. "It is your bed. At least it used to be. It can be again."

"I need some time."

His sigh told me it wasn't fair to keep him waiting. I should open a vein and tell him where I stood. But once the words came out of my mouth, things between us would change. I wasn't ready for that.

We stopped by his house first. I stayed in the car while he went inside and got Felony. He laid the dog on my lap, and I let him lick my face on the ride home. It felt good to hold him in my arms. I'd never give him up. I knew that much. "How much damage to the bathroom?"

Betz laughed. "Been meaning to redo it, anyway."

I cringed. "Sorry."

"Doesn't matter." He reached over and gave my knee a gentle squeeze. "Nothing matters except that we get to live another day."

"True," I said.

When we got to my house, we sat for a minute, idling at the curb. Betz turned off the ignition and sighed. He looked tired. More tired than he did on the last day of our marriage, and that was saying something. "I'm not leaving until I clear the house."

"Fair," I said. But knowing the major players were all guests at the Maricopa County Jail made my house feel safe again.

Since the investigating detectives kept his gun—the one I'd used to shoot Luigi—Betz pulled another from a locker in the back and slid it into his empty holster. I followed him inside and stayed by the front door as he went from room to room. Once he declared the house safe, I let Felony off his leash. He ran straight for the water bowl, which I scooped up and refilled.

Gun holstered, Betz stood before me, rocking back on his heels. "You gonna be okay?"

I stifled a yawn. "I'm gonna crash."

"We still need to talk."

"I know. We will. Soon, I promise."

He leaned forward and softly kissed my lips. I breathed him in. And he left, taking my resolve to decide our future with him.

Felony followed me into the bedroom. I plugged my phone into the charger and checked for messages. Seven. All from Marcus. The last, *give me the green light, and I'll be right over. Or are you with him?*

My finger hovered over the keypad. *I'm home. Alone. I need sleep.*

He responded before I could put down the phone. *Headed your way.*

I could have stopped him. But what was one more night?

I changed into an oversized Counting Crows concert T-shirt. Not so sexy, but that wasn't the look I was going for. By the time I brushed my teeth and ran a comb through my hair, there was a knock at the door.

Felony beat me to it as I zombie-walked across the living room floor.

Just in case, I checked the peephole. Marcus stood there, roughed up but still irresistible. Longing for him threatened to quash my fatigue. I opened the door and stepped back as he came inside.

Giving Felony a quick tap on the head, Marcus crossed the space between us, kicking the door shut behind him. My "decision" shifted to the back of my mind, and I welcomed his lips, warm and soft against mine.

I backstepped toward the bedroom, and he came along with me, his kisses more and more insistent.

I was so lost in him, I almost discounted Felony's no-nonsense growl. I pulled back and looked down at the dog, barring his teeth. He held his tail high, and the fur on the back of his neck stood on end. I followed Felony's gaze, stopping at the giant chicken standing behind us.

A gloved hand held an ax.

"Betz isn't enough for you? Does he know you've got this hottie on the side?"

Suzy.

All this time, Suzy.

Chapter Fifty-Seven

Suzy raised the ax and took a swing at Marcus. He jumped back, lost his footing, and stumbled against the fireplace. I reached for him, but he fell, his head hitting the mantel before he slumped to the floor, banging his head for the second time on the brick hearth.

He went limp.

For a moment, I froze, but then started toward him.

Suzy turned her attention to me, upping her grip on the ax.

I twisted out of reach, ducking as she swung my way, slicing the air between us. I stepped back, and she narrowly missed me. I moved to the side. Got the couch between us.

Reaching behind me, I felt for the fireplace poker, got it in my hand, and held it in front of me like a lightsaber.

Suzy laughed. It was a nails-on-the-chalkboard cackle.

She adjusted her grip, dancing on her chicken feet from side to side.

The poker was no match for the ax, but it was all I had. That and my words.

"Why?" I said. "Why are you doing this?"

"You thought you could take everything from me. Not only Betz, but my biggest source of income."

So, money trumped any feelings she had for Betz. "You're involved with Diablo? With Luigi?"

She pushed a wayward feather out of her eye and shrugged. "What can I say? I followed the money trail. I've known Luigi for years. I'm an award-winning journalist, and I knew he wasn't getting paid enough by the county to cover his lifestyle. When I threatened to out him, to use my clout as a reporter to expose his community service scam, he offered me a piece of the action."

I chanced a look at Marcus. He remained slumped on the floor. I had to get him help before it was too late.

Suzy took another swing and barely missed me. "And now you're trying to ruin everything. Sticking your nose where it doesn't belong. Jailing Diablo, so I don't get my cut. But I know one thing. You can't testify if you're dead."

"Why the chicken suit?"

"Everyone has security cameras these days. I figured it was a good disguise, and Brian Johnson didn't need it anymore." She sniggered. "Are you satisfied? Now you know everything. I should have known Luigi and Diablo would mess things up, and I'd have to take care of you myself. I never could count on a man.

"Too bad you won't live to share what I told you. Betz won't find you so attractive when you're chopped into little pieces."

She took another swing, so close I felt a breeze. I waited for her to follow through, then brought the poker down as hard as I could. She jerked away, but I managed to whack her in the side.

She yelped and jumped back.

I was awake. More awake than I'd ever been. I charged forward, the poker held in front of me like a sword. I aimed for the fluff of feathers at her chest, but the wooden ax handle met my strike and blocked it. The poker fell from my hand, clattering to the floor.

Suzy kicked it out of the way. "Your luck just ran out."

She shortened her grip on the ax and came around the couch. Her crazed eyes spun like saucers. Another swing, and I ducked, feeling the air slice above my head.

She swung wildly now, not taking a break and coming at me with repeated blows. Backed into a corner, I braced for impact, shielding my face with my hands. The ax handle came down against my forearms, stopping the blade just before it connected with my skull.

Pain exploded and ran up my arms like an army of red ants. I tried to ignore it.

Before I could come up with my next move, Suzy cried out and stumbled backward.

Confusion slowed down the action as I fought for breath.

Then I saw Felony latched onto Suzy's feathered ass.

With her attention on the dog, I charged at her, knocking her off balance. Candles and magazines tumbled to the floor as Suzy landed with a thud on the coffee table. Felony scampered out of the way as the ax flew into the air before banging against the tile.

I threw myself on top of her. We rolled, and both landed hard on the floor. As she tried to crawl away, I slipped my arm around her neck, squeezing it in the crook of my arm.

Using all my strength, I pressed down. Feathers flew, and I got a mouth full of them, but I didn't let up.

Bird legs kicked as she squirmed against me. I held on.

It felt like forever, but eventually, she went slack in my arms. Loosening my grip, I lay still for a moment, making sure she wasn't getting a second wind.

When she didn't move, I pushed her off me, kicked the ax under the sofa, and propelled myself to my feet. Out of breath, I staggered toward the garage. At the door, I flipped the light switch on and went to the shelf across the room. I found a bungee cord, grabbed it, and ran back to where Suzy lay—almost plucked clean in a pile of discarded feathers.

She groaned as she started to come around. I had to work fast.

I tied her hands to the sofa leg and then sat back, taking a minute to catch my breath.

Marcus still lay where he fell.

Getting to my feet, I stumbled down the hall, grabbed my cell off the charger, and then rushed back to the living room.

Suzy moaned as she rolled from side to side. But tied up, she wasn't going anywhere.

Scooping the poker off the floor, I kept it with me for protection, just in case. I dropped behind Marcus and settled his head in my lap. My fingers rested on his neck while I used my other hand to punch in 911.

Getting a pulse, I waited for the dispatcher to come on the line.

"Please send help." I gave my location and then dropped my lips to Marcus' forehead and prayed.

Chapter Fifty-Eight

Two weeks later

K ate held Ethan on her lap while Ashley played tug of war with Felony.

I took the last stack of books off the shelf and placed them in the moving box on the floor. Tomorrow, the house would go on the market, and the real estate agent had asked me to declutter, staging it for a quick sale.

I couldn't live here anymore. Too much had happened, and I flashed back to it every time I walked into the living room. No matter how many times I vacuumed, I continued to find feathers. They were endless.

There weren't many Diablo members left in the community, but those who were around knew where I lived. I was no longer safe here.

Suzy and Luigi were tucked away in the county jail, awaiting their trials. Justice was slow, and the hearings were months off. But they weren't going anywhere. Not anytime soon. Not with three murders, numerous assaults, and drug and conspiracy charges holding them.

Joy and Jerski got an apartment together, while Felony and I stayed in my dad's guestroom. A good excuse not to have male company.

Not that Marcus was up to it.

Betz was another story, but he seemed to understand that I needed time. I'd almost lost both of them as fate tried to make my choice for me.

I taped the box shut and checked my watch. "I need to go to the hospital."

Kate insisted she accompany me wherever I went. But as a germaphobe, she wouldn't bring her kids to the hospital. It was the only place I was allowed to go alone.

I appreciated her looking out for me, but I craved time by myself. Even if that was only a twenty-minute drive in my Jeep.

Kate got to her feet, balancing Ethan on her hip. "Okay, but be home for dinner. I threw a lasagna together this morning, and I'll bring it over to Dad's around five."

I was deeply moved by my family's support and delighted to see my dad so happy now that Millie was a permanent part of his life.

I walked Kate to her car and secured Felony in the rear compartment as she put the kids in their car seats. I promised to come home as soon as I could.

Home.

I'd have to find a new one soon. My life had been turned upside down. I didn't know what the future held, but one thing I had was time. And I was going to take mine.

Marcus sat propped up in the hospital bed, a bandage worn like a cap on his head. It had been a frightening few weeks. Words like brain bleed, blood clot, and surgery were tossed around like a chopped salad. Recovery percentages weren't good. We were warned about possible side effects of paralysis, brain damage, and lifelong disabilities.

But Marcus was a fighter—and one of the lucky ones. He got stronger every day. It was theorized that his condition started at the warehouse in the hands of Diablo, and he shouldn't have been walking around when he came to my house that night. Whacking his head on the fireplace had probably saved him. If he'd just gone to sleep that night, he might have died. Probably in my bed.

That wasn't lost on me as I came into the room. His face lit up when he saw me. At his bedside, I took his hand.

"Looking better every day," I said. The bruises around his neck and face had almost faded away.

"So are you," he said. "Then again, you always look good to me."

I pulled up a chair. "You didn't eat your Jello."

Marcus made a gagging sound. "All yours."

"Thanks, I'm good. Want me to get you something better?"

He squeezed my hand. "I want you to talk to me. You seem like a scared bird about to take flight if I come on too strong. Is it Betz? Did you choose him?"

I laid my other hand over his. "I choose me."

"What does that mean?"

I broke contact and settled back in my seat. "I'm selling my house. I took time off work. I need to spend some time in my own company before I commit to anyone else. I know it's not fair, making you wait. So, I'm not. I'm setting you free. Go out, have a life." I choked on the last part, my words sticking in my throat like dry burnt toast. A tear splashed down my face, and I swiped it away.

"I don't want a life," he said. "I want you."

I snuffed back more tears. Grabbed a tissue and blew my nose. "Yeah, and that's about how it works. You can't have both. I'm a disaster. Felony doesn't follow me around as much as trouble does."

"You," he said with a grin. "Are my favorite disaster."

"And you're mine. I'm just not sure I can handle any more. I almost killed someone. Hell, I almost killed three people. I need to take some time…. Digest everything that's happened. I care too much about you to make you wait."

He shrugged. "That's not up to you. I know what I want, no matter how long it takes. Anyway, it's gonna be a while until I'm back to normal. Doc says I should be my old self in a few months. So, take your time. You work on you, and I'll work on me. Deal?"

I reached out and shook his hand. "Deal."

I had to share my decision with one more person. With a few hours to go before dinner, I swung by Kate's, picked up Felony, and went to the dog park where Betz and I had agreed to meet. He waited on a picnic table in the far corner of the park.

Once through the gates, I let Felony run. He made a beeline for Betz, who fluffed his ears as the dog danced before him.

As I crossed the field, my resolve grew stronger. If I didn't know myself, what I wanted, I couldn't expect anyone else to know. I wasn't the same Casey. Near-death experiences will do that to a girl. And I wasn't sure if this new Casey—a work in progress—was what anyone expected me to be.

A Golden Retriever loped past me, introducing himself to Felony, who took the invitation to play. I stepped on the picnic table bench and settled on the tabletop next to Betz.

"Beautiful afternoon," he said.

I nodded.

"You've been quiet. You doing okay?"

Why did this have to be so hard? "I'm going to be alright, but we have to talk."

"Ah," he said, clasping his hands together and sliding them between his knees. "You've come to let me down."

"Not exactly…. I mean maybe. It's up to you. I need time to think…to figure out what I want my future to look like. But I understand that you probably want to get on with your life."

Betz laughed. "Like I know how to do that."

"I'm taking a vacation. Me and Felony. We're heading to the coast in the morning." It had been my mom's favorite spot, and it was mine, too. It was the only place where I felt close to her.

"Will you let me know you made it safely?"

I nodded. "I can do that. But mostly, I plan to disconnect. Turn off my phone. Jog and go through my to-be-read pile. I want to enjoy some seafood and good wine."

"Sounds like heaven. And it's overdue."

"Yeah," I said. "Maybe a little self-care is in order."

Betz reached over, took my hand, and squeezed it. "I think that's a wonderful idea." He leaned over and lightly kissed my cheek. And then he stood and walked away.

I watched him go, leaving his love for me behind. Not all of it, but enough for me to hold on to, knowing it would get me through whatever came next.

Acknowledgements

There are many who encouraged me and offered critiques and advice on my journey to publication. First off, I'd like to thank Mary Keliikoa and Dawn Ius for being early readers of this book and providing valuable feedback. And to my writer's group, Laurie Cutter, Keli Esser, and Rod Langer, for keeping me on task. Good friends Deneen Bertucci and Jennifer Vaughan, and my aunt, Carole Willson, have also offered feedback, reading an early draft. Special thanks to my daughter, Brittany Goyette, for pointing out the lines that made Casey sound old like me so I could change them and not embarrass myself. And to all the other people who have supported me on this incredible journey, even if it was just listening to me talk endlessly about writing and my dream of seeing Casey's story in print. You know who you are!

To Harriette Sackler who believed in this series and signed me with Level Best Books and to Verena Rose and Shawn Reilly Simmons and the people behind the scenes for helping me elevate this book to its best version.

And Michael Verdun for designing another fabulous cover.

The support I've received for book one, OBEY ALL LAWS, from coworkers, friends—old and new, and book clubs has been a nice surprise. The writing community and local bookstores have also been fabulous. And my readers! Thank you for all the wonderful reviews and feedback. You are what it's all about!

Without the support of my family, especially my husband Paul Hummel, daughter Brittany Goyette, son-in-law, Michael Verdun, and my mother, Beverly Schmidt, I never would have seen Casey's adventures in print. You have always had faith in me, even when I didn't have it in myself. I love you all. Thank you for understanding why I'm always on my laptop and for riding this wild wave with me.

About the Author

Cindy Goyette is a former probation officer who had a front row seat to the criminal justice system. She kept her sanity by finding humor in most situations. A mix of these things helped her create The Probation Case Files Mystery Series. After spending over twenty years in Arizona, Cindy lives in Washington state with her husband and two Cocker Spaniels.

AUTHOR WEBSITE:
  ccgoyette.com

SOCIAL MEDIA HANDLES:
  Twitter: @cindy_ccgoyette
  Facebook: (Cindy Goyette)

Also by Cindy Goyette

Obey All Laws, book 1